# SANTA &
# COMPANY

# FERN MICHAELS

# SANTA & COMPANY

**KENSINGTON**
PUBLISHING CORP.

www.kensingtonbooks.com

KENSINGTON BOOKS are published by

Kensington Publishing Corp.
119 West 40th Street
New York, NY 10018

All Kensington titles, imprints and distributed lines are available at special quantity discounts for bulk purchases for sales promotion, premiums, fund-raising, educational or institutional use.

Special book excerpts or customized printings can also be created to fit specific needs. For details, write or phone the office of the Kensington Special Sales Manager: Kensington Publishing Corp., 119 West 40th Street, New York, NY, 10018. Attn. Special Sales Department. Phone: 1-800-221-2647.

The K logo is a trademark of Kensington Publishing Corp.

Library of Congress Control Number: 2023938814

ISBN: 978-1-4967-3716-8
First Kensington Hardcover Edition: October 2023

ISBN: 978-1-4967-3720-5 (ebook)

10 9 8 7 6 5 4 3 2 1

Printed in the United States of America

# SANTA &
# COMPANY

# Chapter One

It had been two years since the class reunion of Ridgewood High School, when four friends reunited and made a pact to go on a singles' cruise if they hadn't secured a date for New Year's Eve.

The anxiety-producing holiday was six months away, so each of them thought they might be saved from the dreaded ship of lonely, desperate fools. Fortunately, the cruise wasn't the disaster they had thought it could be, and each of them began new chapters in their lives.

What all four women had in common besides graduating from the same high school was their passion for their work. Most men found it intimidating to be with a woman who was smart, successful, and attractive, leaving just a handful of eligible men who didn't feel threatened or overshadowed by their partner.

The four friends approached the high jinks on the high seas as an entertaining escape, if nothing else. Yet each of them had experiences that changed the course of their lives. Maybe not forever, but at least up until now.

The instigator of the cruise, Francesca (Frankie) Cappella, discovered romance was right around the corner from her

Manhattan apartment. Giovanni Lombardi, brother and partner at nearby Marco's Restaurant, offered to look after her cat Bandit while she was on the cruise. Across the sea and thousands of miles away, the universe was working behind the scenes to bring Frankie and Giovanni together upon her return.

For Frankie, it was a wonderfully comfortable relationship. For the most part, Giovanni was as married to the restaurant as Frankie was to her publishing career. Both appreciated the affection and attention of the other without the insecurities and demands other partners had put on them. Frankie knew the elephant in the room was the word *marriage*. Neither broached the subject, and their friends and family had the good sense to keep their lips zipped.

Rachael Newmark, the second member of the foursome, had the reputation of being a major flirt. "Boy crazy" was often used to describe her, despite her protestations. She was coming off a messy divorce followed by a string of unhappy relationships. But it was her passion for dancing that recharged her self-worth when she opened a dance studio in Ridgewood, New Jersey. Her talent was her introduction to Henry Dugan, a dance virtuoso who spent every year on the cruise ship raising money for his organization, Let's Dance, a program to enrich the lives of underprivileged children. He was more than a decade older than Rachael, but that seemed to be working for her.

Nina Hunter was starring in an extremely popular sitcom when she was told the series was canceled while she was aboard the ship. Fortunately, her writing talent caught the eye of a colleague, who opened a new and exciting opportunity for her. The stipulation was she had to move from LA to New York. It took two blinks, and she was ordering packing materials. She was ready for a big change. While she convinced herself she wasn't ready for romance, it, too, presented itself. What began with snarky banter at the opening cocktail party became the basis for interesting, deep, intellectual, and often hilarious conversations. They say the way to get into a woman's pants is through her brain. Make her laugh. Seal the deal.

Nina and Richard shared a similar interest in the arts, theatre, books, and music. He was an attorney in Philadelphia, which allowed them to continue their new relationship. He was only an hour drive or a train ride away.

Amy Blanchard was a brainiac. She worked as a bioengineer at a firm in Silicon Valley, but academia was her true love. She applied for a position at MIT as an associate professor. It would mean a major move across the continent and a decrease in her salary, but it was her dream job. Eventually she would figure out her finances with the help of Peter Sullivan, an accountant she met on the cruise. He lived in Connecticut, a much shorter commute than Northern California. In Peter, Amy found someone who loved solving math puzzles, whether they were business-related or for sheer entertainment. It was true nerd love.

Nina, Frankie, and Amy agreed they had almost perfect situations. No one was smothering them, yet it was comforting to know there was that one special person out there. As for Rachael? The jury was still out. No pun intended. Richard once referred to Rachael's relationships as "one mistrial after another." Sure, it sounded cruel. But Richard was a pragmatist. His assessment was remarkably close to the truth.

Amy's father, William Blanchard, had not been part of the original plan, but after his golfing buddies canceled their weekend in Florida, he decided as long as he was already there, he might as well take advantage of the opportunity to see a few sights, eat, drink, and socialize. A cruise sounded like just the ticket. His daughter was off with some friends, and his ex-wife? Well, who cared? He booked his ticket to the ocean air and relaxation.

The day the women boarded the ship, Amy thought she was having "dad sightings," but Frankie convinced her it was just guilt about leaving her father alone for the holidays. While on the ship, the four gal pals became acquainted with a slightly older woman named Marilyn. One evening, Marilyn canceled their dinner plans, saying she was "meeting someone." The women were concerned she might be seduced by a charming lothario looking for a rich widow, so Amy and Frankie stalked Marilyn, only to discover the "someone" was Amy's father. Surprise!

A year after the cruise, the five couples, including William and Marilyn, met for New Year's Eve at The Ridgewood Country Club. As they reminisced, they agreed the trip had been a magical adventure, but one never to be repeated. And yet . . . "never say never" had always been one of Frankie's favorite expressions.

# Chapter Two

*Present Day*
*New York City*

After the New Year's Eve "reunion-reunion," as Frankie liked to call it, everyone promised to see each other more often, but time slipped through their fingers as jobs, family, distance, and other obligations demanded attention. This year, Frankie vowed to bring the crew together again, even if she had to drive everyone to . . . where? That was the big question.

It was two weeks before Thanksgiving when Frankie pulled open her laptop and sent a Zoom call invitation to her friends with a note: *Make yourself available! Love ya, miss ya, Bossy Pants.*

The following evening, people were dialing in. Amy's face was the first to pop onto the screen, then Nina's. Frankie was already online.

"Hey, girls!" Frankie smiled and blew kisses with both hands.

Amy and Nina returned the affectionate gesture, and then Amy asked, "Where's Rachael?"

Nina shrugged.

Frankie pursed her lips. "I think it was me."

"What do you mean, it was you?" Nina leaned into her camera so that her face filled the little box on the screen with her name under it.

"Yeah? What?" Amy echoed.

"About six, maybe eight weeks ago, she left me a voice-mail dump. You know when someone leaves a three-minute message about everything that's going on in their lives? And then they end it with something like, 'I want to know what's going on in your life, but I need to find a plumber, so I won't have time to talk to you for a few days.'" Frankie mimed a double take with her phone. "Seriously? You want to know what's going on with me, but I have to make an appointment? I found that quite irritating." Frankie paused. "And self-serving." She bit her lip, as she often did when in deep contemplation.

Nina was nodding in agreement. Amy's head was cocked to one side, the light shining on the purple streak in her hair.

Frankie continued. "I cannot tell you how many hours I listened to tales of her boyfriend woes, down to the minutiae of each relationship." Frankie let out a huff. "I know. I must sound mean, but for criminy sakes."

It was Amy's turn to lean into the camera. "So what did you do?"

Frankie raised her eyebrows. "Well . . . I left her a message saying I could not believe I had to make an appointment to speak to her. And then ended it with, 'what if I needed you now?'"

"Good point. We're supposed to be here for each other," Nina said. "Have you heard back from her?"

"Nope. Nothing. Zero. Nada. Niente." Frankie rapid-fired her response.

"Not even a text? Geez, even Blinky and Gimpy can send a text. Well, almost." Amy grinned at the mention of her cats. "I'm still working on it." It caused a little chuckle but did not change the indignant mood.

"No. No email. Absolutely nothing."

"You would think she would reach out to see if you were all right?" Nina said sharply.

Frankie continued. "A few weeks later, I sent her a beautiful e-card for her birthday. I know it was delivered, but still nothing." Frankie folded her arms. "So?"

"Wow. And she didn't respond to the card, either?" Nina said, staring at the screen.

Frankie shook her head. Her eyes were welling up a bit. "I know. Like I said, it may sound mean, but she has a slew of support people who can jump through hoops for her. I'm no rocket scientist, but it seems our friendship isn't that important to her." Frankie wiped the one tear that escaped and was running down her cheek. "Each year, when I add another candle to my birthday cake, I try to add one line of wisdom. This year it was to simply lower my expectations."

"How sad is that?" Nina winced.

"Anyway, let's move on, please," Frankie said.

"Agreed!" Amy said, with her usual big grin.

Frankie began to discuss her idea. "It's been a year since we have all been together in the same room, and two years since our wild and crazy escapade."

Nina and Amy were nodding in agreement, and then Nina's eyes brightened. "Are you thinking what I'm thinking?"

"Which I might be thinking, too?" Amy added. "But wait. What are we thinking?"

Frankie started. "Meet up somewhere between Christmas and New Year's. Four, maybe five days?" Frankie cocked her elbows and turned her palms up. "Yeah? Maybe?"

Nina squinted. "I have to go out to LA to finish the last season of the sitcom. My agent is leaving town on the twenty-seventh for Hawaii, and we have to wrap up some details. So I'm flying out on the twenty-sixth to sign papers and go over the audition tapes for the final episodes."

"How are you doing with all that?" Frankie was referring to the fact that Nina's show had been canceled after two seasons.

"That's two for two. First acting, and now writing." Nina shrugged. "That's showbiz. I know this will sound cliché, but I genuinely appreciate the experience." She took a bow.

"Got any ideas floating in that creative head of yours?" Frankie gave her a smile of encouragement.

"Ooh. Maybe a tell-all," Nina said sarcastically. "Except the story has been told repeatedly."

"Don't the networks always say they're giving people what they want?" Amy asked innocently.

"No, honeybunch," Nina corrected her. "They are *telling* people what they want to watch. It's no surprise streaming makes up almost forty percent of television viewing. But please don't get me started." She held her hands up in a "time out" gesture.

"Right," Frankie broke in. "Amy? What's your schedule?"

Amy lowered her head. "I have an interview at Stanford. They called me about a professorship, but the only time I had available was during the holiday break. I offered to do it on Zoom, but they want to show me all the amenities. Wine and dine me, I suppose."

"Wow! Amy!" Frankie shouted.

"Whoa. Wait." Nina jumped in. "As in moving back to California?"

Amy blinked. "Yes." Her expression was odd. It was as if it had suddenly occurred to her. She would have to move three thousand miles away.

"Amy?" Frankie asked softly. "You okay?"

She blinked again. "Yes. Yes, I'm okay. What was I thinking?" She made a funny face and slapped her hand against her forehead. "Duh."

"Back up," Nina said. "You have an interview at Stanford?"

"Yes. At one time I thought it would be the highest level of accomplishment for me, but now, I'm ambivalent. I actually love my job at MIT. And my friends. And my life. I was so flabbergasted and flattered at the sheer thought of being considered, I didn't think the offer through. But the more I'm deliberating, it's really not as wonderful as I had imagined." She shut her eyes, furrowed her brow, and pouted her lips.

Frankie chuckled. "You are the epitome of the absent-minded professor. You get an interview, but the scope of the situation escapes you?"

"How have you made it this far without getting hit by a bus?" Nina laughed.

"I take taxis." Amy giggled. "Kidding. So I suppose I should cancel the interview."

"No. Don't do that. If they are paying your way, you should go. See what they are offering. You don't have to say yes, but it might give you some bargaining power to get a raise at MIT, or a grant for a special project." Frankie was now wearing her negotiating hat. Yes, being an editor required a lot of that. With agents, authors, publishers, salespeople.

"I have an idea." Nina jumped in. "Why don't we meet in Tahoe? I can drive up from LA, and Amy can drive in from Stanford."

"Sure! That would be fab! I haven't been to Tahoe in a long time." Amy clapped her hands.

"I can't remember when I was last there." Frankie thought back to the time when she and her now ex-boyfriend Scott spent their last romantic weekend together in Lake Tahoe. Shortly thereafter, everything fell apart. Too much drama with the ex-wife, the kids, the house. All of it. As her dad put it, "You can't fault a man who wants to be with his son."

Sadly, Frankie agreed, and for the past ten years, Scott had called to wish her a happy birthday.

Amy's eyes got wide, recalling Frankie and Scott's break-up. "Oh, wait. Isn't that the last time you and Scott were together?" She paused. "If it will bring up bad memories, we can pick another place."

"No. Actually, it's fine. I am *so* over it. It will be a new experience in a gorgeous setting." Frankie remembered the clean air and beautiful landscape, although in all honesty, she would have preferred somewhere warm, with beaches, and palm trees.

"Yay!" Amy clapped her hands again. "What about Rachael?"

Frankie sighed. "I have no problem with her joining us, but I am not going to be the one to invite her."

"Harsh?" Nina raised her eyebrow. "It's not like you to cross someone off your list."

"No, not harsh, but yes, it is like me. I let people push me over and over, and then when my back is against the wall, I put my foot down. If they're lucky, that's the only place I put my foot."

Amy couldn't help but giggle.

Frankie smirked and continued. "If she really wanted to know what was going on in my life, she would have contacted me."

Nina continued. "Here's what we'll do, Frankie. Amy and I will give you available dates; you set it up for a four-bedroom cottage, townhouse, or whatever is available. It's a little short notice, but I trust you'll work your magic." She paused to take a breath. "Once we have the info, Amy and I will send Rachael the deets. I'll act as if I know nothing about your situation. If she brings it up, I'll tell her it's between the two of you. If she wants to come, she will be welcome."

"That sounds very reasonable. Thanks," Frankie said.

"It *is* very reasonable," Amy agreed.

Frankie let out a sigh of relief. "Okay! We're going to Lake Tahoe." Then she burst out with, "Oh, by the way, did I ever tell you I don't know how to ski?"

Nina and Amy let out raucous guffaws, *yippee*s, and *woo-hoo*s. They were so loud, it startled Bandit, who had been sleeping comfortably on his big cushion in the corner. Frankie turned to the cat with his puffed-up tail. "It's okay, bubbie . . . just us girls getting excited." He blinked, stretched, got up, and circled the bed twice before he got comfortable again.

"I'll start looking into it. Nina's right—we're kinda late in the game here, but I'll see what I can do," Frankie said.

Amy jumped in. "Wait! Aren't you forgetting something? What about the guys?"

Nina and Frankie started to laugh. "Oops."

"Richard isn't expecting me back until after the first," Nina said.

"And Peter wants to visit his brother in Harrisburg. I already told him I'm not ready for the big family whatever and want to spend time with my family." Amy nodded. "To be honest, I said I might go to some reunion, but didn't tell him about Stanford."

"Why not?" Nina looked surprised. "How long have you known about this interview?"

"Just a week, but it would have started a conversation I'm not ready to have. I was enjoying the fantasy, I suppose. And I wasn't thinking about anyone else. It's that big picture thing I don't seem to have."

"Because you spend too much time staring into a microscope," Frankie noted.

Amy looked up. "Good point. I'll continue to use it as my excuse." She giggled. "Okay, so where were we?"

"Planning our girls' getaway." Frankie's eyes sparkled. "Giovanni can't leave the restaurant. It's crazy busy with holiday dinners. So? Looks like we are on our own!"

"Uh-oh." Amy snorted.

"We are doing this!" Frankie's smile was gleaming. "Get me those dates before you go to bed tonight."

"You got it, kiddo." Nina gave her a two-finger salute.

"Yessiree Bob!" Amy's exuberance could be either exhilarating or exhausting. It depended on what time of day it was.

They said their goodnights and hit the button that ended the meeting. Frankie leaned her back against the bottom of the sofa. Bandit stretched and sauntered over to where she had been sitting on the floor with her laptop on the coffee table. She scratched his neck. "Sorry, pal, I should have checked with you first. I am sure Giovanni will take good care of you. I will only be gone for four darks." She always spoke in terms of *darks* and *lights* when explaining her absences to him. She leaned over and gave him a kiss on the head. "You need a playmate. I know, I know, I keep saying it. I'm such a loser." He rolled over onto one side so she could stroke his belly. "Mommy's not a loser?" She scratched him under his chin. "Okay! When I get back from Tahoe, we will find you your own little pal." Bandit seemed to agree as he rolled over to the other side. Then he gave her a look as if to say, *I'm holding you to it, lady.*

# Chapter Three

Frankie pushed herself away from her desk, stretched her arms as high as she could, and tilted her head from side to side. She looked down at the right corner of her monitor. It was already 8:30 p.m. An exceedingly long day. She wondered how everyone was enjoying the traditional lighting of the Rockefeller Christmas tree.

Her team was on a very tight deadline to get the final page proofs to the production department before everyone scattered over the holidays. Frankie recalled the dozens of times she'd observed the tradition of the lighting of the glorious tree at Rockefeller Center. It was the best kickoff to the holiday season. Some of her staff had never experienced this celebration, so Frankie volunteered to stay late and get the pages turned in, allowing her colleagues to join in the merriment.

Frankie loved the holidays, but with her family scattered across the country, it had become more stressful to try to accommodate everyone's schedule. Instead of the big Italian family gathering for a five-hour feast, now her parents would drive into the city and enjoy their Christmas dinner at Marco's. The one thing Frankie's mother didn't miss was all the work involved in preparing two big meals. It was fun when there were a half-dozen people to whom she could assign duties: Frankie grated the cheese and set the table; Aunt Millie made the meatballs and the braciola; and her two grandmothers made the pasta, laying out the cut dough on a piece of plywood Frankie's father would place on top of the bed to allow the pasta to dry. Now the group was smaller, and there were fewer hands to pitch in.

But this new arrangement suited Frankie's parents fine and included Christmas Eve dinner when they celebrated with the Feast of the Seven Fishes, known in Italy as *La Viglia*. It wasn't necessarily a religious thing unless food was your religion. And most of the time it was Frankie's. At work, she was often described as the "Big Cheese," ever since she brought in the major best-selling cookbook, *Formaggio Mio!*

It began as a joke when she was having dinner at Marco's, her boyfriend's family's restaurant. Without fail, each meal started with an antipasto served on a wooden plank; the dish consisted of cured meats including prosciutto, salami, and capicola, or as some pronounced it, *gabbagool*. In addition, there would be a variety of cheeses from sharp provolone to creamy burrata. And no respectable meal would be without crusty bread, olives, and extra-virgin olive oil for dipping. If you wanted to get fancy, you might add grilled artichoke hearts and roasted peppers.

One evening, a new busboy tried to remove the platter with a few pieces of remaining cheese. Without any hesitation, Frankie let out a loud, "Formaggio mio!" causing the young man to drop the platter back on the table. She and Giovanni looked at each other and howled. Once they regained their composure, they formulated the idea of a book about cheese. It wouldn't be fancy, but a fun look at the history of cheese, the different varieties, simple hacks to make a meal better, and ways to serve.

Frankie hit up her list of favorite gourmet aficionados and asked them to contribute a recipe, offering to donate a portion of the profits to either a food bank or an animal shelter of their choosing. She handpicked the chefs and restaurateurs to form her dream team and purposely passed on the prima donnas. A little over a year later, the contributors supported Frankie's vision of "giving back" and made as many personal appearances as their schedule permitted. It became a *New York Times* bestseller, the easiest and most satisfying publication she'd ever worked on.

Frankie's stomach growled, reminding her she hadn't eaten anything since noon, and she was salivating thinking about the meal she'd had the night before. Once a week, she and Marco's brother, Giovanni, would meet for dinner at the restaurant. It was usually on Tuesday, when everything was freshly delivered that morning. Of course, more purveyors would bring goods every day, but even the chef was more refreshed after taking the traditional Monday off.

She looked at the clock again. It was 9:00. She had been daydreaming and reminiscing for half an hour. No wonder her stomach was growling. Time to order something to take away from Marco's. She flipped her phone open and hit the speed-dial button for Giovanni.

"*Buona sera, mi amore!*" Giovanni always sounded as if he were about to break out into an Italian aria. His English was impeccable, with just enough of an accent to make him even more charming.

"*Ciao*, Gio. *Che cosa?*" she responded, asking what's up.

"I'm waiting for my beautiful friend. I remember you work late tonight, so I saved a portion of the special, Gambero Scampi, and of course a glass of vino," he replied.

She could almost smell the garlicky shrimp through the phone. "With capellini?"

"Of course, with pasta! But tonight it's linguine."

"Well, you can just forget about it," Frankie teased.

"Oh, *cara mia*, do not make me weep." He tossed it right back at her.

"If you insist. See you in a half hour." She made the sound of a kiss as she ended the call. Her relationship with Giovanni was steady. In addition to their weekly dinner, they would have date night on the evenings Giovanni was off. When her schedule was frantic, as it currently was, she would pick something up on her way home, or Giovanni would deliver it if the restaurant wasn't busy. It varied every week. "You will eat here tonight?" he asked.

"It's getting late. I don't want to keep anyone."

"*Cara*, it's not a problem. I will wait for you. Marco and I still have to check the pantry and make orders for the weekend."

The restaurant business was grueling, and during the holidays it was chaos. That, too, mirrored her life. As an executive editor, she was always on call to the high-maintenance celebrity-chef authors, especially those with a TV show. Pulling a book together took about a year with changes, rewrites, and revisions. Then there was planning the media tour. That was another nightmare of demands until the book release, when the publicity was in full swing. It was probably the most challenging time of the entire publishing process, those first months when the book was on sale. If the author's niece's mother-in-law's sister's daughter couldn't find the book in Tupelo, Mississippi, the phone would ring off the hook.

For the most part, she wasn't a fan of the celebrity cookbook, but a bestseller could bring in a lot of sales, unlike most of the other celebrity tell-alls or memoirs. *Memoirs.* Frankie wanted to grimace at the word. Most of what was between the pages of the typical memoir had already been splashed across the electronic media universe, leaving little to reveal. But a cookbook gave the customer something of value. Food and the opportunity to create something to share.

Frankie counted her blessings. In Giovanni, she'd found someone who had a mutual passion for food, and the tradition and appreciation of family, even if some of the people in her circle weren't related by blood. Frankie referred to them as "framily." There are those who share DNA, and there are others who share LOVE. Whenever Frankie's cousin Betty would snub her in high school, Frankie's mother would remind her, "Friends are God's apology for family."

Frankie smiled at a photo on her desk, one of her parents when they were chaperones at her junior prom. In spite of the screaming matches she'd had with her mother when Frankie was a teenager, she had to admit her parents were probably the coolest of her classmates' moms and dads. Maybe that was because they were older when they had her; ten years older than most of her friends' parents. At first, she was horrified when she found out their real ages, but then she was thrilled they were so cool.

Again she checked the time. She had to get a move on. She cleared her desk, put on her coat, straightened her long, black ponytail, and carried the armload of collated pages to the production office. Even though everything was done on computers, Frankie insisted on seeing the final page proofs in hard copy. She wanted to imagine the experience of the person who either got the book as a gift or bought it for themselves. She wanted it to be an immersive experience, from page to plate.

As she maneuvered around decorated trees, menorahs, Kwanzaa candles, and a variety of other decorations celebrating the end of darkness, she considered it might not be a coincidence that these special holidays were all close to the Winter Solstice, the day when we begin to see more sunlight. Her musings were halted when she heard voices coming from an office farther down the hall. The publicity department was buzzing with the latest challenges of delayed flights due to a storm in the Midwest. It was a big week for daytime television and shameless self-promotion. Thankfully, her books had been on sale since early October, and two chef/authors lived in the New York Metro area. One of them was Mateo Castillo.

Mateo had had the opportunity to become a celebrity chef, but decided to do something more meaningful with his culinary talents. He was inspired by José Andrés and his work with the World Central Kitchen and began a movement called Share a Meal with the intention of helping people help others through food.

Mateo and a small crew would go to underserved parts of the country and gather members of the community to share a meal. He would do a cooking demonstration, encouraging and teaching techniques for serving healthy and delicious meals to large groups of people such as the residents of nursing homes, shelters, and church organizations. The only prerequisite was that participants had to sign up two weeks in advance. Word spread quickly, even without social media, and folks would camp out overnight to be sure their names were on the list. In a noticeably short time, Mateo became a folk hero known for sharing a meal with anyone in need of home cooking. Frankie had high hopes for his book, as the proceeds would benefit the Share a Meal Foundation.

Mateo was a handsome man in his late thirties. His biological parents were unknown, but his 23andMe results showed he was Mexican and Dutch. His adoptive parents were immigrants who'd barely escaped from the Medellín drug cartel in Colombia. He had a unique story to tell, and audiences were eager to listen. Frankie set her phone to remind her to tune in to *The Today Show* in the morning. He was scheduled to be on air in the second hour. It wasn't as if she would forget to tune in, but the phone was always ringing, and she didn't want to miss the show if someone was talking her ear off.

After she dropped the pages off, she stuck her head into Liz's office. "How is it going?" Frankie rolled her eyes in anticipation of the response.

"Oh, you know, the usual. I have an author scheduled for *GMA* tomorrow, here, in New York City, and he is sitting in an airport in Albuquerque. Then another one is scheduled for *The Late Show,* and she is also late, but not the good kind of late." Liz plopped back into her chair. "Tell me, Frankie. Why do I do this to myself?"

"Because you love it. And you're brilliant at it." Frankie gave her friend a big smile. "Everything set for Mateo's appearance tomorrow?"

"All set. I wish all our authors were as easy as he is." Liz picked up her ringing phone, made a goofy frown, and gave Frankie a wave.

"Good luck with everything! *Ciao!*" She turned and walked toward the bank of elevators. When the car got to her floor, several people were already onboard, grumbling about how they had to work late. *They don't have a super boss like me.* Frankie silently patted herself on the back.

She walked along Forty-seventh Street toward Fifth Avenue, where she could get a peek at the Rockefeller Christmas tree on her way to the bus stop. The crowd of over ten thousand people had thinned following the earlier celebration, which was considered the best tree-lighting ceremony in world.

She took a quick left at the intersection where the street met the plaza. Only a few hundred feet ahead stood the eighty-foot-tall tree, with over 50,000 LED lights and a star encrusted with three million Swarovski crystals placed on seventy spikes. It was magnificent. And heavy, weighing 900 pounds. The detail, time, and skill it took to produce such a dazzling spectacle gave her goosebumps.

She approached the promenade that ran from the area

overlooking the ice-skating rink to Fifth Avenue. Down the middle was the meticulously kept Channel Garden. Twelve eight-foot-tall white angels infused with twinkling lights flanked the sides of the garden, each holding a six-foot-long golden trumpet, all slightly angled toward the spectacular tree. Frankie stopped for a moment. The holiday spirit engulfed her entire being. This particular place was truly magical. *No wonder half a million people stop by every day.*

As she neared the avenue, she looked across the street, where the famous Saks Fifth Avenue Department Store exuded more holiday dazzle. Just then, Frankie felt a pang of guilt about Rachael. Maybe she should give her friend another chance? But then an obnoxious, overzealous merrymaker bumped into Frankie, slamming her into the person in front of her in the bus line. Frankie grabbed onto the person's sleeve to keep the elderly woman from toppling over. Frankie apologized profusely. "I am so sorry." Frankie looked around for the bungler as she steadied the woman. "Are you all right?"

The woman gave her a sour look and stomped the tip of her folded umbrella on the sidewalk. "Watch where you're going, girlie."

For no apparent reason, Frankie burst into laughter. She didn't know which was funnier, the lady being snarky or calling her "girlie." Perhaps it was the dichotomy of the tree's stunning beauty and the stranger's rudeness all wrapped into the same moment. *Only in New York, kids, only in New York.*

Frankie stepped back and motioned for the person behind her to move ahead. His eyes grew wide, and he shook his head, and then glanced down at the woman's large, very pointed umbrella. Frankie understood and politely stepped out of the line. *People are also very touchy this time of year.*

By the time she got on the bus, there were no empty seats. Actually, there were never any seats at this point on the bus's route. Her stop was just twenty-three blocks away and should take about fifteen minutes. She was happy to stand and gawk at the brightly decorated stores they passed along the street. She also made sure she wasn't within striking distance of the cranky umbrella lady.

Traffic was slow, and she arrived unscathed a block from her apartment. She gave Giovanni a call to let him know she was going to feed Bandit and then meet him at the restaurant. "Shouldn't be more than ten, fifteen minutes." When she got to her apartment building, the super and his wife and children were decorating a small tree in the foyer. Their six-year-old daughter was handing out holiday cookies. "Hi Miss Frances-ka." She liked to emphasize the end of Frankie's name.

Frankie responded with, "Why thank you, Miss Christin-ah! You're up past your bedtime, aren't you?" The little girl giggled and wrapped her arms around Frankie's legs. "Mommy said I can help decorate the tree." *If only kids could stay this young and innocent.* Frankie remembered a book idea she'd once had called *What a Cute Baby!* The twist was that the collection of sweet baby pictures depicted the most notorious criminals in history. Frankie was an optimist, but a cynical one if there was such a thing. Whenever people would say, "What a cute baby!" Frankie's thought balloons would reply with, *"I bet they said that about Al Capone,"* as a list of others ran through her mind. But none of the publishers wanted to touch the subject, so it went into Frankie's file of "Brilliant Ideas That No One Understands."

Christina was clinging to Frankie's coat. "Sing me a song?"

"Oh honey, I can't right now, but I promise I will. Maybe next week?"

Christina held out her pinkie. "Pinkie swear!" Frankie smiled. Christina was really a cute kid. And sweet. Frankie hoped for the best outcome of this young girl's development into a woman. Her parents seemed kind and attentive, so Christina was off to a good start. She smiled at the family. "The tree is looking beautiful. Can't wait to see it when you're all done!" She raced to her front door, knowing the scampi was waiting at Marco's.

Bandit was already pacing the floor when Frankie unlocked the door. He seemed to know when Frankie entered the building. "Hey sweetie. How's my boy?" She dropped her tote bag and picked up the purring ball of fur. She didn't bother to remove her coat, since she was going right back out the door. Frankie was starting to feel guilty about all the time she spent away from her fur baby. She kissed him on the top of his head and put him down, and the two moved into the kitchen as she resolved to adopt a rescue kitty when she returned from her trip. Lord knows, there were plenty out there who needed loving homes. She felt good that she was finally putting it at the top of her to-do list for the New Year. Even cats know when you drop the ball, and after that look he gave her the week before, Frankie could swear he was keeping track.

Frankie put Bandit's food in the dish and sprinkled a special digestive powder on top of his dinner. Instead of snubbing it, Bandit went crazy over it. Whenever Frankie forgot the special topping, he would sit on his hindquarters and stare up at her. "Sorry. Forgot the Kitty Crack," Frankie would laugh. They might not speak human, but their expressions and behavior were great indicators that cats were no dummies. She rinsed the fork designated for Bandit's food, placed it in the rack, and dashed toward the door. "Be back soon!"

Frankie heard the clock on the Met Life building signal it was 10:00. She was late. Most of the kitchen staff would be gone and the waitstaff would be leaning on one of the stations hoping their customers would finish and get out. She made her way to the back of the restaurant as she spewed numerous apologies to everyone. Giovanni got up from his seat and pulled the chair out for her. A kiss on both cheeks was the customary greeting. Marco poured her a glass of wine. "You look like you had a very long day, Francesca."

"It was." She sighed as she felt the warmth of the room engulf her. "It's so nice to be here." She lifted her glass and clinked Giovanni's. "*Cent'anni!*"

"*Salute!*"

Frankie's trip to Lake Tahoe was becoming the elephant in the room. When she'd first mentioned it to Giovanni, he was happy she and her friends were getting together. But the next time Frankie brought it up, Giovanni was pouty. Tonight she could sense a bit of tension, as well. Marco also sensed he should become invisible so his brother and Francesca could have some privacy.

Frankie took his hand. "*Che cosa c'è?*" she asked, inquiring what was wrong in Italian.

Whenever Giovanni got emotional, his accent increased. "*Per favore*, don't misunderstand me. I do not want you to think I am being the big boss man. But I feel bad you don't wanna to spend the New Year's Eve with me." He was hurt that she hadn't discussed it with him first.

"Oh, Giovanni. I am so sorry. It was one of those spontaneous things. We got caught up in the moment, and before we knew it, we were planning a trip." She squeezed his hand. "New Year's is only a date on the calendar. We can celebrate any time we want."

Giovanni kissed the back of her hand. "*Bene!* Tell me more."

Frankie told him it had taken many calls for her to find a place, and she'd almost given up when one of the authors gave her the name of a concierge in South Lake Tahoe who found a three-bedroom suite with a lake view. It was pricey at $1500 per night, but split three ways, maybe four, it wouldn't be too bad. It was at La Spa Resort with day passes for skiing, snowshoeing, snow-tubing, or doing absolutely nothing. It was also within the village, which offered fine dining, shops, and art galleries. It was perfect for Frankie because she knew she wasn't going anywhere near the slopes. Maybe snowshoeing but nothing that involved moving fast downhill. Nina was an accomplished skier, as was Amy, but Rachael was by far the most experienced of them all. Her family owned a house in Aspen, where she had spent all of her winter vacations. It didn't hurt she was petite and agile and her center of gravity was much closer to the ground than Frankie's.

"So, tell me. You are inviting Rachael, yes?" Giovanni asked in his sometimes-backwards sentence structure.

"No. I am not inviting her, personally," Frankie said with complete assurance. "I am also not *not* inviting her," Frankie returned.

"*Non capisco*. You are not inviting her? Or you are inviting her?" Giovanni's deep, dark brown eyes revealed his confusion.

"I, as in me, am not inviting her. I told Amy and Nina I was okay with her coming, but the invitation would not come from me." Frankie took another sip of her wine.

"Ah. You are going to be *testarda*?"

"Stubborn? Me?" Frankie let out a guffaw. "No, Gio. I am being realistic. She has not shown she cares about our friendship so, *abbastanza*! Enough!" She lightly slapped the table.

Giovanni flinched and then pursed his lips. He knew Frankie well enough to understand how she felt. Frankie was always one to give people enough rope to hang themselves. And then they would act shocked. When people disappointed her, she would let it go. Up to a point. "Time to have the 'Welcome' tattoo removed from my back," was her answer. It took a little explaining before Giovanni understood what she meant. Americans had a lot of expressions with which he was not familiar. But then again, so did the Italians. It was fun learning the phrases and jargon her grandparents used to say but would never explain. She could attempt an interpretation but didn't get the true meaning until she spent time at Marco's Restaurant.

"So, Amy and Nina, they will invite Rachael?" Giovanni figured he had it right.

"Correct-o-mundo," Frankie replied. "There's a sofa bed in the living room with a fireplace and a view of the lake. I reserved a suite large enough for four of us."

"Of course you did." Giovanni patted her hand. "You are special, Francesca. You are angry with a friend, but you still make room for her. In your plans, and in your heart."

"Whatever." Frankie didn't want to admit she was deeply hurt by Rachael's cavalier attitude. Frankie often thought about writing Rachael a letter telling her how she felt, but the pragmatic side of Frankie told her if Rachael really cared, she'd show up. Either by phone, text, email, or in person. There was a Buddhist saying that you mail the letter once. It didn't necessarily have to refer to a letter. It could be any kind of communication. Frankie had sent a message via a birthday card that showed she cared about Rachael. Over the decades of friendship, Frankie had discovered Rachael could be self-centered, but she wasn't oblivious. Or was she? Had so much time passed over the years that Frankie simply accepted Rachael for Rachael? The essence of people didn't change. Maybe the way they handled things did, but not their core. That was, unless they had some kind of epiphany, which most people didn't. *Lowered expectations is the sensible way to go.* Frankie pulled off a hunk of crusty bread and dipped it in the family-made olive oil.

Frankie glanced around the traditional white-tableclothed dining room. Two years before, the brothers had planned on opening a second restaurant in New Jersey, but the pandemic snuffed out that dream. Fortunately, it was before they signed the final contracts, and they didn't lose any money.

Not even the $10,000 deposit. It was a hard time for every small business owner, and the landlord was sympathetic and astute. He returned the deposit, hoping they could come to an agreement in the future when the world stopped spinning out of control.

For Marco and Giovanni, there was an up-side to the shutdown. They had enough cash to keep the restaurant supplied while they maintained a steady takeout and delivery business until the worst of COVID abated and they were able to open to the public again. It was challenging, but they stuck together and made it work. They even delivered free wine to some of their regular customers. Each time someone placed an order, Marco or Giovanni would bring a fresh carafe of wine in exchange for the empty one from a previous delivery. It was against the law to give free alcohol to patrons, but at that time, when it seemed that the apocalypse had descended upon the world, no one was going to go to the trouble of arresting them.

As it turned out, a few of their patrons were employed by the city and helped Marco and Giovanni get a license to sell wine and beer when they reopened. "Ats-a because-a good customer service, no?" Marco rejoiced when the certificate arrived. Giovanni reminded him that what they had been doing wasn't legal, and everyone involved could have gotten into a lot of trouble.

"*Una benedizione*! A blessing." Marco would respond.

It was some time now since businesses had fully reopened— those that had survived. During the time the restaurant was shut down, Frankie helped them with a bit of remodeling. It was she who suggested ditching the red-and-white checks for plain white cloths with a simple votive candle and a bud vase. Marco frowned, reminding her that using fresh flowers could become costly and it would add another chore every day, so Frankie learned how to make faux flower arrangements in glass vases. She purchased three dozen four-inch vases, floral wrap tape, wire cutters, and Quick Water. With the office closed down, she didn't have to go back and forth every day, giving her more time at home. Each night, she made two until she got the combination right, and then she set down to complete her mission, working on three or four every evening. When the long lockdown was finally lifted, she presented the arrangements to Marco and Giovanni. A simple act of kindness, a little ingenuity, a fresh coat of paint, and new upholstery on the chair cushions transformed the original pizza restaurant into a lovely, relaxing romantic setting.

"*Bellissima*!" Anita, Marco's wife, exclaimed on opening night. Anita had been busy homeschooling the kids during the lockdown and had little time to help at the restaurant, even though it was just below the apartment where they lived. She fretted about the family's future, but Frankie always made a point to visit Anita and give her a pep talk. She hugged Frankie so hard, Frankie thought she might crack a rib. "*Grazie. Grazie.*" Her appreciation brought tears to everyone's eyes.

That particular day was over a year ago. Now, she and Giovanni had been together for almost two years. She sighed.

"*Cara mio?*" Giovanni noticed Frankie's pensive mood.

"Oh, nothing." But it *was* something. They never discussed their relationship and where it was going. *If* it was going anywhere. They'd fallen into a routine, and it was a good routine. *But is this it?* she wondered.

"Oh, you know," she went on. "I get sentimental during the holidays." Frankie gave him a warm smile.

"But you should be happy. You have many people who love you and want to be with you." He kissed her hand. "*I* want to be with you." He looked deeply into her eyes and brushed her cheek. Frankie got a bit of a shiver up her spine and waited for him to move on to the next sentence, whatever it was. Then nothing. She resisted the temptation to say *And?* But the conversation ended.

Frankie leaned against the back of her chair, cocked her head, and smiled. She didn't really need to say *And?* Even though she was relaxed, her mind was bouncing from *Why didn't she press him to say more?* to *Weren't his actions enough?*

Frankie was certain about her feelings toward Giovanni. They ran deep. And she knew he felt the same way. But they never broached the subject of marriage. The first year, they were getting to know each other through the ups and downs of COVID. The second year, they were readjusting to some kind of normalcy in their jobs. It had been a growing process. For a long time, Frankie had yearned for a partner in romance. In life. *Yes, marriage is a partnership, but did you have to be married to be someone's partner? Who made up those rules, anyway?* In her mind, a relationship meant trust and integrity. You didn't need a marriage license for either of them. Plus, a piece of paper was no guarantee your partner wouldn't cheat on you or steal your money. A relationship was about mutual respect. But then, this tiny voice in her head would make her second-guess herself. *Why wouldn't he want to make a commitment to me?* Those last two words were probably the most important part of that sentence. The "to me" or "to you" part, depending on who was talking.

Frankie remembered a conversation she'd once had with her pal Gerry. It was about a mutual friend Frankie had been seeing. Frankie told Gerry, "Ron said he isn't ready for a commitment."

Gerry shocked her with, "A commitment to *you*."

Frankie was taken aback. "Is he seeing someone else?"

"No, but when you're ready for a commitment with a particular person, then you're ready," Gerry said wisely. "It isn't a hard-and-fast rule. It's flexible."

That's when the word *commitment* became a dirty word.

She feared it from both ends. Being rejected, and conversely, being obligated. That fear explained her last few boyfriends. None of them were emotionally available. That got her off the hook, even if it meant they usually broke up with her. But now her love life was different. It was solid. *But still . . .*

Giovanni broke her reverie. "*Cara*, you are so distant tonight."

"Just a lot on my mind. I have an author who is going to be on *The Today Show* tomorrow morning. He is going to do a cooking demonstration and promote his cookbook."

"Ah, the one promoting Share a Meal?" Giovanni wasn't sure if he was jealous or in awe of the young chef who'd walked away from fame to do something selfless.

"Yes, Mateo Castillo."

Giovanni stiffened. Castillo was also an immigrant. They were both in the restaurant business. The difference was Castillo was feeding a lot of people and not making money. It was admirable. Maybe Giovanni felt a pang of guilt.

"Now it's my turn to ask you what's wrong?" Frankie sensed the subtle change in his posture.

"Nothing. The man is doing commendable work." His gaze flickered around the restaurant he and his brother owned.

Frankie immediately chimed in. "You are also doing commendable work." She waited a beat before she went into full cheerleading mode. "You and your brother prepare wonderful food and provide a beautiful atmosphere so people can experience a fantastic dinner."

"And this is why I love Francesca Cappella." He kissed her hand again.

Then Frankie heard her grandmother's voice in her head. "What will be will be."

Frankie finished her pasta and wiped up the remaining garlicky sauce with the toasted ciabatta bread. The olive oil dripped down her chin.

"Another reason why I love Francesca Cappella." He handed her his napkin. "*Ami il cibo*! You love food."

She dabbed her chin and gave him a wink. Maybe this little separation vacation might move the needle on their relationship. He already showed a tinge of jealousy about Mateo, and Frankie knew it wasn't just because of Mateo's career. Mateo happened to be as easy on the eyes and as physically fit as Giovanni. Their melodious voices with the hint of a romance language added to their quixotic, tall, dark, and handsome appeal. They could almost be rivals. Almost. But Frankie had a rule about fraternizing with authors: you simply did not. But Giovanni didn't have to know that. Even though Mateo wouldn't be anywhere near Lake Tahoe, the idea of Frankie's admiration for another man was enough to get the fire started. It didn't hurt that the respect was mutual between Mateo and Frankie. *Yeah, let him sweat wondering who might find me alluring while I am so far away from home.*

Giovanni walked Frankie home, but she stopped him at her building's front door. "I have to get up early. Tomorrow?" She lifted her face for him to kiss her, but he didn't. She bit her lip trying not to smile. She knew he was brooding. Frankie kissed him on the cheek. "*Domani. Ciao!*" She pulled out her keys and made her way into the foyer. Again she stifled a grin. This trip was going to be even more fun than she'd planned. "*What will be will be.*"

# Chapter Four

*Cambridge, Massachusetts*
*Amy Blanchard*

Having a boyfriend helped Amy navigate the holiday visitation schedules between her and her divorced parents. For several years, her mother made things difficult because she refused to keep her mouth shut about her father. "Mom. It's over. Stop dwelling on the past." Then there was her mother's boyfriend Rusty, who claimed he was related to the wealthy Jacobs family in Switzerland. But when Dorothy Blanchard was faced with her attorney insisting she ask Rusty to sign a prenuptial, good old Rusty took a powder. Amy referred to that experience as "Mom's brush with being a potential *Dateline* episode."

Amy could sense it from Rusty. He was the epitome of a grifter preying on older women with money. Amy supposed her mother had been lulled by getting so much attention from a younger man. But still. *Doesn't anyone watch* Dr. Phil *anymore?* Fortunately for Dorothy, her lawyer, Lloyd Luttrell, came through for her in more ways than one. The ill-fated romance between Dorothy and Rusty was a wake-up call for Lloyd and Dorothy, and they'd been dating ever since. Maybe a couple of days with her mother wouldn't be so bad now. She liked Lloyd, and her mother's mood was much better when they were together.

Her father, William, had married Marilyn Mitchell, the woman he'd met on the cruise. Amy snickered. So far, they were the only couple that had taken the plunge. When William told Amy he planned on asking Marilyn to marry him, Amy was surprised. "You've only known each other for about a year."

Her father smiled. "And time's a-wastin'."

That's when it hit Amy that after a certain birthday, there are fewer years ahead than there are behind. A chilling thought. But it was also a reminder to Carpe Diem. Seize the Day. Try to put joy into everything you do. Having a philosophical moment, Amy realized moving to Stanford would not guarantee joy. Where she was at this time in her life was joyful. She loved her job. She loved her townhouse. She kinda thought she probably loved Peter. One thing for certain was how much she loved Blinky and Gimpy, her two fluffy cats.

The letter from Stanford was sitting on the dining room table when Blinky jumped up and decided to lie on top of it. "Does this mean you want to go?" He blinked rhythmically, living up to his name. "Well? What do you have to say about this?" Gimpy was sitting on the floor, looking up at Amy. "Okay. What are you guys trying to tell me?" Blinky got up and began to slowly paw at the letter, making tiny paper cuts. "Hmm. Does that mean you don't want to move?"

Amy could have sworn Blinky and Gimpy gave each other an eye roll. She pulled one of the chairs out and sat. "You're right. Bad idea." Blinky laid down on the paper again, punctuating his thoughts. For a moment, Amy thought Blinky might really convey his objections by doing his business right then and there. On the dining room table. He never went outside the litter pan, but this situation might be the exception.

She scratched him under his chin. "I haven't even discussed this with Peter." She frowned. "Could there be something wrong with me? Am I losing the plot? Am I really a space cadet?" The phone rang, and Amy jumped.

"Hey, Dad! What's going on?" she asked happily.

"Hello, dollface. How's my girl?"

"I'm good!" she said with gusto. "And you?"

"Fine. Doing fine." He hesitated a moment. "Honey, I know we don't make a big deal about the holidays anymore, but I wanted you to know Marilyn and I are going to Turks and Caicos for Christmas."

"That's great, Pop!" Amy was relieved this plan would whittle down available visitation dates.

"We got a great deal on a cottage right on the beach."

"Sounds divine." Amy imagined the balmy breeze and the warm sun.

"But we have to travel on Christmas Eve."

"That's fine, Dad. Peter and I were trying to figure out our schedules. He wants to visit his brother, and I'm not ready for a big getting-to-know-you holiday extravaganza." Amy realized she hadn't told her father about Stanford, either. "And I received a letter from Stanford requesting an appearance to interview for a position on the faculty."

"That's marvelous!" William Blanchard cheered.

"It's Stanford, Dad. As in California." Amy wondered if he suffered from the same malady of "big-picture blindness" as she.

"Oh. Right. But you always dreamed of teaching there."

"I know, but that was a few years ago when I thought it would be my career's crowning glory."

"I see. I know you love what you're doing at MIT."

"I do. And I have a life here now. I get to see you more often, I see Peter every weekend, Blinky and Gimpy have more company."

"So you aren't going to the interview?"

"Frankie made a particularly good suggestion. I go to the interview and find out what they have to offer. Then I come back and see if I can leverage something with MIT. Maybe a special project."

"You are one smart cookie."

"It was Frankie's idea."

"Well, you're smart to have a friend like that."

"So you and Marilyn are leaving on the twenty-fourth. When are you getting back?"

"January third."

"Sounds nice. When do you want to get together for dinner?"

"When can you come down here?" William and Marilyn lived in Fair Lawn, New Jersey, not far from Ridgewood.

"MIT staff is off from December twentieth until January tenth, so how about I get down there on the twenty-third? I'll stay through Christmas, spend time with Mom and Lloyd, and then fly to San Francisco from Newark."

"Excellent." He paused. "I'm glad you're not going back to the city of smog and glitter."

"And silicon and chips." Gimpy rubbed his head against Amy's ankle. "The fur babies are in agreement."

"Good thing. We wouldn't want Blinky or Gimpy to wreck the house."

"Yeah. They're good until they're bad." Amy laughed. Lately it was toilet paper. She wasn't sure which one recently developed a desire to unravel the entire roll.

"Gotta go, Dad." Amy put on her pink and black plaid jacket and dangled her pink backpack on her shoulder.

"Okay, honey. Looking forward to seeing you," her father said.

"Me too. Love you!" Amy signed off. On her way out, she grabbed the matching beret and placed it on her head in a jaunty fashion. She cocked her head as she inspected her attire. "Maybe ditch the purple streak. That was so last year!" She opened the front door and stopped mid-step. "Keys!" She laughed at herself and what Nina had said about not being hit by a bus. She really should pay more attention to her surroundings and "the big picture."

Amy had a very youthful way about her. At thirty-seven, she could pass for a college student, especially the way she dressed. No one gave her any guff at the school, but maybe it was time for a change. They say you should dress the part you want to be. Even though she was happy in her current job, she could use a step-up in her wardrobe. If she was going to come back from Stanford to negotiate with MIT, she had to look more academic, less like an array of paint samples carelessly placed on her clothing.

Marilyn was very fashion-forward and would probably enjoy helping Amy pick out a few items to add to her closet. On her way to her first class, Amy hit the speed dial on the dashboard. If Marilyn were available, maybe Amy would take the train down one or two days earlier to go shopping, although it wasn't the easiest time to visit stores with the throngs of last-minute Christmas shoppers. The phone rang twice.

"Amy! Everything all right?"

"Yes! Fine. I hear you and Dad are off for a tropical getaway."

"We are! I am thrilled. But I'm sorry we won't be here for Christmas."

"I just spoke to Dad. I told him I'd come down on the twenty-third, but what if I made it the twenty-first or twenty-second? I need some help." Amy's voice was steady. "With my wardrobe."

"Why, I would be delighted! What do you have in mind?"

Amy told Marilyn about her interview in California and how she planned to use it as leverage. "But I need to look less spunky and more polished."

"I don't think clothes will camouflage your spunk, dearie."

"Thanks. But you know what I mean. Nothing binding or stiff, but mature without being too mature." She giggled.

"I totally understand." Marilyn hesitated. "Do you think your mother would mind?"

"Mind what? My changing up a few things?"

"Mind that you and I are going shopping. Do you think her feelings will be hurt?"

"Not if we don't tell her," Amy said conspiratorially.

"Ah. I see."

"I'll tell her I'm going to have dinner with you and Dad on the twenty-third. She doesn't have to know when I get there."

"I see." Marilyn's wheels were already turning. "What kind of look are you going for?"

"What do they call it—business casual?" Amy's choice of clothes was more Betsey Johnson than Ann Taylor.

"We can go to Chico's in Short Hills. They have a lot of mix-and-match patterns. Tunic, leggings, boots?"

"Ha. That's Frankie's uniform," Amy said.

"And she works in an office, correct?"

"Yes, she does. I always thought of myself as skirts, dresses, and sweaters."

"They also have some stunning jackets you can wear with a long skirt and turtleneck. Oh, this is going to be fun!"

"Great! Listen, I'm in the parking lot at school. So should I come down on the twenty-first?"

"Absolutely. I'll let your father know, and mum's the word for your mum!"

Before she got out of her car, Amy Googled Chico's and fell in love with the first thing she spotted: a red rose soutache and black open-front duster jacket. Marilyn was right. This was going to be fun. The next item was her hair. What to do with it this time? *Leave the pastels out of it* was her first thought.

# Chapter Five

*Nina Hunter*
*That's Showbiz*

Nina Hunter had been acting since she was in high school—make that since she could remember. When she was growing up, she and her friends Sandy and Chrissy would dress up and pretend they were famous actresses.

Then she met Frankie and Amy in high school, where they bonded during the school plays.

When she graduated from high school, Nina stuck close to home and enrolled at Drew University, considered one of the best for theatre. It was only a thirty-minute drive from her parents' home, so they saved money on room and board.

The Hunters lived in a large ranch with the master bedroom separated from the other side of the house, leaving Nina and her brother's room very private. She had a good relationship with her parents, and she could come and go without disturbing them and vice versa.

Although she was enrolled in a Bachelor of Arts program, in order to be considered for The School of Drama, she had to audition numerous times, often with another student. Most of the parts she'd had in high school were in musicals, but now she was auditioning with a dramatic script, and she was beyond nervous. She took a deep breath, reached into her well of creativity, and forged ahead, stepping into the role and becoming that character. When the scene was over, she realized she had nailed it. It was almost an out-of-body experience. The professor was impressed and sent her off to her second round; this time, the play was a comedy. With her newfound artistic freedom, she quickly read through the script and saw an opportunity to take it over the top. It was risky, but her instincts told her to go for it.

The scene required her to accidentally bump into someone walking on the street, but instead of reading the lines as they were written, she decided to ad-lib and take a pratfall, landing on her behind. It was a perfect *I Love Lucy* moment, creating a burst of laughter from the jury. They were so impressed with her ability to improvise, they immediately enrolled her in the drama department. But it wasn't all acting. Building sets, pulling nails out of old wood, sewing costumes, and learning everything about theatre was part of the curriculum.

The one thing Nina was very self-conscious of was her mane of long curly hair. She was forever chemically straightening it until her hair was damaged beyond repair. During the time she was letting it grow out, she wore wigs; anything to keep it under wraps.

One afternoon, while the students were building a set for a new play, her wig caught on a wire and was unceremoniously yanked off her head. The stage manager ran over to help her unhook the dangling wig and stopped short as Nina shook her head of beautiful locks. "Nina, honey! What are you doing hiding all that fabulousness?" He fussed with some of her curls. "Sweetheart, this can be your calling card!"

Nina was stunned, both by embarrassment and the revelation. "You really think so?" She pulled a few strands in front of her face, examining her long-hidden secret.

As each semester passed, Nina got increasingly more important roles, letting her hair be her hair. If the role called for something else, she would adjust. But her hair was no longer an issue, until one night during a performance when the set was lit with real candles. One of the cast members got a little too close and set Nina's hair on fire. The audience thought it was all staged, partly because Nina made such a dramatic exit. She was the consummate professional.

By the end of her first two years, Nina was considered the most versatile actor in the entire school, but there was a new kid in town, and her name was Jane Douglass. Jane was a few years older than the other students and much more experienced in acting and in life. At twenty-four, she was already married and divorced, and the four years between the two of them made a huge difference at the time. Jane was as charismatic as she was beautiful, and Nina became enthralled by the other woman's confidence.

Nina's first recollection of Jane was the day she pulled up to the theatre in a Jeep convertible with her equally beautiful boyfriend. Jane bounced out of the car wearing tight jeans, braless in a white shirt, with a red bandanna wrapped around her forehead and tied in the back. It was a look everyone ultimately copied, including the big hoop earrings. The beautiful boyfriend looked like he, too, just walked off a movie set. Before he pulled away, Jane walked over to the driver's side and gave him a kiss that was inches away from pornographic.

It was a dramatic entrance, to say the least. Nina's classmates looked on with awe, disgust, fear, and envy. At that moment, each of them decided if they wanted to love or hate Jane. Nina took the side of love and admiration. There were many times when their friendship and rivalry were precariously at odds. But Nina looked to Jane as a mentor and acquiesced at every turn. After graduation, they drifted apart when Jane moved to Los Angeles and Nina ventured into the theatre world of New York City. Nina was tempted to follow Jane, but her parents gently talked her out of it, reminding her she was just miles from The Great White Way of Broadway.

Right after college, Nina auditioned for summer stock productions in the Catskills. She did three in a row, taking the lead of Sally Bowles in *Cabaret*, Miss Adelaide in *Guys and Dolls*, and Marilyn the Librarian in *The Music Man*. It was a grueling schedule, but she knew if she could cut it, she would be well prepared for anything.

She got a professional photographer for her eight-by-ten black-and-white glossy headshot and was able to put a few more credits on her résumé. When the last play closed, it was time to set off to the big city, where she got her first taste of how tough the business really was. Being on stage was exhilarating, but getting there was a hard road. Unlike the university atmosphere, where the competition was limited, and she knew everyone in the theatre department, New York was filled with a thousand strangers, all vying for stardom. It was a magnet for every wannabe actor, musician, and dancer.

The first open call was a kick in the pants. The announcement in the trade papers said it was from 11:00 a.m. until 3:00 p.m. She arrived an hour early to put her name on the sign-in sheet, only to discover she was number 273!

"First time, huh?" one of her fellow hopefuls asked, tipped off by the look on Nina's face. She then informed her, "You need to be here by eight o'clock if you want to be in the first hundred."

Nina looked at the line of auditioners. She wanted to cry.

"Don't worry. The line moves fast once they start." She continued to explain the process. "They usually take ten people at a time. They line you up in front of a table where the casting director and some other production people sit. Then they point and say, "You, you, and you." The young actress folded her arms. "Then they say goodbye to the other seven people."

"I'm not quite sure I understand." In college, you got the script and you auditioned for the director. This was an entirely new experience for her.

"It's called getting 'typed-out.' "

Then it dawned on Nina. "Oh, I see. If I'm not tall enough . . ." Her voice trailed off.

"Yep. And more. But they can't put that in the paper. Singers who act, actors who sing—that's about all you'll see in the announcement. So you really don't know if you're the type they are looking for until you walk into the room."

"Well, that stinks." Nina frowned.

"Yep. That's showbiz."

Nina realized the old adage was true: *It's not what you know; it's who you know.* Determined not to be deterred, Nina phoned one of her former professors and asked for some advice. "Get an agent. And a good one."

"How do I do that?" Nina asked.

"Well, it's a catch-twenty-two. Agents don't want to take on clients unless they have a job, and you can't get a good job without an agent. And the Screen Actors Guild has a similar policy." He paused. "Getting involved with some seasoned people could be immensely helpful. I'll make a few phone calls and see what I can do. Maybe put you in touch with a group that does backer's auditions."

"Backer's auditions?" Nina needed some clarity.

"When a writer, songwriter, or producer wants to produce a musical, they need to get the funds. What they do is hold auditions in front of potential financial backers. It's not a paying gig, and there is no guarantee that they'll get the money for the production, or that you'll even get a part in it, but like I said, it could get you in front of a lot of influential people."

"That would be wonderful. Thanks so much." Nina was relieved. "So no extra work for me?" Nina was asking about playing an extra in a film or television show.

"Nina, you have a lot of talent. Doing extra work might get you from one rent payment to the next, but you need to pursue serious acting."

"And that is exactly what I want to do." Nina pursed her lips; her mind was racing. She had to get to the head of the line if she wanted to succeed.

There were so many, too many, people who thought a career in entertainment was a viable option, and a lot of them were willing to compromise their morals to get there. Every day was a field day for casting directors, but Nina refused to go down that road, and it cost her a few roles before she found an agent who was willing to represent her. Not that it made much of a difference when she was alone with a man for an audition. She told a friend she considered putting "Karate Black Belt" on her résumé just to scare them off, but if she should be called to demonstrate her skill, she would be out of luck.

After several months of determination and grit, Nina was spotted by an agent during one of the backer's auditions. The agent saw something in Nina. She was versatile and charming, and he offered to take the young actor on as a client. "No guarantees, but at least you'll have a shot at a few things."

Nina was downright relieved. This was the first break in her career. Some people think it's securing that big role, but securing an agent is probably the most important step in getting there.

The agency sent her for a part that was referred to as an "under five," which meant it had under five lines. It was not *Black Swan* or *Silence of the Lambs,* but it was a shot at some camera time and expanding her circle of professional contacts. This particular show was part of a franchise of spin-offs, similar to *CSI, NCIS,* and *Law and Order,* which could mean a bigger step for her, and it was. Even though her on-screen time was less than five minutes, her agent called her with an offer to audition for a national toothpaste commercial. There was something about her smile that got her the job.

A year later, with many more credits added to her résumé, her agent sent her to Los Angeles to audition for the family-oriented situation comedy, *Family Blessings.* She held that role for almost five years until the show wrapped up its final season.

Shortly thereafter, a colleague contacted her to co-write a pilot for a new sitcom, and it was picked up by a network. But after two years on air, the network executives decided it was much cheaper to put another game show in that time slot.

Nina bemoaned the direction television was taking. On a game show, only one celebrity was required, there was no scriptwriting or need for a large staff, and usually only one cheesy set. Sure, they gave away money, but the prizes were provided by the manufacturers. The setup was a bean-counter's dream: a cheap way to fill the airwaves. Even if the show had the word *Celebrity* in it, most guests made you scratch your head and ask yourself, "Who are these people?" She vowed never to be one of them. She wasn't bitter, just exhausted and frustrated by the emotional teeter-totter.

Nina had always been a realist and knew she had to devise a new plan now that acting and writing didn't appear to be "in the stars." She guffawed at the thought. Then she sighed as the words, "That's showbiz," echoed in her head. But she was more than an actress and a writer. She was a creator, and she was going to create something for herself. Even if she had no idea at the moment what that might be.

# Chapter Six

*Rachael Newmark*
*Back to Square One*

When Rachael heard about the trip to Lake Tahoe, she was upset that Frankie hadn't invited her personally. She was still angry at the message Frankie had left about having to make an appointment to talk to her. Didn't Frankie know how stressful Rachael's life was? Finding a plumber was next to impossible, and her ex-husband was no help. The only time they spoke was to confirm visitation plans, and that was usually done by text, which suited her fine. She couldn't stand the sound of his nasal voice. How could she have married him in the first place?

Her parents, that's why. They were desperate to reel her in. If she kept up the pace of her spending after she graduated from college, she would have no money left in her trust fund, and they surely didn't want her to move back home, so they pressured her to "find a nice boy."

The word *boy* summed it up. Greg came from a middle-class family whose mother smothered him. One evening when they were having dinner with his folks, Rachael couldn't help noticing his mother was cutting his food. At first, she didn't know if his mother was trying to be funny, but it didn't take more than a few minutes for Rachael to realize the woman was seriously carving his steak. She couldn't decide if she should laugh or cry, especially when Greg didn't seem to think it was unusual.

*If she puts the meat on a fork and pretends it's an airplane, I am outta here.* Rachael tossed the glass of cheap wine down her throat and asked for a refill. At that point, arsenic would have been preferable. But Rachael maintained her manners and avoided staring at this display of an overbearing mother. Her own mother was enough to handle. Now this one was her future mother-in-law. *Laugh or cry?* Rachael consoled herself with the notion that once she and Greg were married, the doting would stop, or at the very least, slow down.

After dinner, Greg drove Rachael back to her apartment. He expected to spend the night, but Rachael put the kibosh on it, stating she had a headache. She wasn't lying. She thought her head would explode. What had she gotten herself into?

She decided to call her pal Frankie for advice. Frankie had always been there for Rachael and let her friend get the steam out of her system. Frankie suggested Rachael have a conversation with Greg. "Maybe he's oblivious. Most men are, you know," Frankie reminded her.

But Rachael knew her parents would never get off her back until she married someone, and Greg was as good as anyone. At least he had a job and his own apartment. But the momma's boy thing? Well, Rachael would have to untrain him.

Rachael huffed. *So where was her good friend Frankie now? How could she be miffed over her message about waiting for a plumber? Didn't Frankie understand trauma?*

*Sure, she sent a birthday card, but so what? She could have called.*

But it wasn't really about the plumber. It was about Rachael's life falling apart again. She was in denial, and she knew it, but she couldn't bring herself to talk about it. Not yet, anyway. All she knew was she was back to square one with her life.

# Chapter Seven

*The Twelve Days of Christmas*

Frankie phoned Giovanni after Mateo's appearance on *The Today Show*. She gushed. "He was incredible. I thought the hosts were going to cry when he said, 'It's wonderful people donate to food banks and work at shelters during the holidays, but we should never forget that people need to eat every day.'" Frankie thought she heard Giovanni grumble something in Italian, but she didn't ask. Nope. She was going to let him stew. If he wasn't ready for a commitment, then she could do whatever she wanted, even if it was simply spending time with friends. "See you tonight?" She asked assuredly.

Giovanni hesitated. "Yes. Sure. Of course."

"Everything all right?" Frankie knew she was baiting him.

"Everything is okay, Frankie. Tonight we will go to see a ballet."

"Really?" Frankie was surprised. They hadn't discussed going to the theatre.

"Yes. Tonight we go to *The Nutcracker Suite*."

Frankie knew Giovanni must have jumped through hoops

to get the tickets. It was a private preview dress rehearsal for the annual holiday production.

"Oh my goodness!" Frankie cooed. "How on earth did you manage that?"

"You are not the only one who knows famous people."

Frankie couldn't tell if he was being facetious or not. She realized she might have been a bit too cheeky, toned it down, and moved on. "This is wonderful, Giovanni. I have been wanting to see that ballet for years."

"You will not be here for New Year's, when I planned to take you, so it's good we can go to this together tonight."

There it was again. That little dig about New Year's. She pretended not to notice. "What time should I be ready?" she asked cheerfully.

"Curtain is at seven o'clock. I'll pick you up at six."

"I guess there won't be any time for dinner," she said.

"The show is one hour and fifty minutes. I made a reservation at Becco for nine-thirty."

"Becco? Lovely!" Frankie was once again impressed. The restaurant was owned by the famous chef and television personality Lidia Bastianich and her son.

"It will be our New Year's celebration," Giovanni reminded her, but in a much softer voice.

"Sounds wonderful. Thank you." For a moment, Frankie felt a little guilty. But only for a moment.

"I will see you later. *Ciao.*" He ended the call abruptly.

Frankie stared at her phone. Either he was going to ask her to marry him or break up with her. She had a flashback from a decade before, when the love of her life at that time invited her for dinner. He had cooked a marvelous meal, served a particularly good bottle of wine, lit candles, the works. Then over dessert, he told her he was moving in with someone else. She was devastated. She rushed to the bathroom and vomited the coq au vin, haricot verts, and roasted potatoes. She knew

Jeffrey had cheated on her in the past, but with all this fan-
fare, she thought an apology would be forthcoming, followed by an invitation to move their relationship forward.
Why go through the ruse of a romantic dinner only to break
someone's heart? It was cruel and hinted at a very dark side
of him. Frankie surmised it was probably the same woman
whose diaphragm she'd found in the linen closet and tossed
in a dumpster a few months before. As she wiped her face
and pulled herself together, she smirked at the brief sense of
satisfaction she felt at her wily behavior. Years later, she discovered Jeffrey lost his license to practice medicine. The *pièce
de résistance*. Ultimately, he'd done her an enormous favor.
Another bullet dodged.

She puckered her lips and shook off her insecurities. Giovanni would never do something so ruthless. He was a stand-
up guy and honest, sometimes to a fault. She could swear he
had some Scorpio in his chart.

Yes, he was moody lately, but who doesn't get moody from
time to time? She recognized his disappointment that she'd
made plans without discussing them with him. Not that she
needed his permission, but a conversation beforehand would
have been the polite thing to do. But she got caught up in the
excitement and gaiety of planning with her friends and made
a spontaneous decision. Amy and Nina were facing big
changes in their lives, and she'd instinctively created an occasion for them to support each other.

She decided to apologize to Giovanni again and reassure
him she would take his feelings into consideration. Plus, it
was the holidays; not only a time for festivities, but also a
time for feeling overwhelmed. The restaurant business was
always in high gear, but the holidays amplified the chaos.
She'd recently read that thirty-eight percent of people feel
more stressed during this time of year, and she counted herself as one of them. Frankie typically had a heightened sense
of empathy, so she made a mental note to be especially mind-

ful of others, and her thoughts moved back to Giovanni. The two of them were solid; that was the thought she decided to focus on for the rest of the day.

Later that evening, Frankie and Giovanni sat transfixed during the ballet. It was glorious. They held hands throughout the entire performance. Frankie couldn't help but wonder how the evening was going to end, and she tried desperately to avoid any negative thoughts. Was it going to be a remake of the Jeffrey debacle? She shivered and silently admonished herself. *Don't be a doofus. Enjoy the now.*

She muffled a squeal of delight when the orchestra began to play the "Dance of the Sugar Plum Fairy." She almost broke a few of Giovanni's fingers, she was squeezing them so tight. She glanced up at him and saw the warm smile on his face. He wasn't going to break up with her.

The production ended with a standing ovation and seven curtain calls. As they waited their turn to exit their row, Frankie was reminded of the moral of the story: *Friends do not hurt each other on purpose, confidence is key, and each of us possesses the power to make our dreams come true.* She began to sniffle. Without missing a beat, Giovanni handed her his neatly ironed handkerchief. He kissed the back of her hand. In that moment, she felt absolutely loved.

As they were leaving the theatre, everyone was buzzing about the marvelous performance. They took a taxi to 46th Street, where Lidia greeted them herself with the traditional kiss on each cheek. Frankie envied her competitors at Penguin Random House, who published Lidia's cookbooks. She would love to work with Lidia at some point in her career.

They were shown to their table in the corner, where they could view the entire restaurant and its patrons. It was the best seat in the house. The dining room was bedazzled with little white lights, beautiful garland, and arrangements made of greens and white birch. It looked like a fairyland. It was unquestionably the perfect setting after the ballet.

Frankie was impressed with the effort Giovanni had made to create an unforgettable night. She reminded herself the night wasn't over yet, and maybe there were more wonderful surprises in store. There were other diners who had also come from the Lincoln Center ballet, and the place was abuzz with excitement. It truly felt as if holiday magic was in the air.

After dinner, they rode back to Frankie's apartment, where she invited Giovanni to spend the night. She gasped when he declined. "Is everything all right?"

"Of course, *cara*. But Marco and I have much to do, and I must have some good sleep." He held her face with both hands. "This is a night I will remember in my dreams." He kissed her lips tenderly, took a slight bow, and walked to the apartment he kept on the second floor above the restaurant.

Frankie's legs were shaking. *What in the world was that?* She hurried to get the key into the main door lock and dashed up the short flight of steps to her apartment. Bandit was waiting inside the door. Frankie burst into tears. She didn't know what to make of any of it. The perfect date, and then *niente*! Nothing!

She didn't bother to remove her coat before flopping face-down on her bed. Bandit looked at his discombobulated mommy, climbed next to her, and placed his paw gently on her cheek. Frankie could not refrain from smiling.

"You are such a mush." She snuggled her face in his fur. "Don't worry. Mommy is going to be fine. For sure. Promise." Frankie could only imagine what was going through her cat's mind. *Humans are rather peculiar.*

She dragged herself off the bed, removed her coat, undressed, washed her face, and put on a pair of lush, soft pajamas. "Much better." She poured a bit of brandy and sat on the sofa. "Bandit, today I had no idea where the relationship was going, and now I am even more confused than ever." He jumped up next to her and started nudging her elbow with his head, telling her it was time for him to get a treat.

"Thanks for putting things in perspective for me." She laughed and grabbed the box of Feline Fiesta, then placed a few pieces in his bowl. When she returned to the sofa, she lifted the brandy snifter. "Cheers! Here's to the here and now!"

The next morning, she phoned Giovanni to thank him for a magnificent night. He replied with his usual, "For you? Anything."

She squinted at the phone. *What does that really mean?* After a few deep breaths, she switched gears.

"Giovanni, I want to apologize again for not talking to you before I made my holiday plans. I was caught up in the moment and excitement of talking with my friends." She paused. "I promise to be more considerate."

"Frankie, do not apologize. You are very thoughtful, and I want you to enjoy your holiday."

"And this is why I love you," Frankie replied.

Giovanni didn't respond right away, which caught Frankie by surprise. After what seemed like a millennium, he replied. "*Ci vediamo dopo. Ciao, mi amore.*"

*Mi amore* was good enough for her. And yes, she would see him later.

She was embarrassed by her ridiculous thoughts of the night before. Why were the holidays so stressful? Because people have huge expectations. Then she reminded herself about her newfound philosophy of lowering them.

Amy was southbound on the Acela from Boston to New York. She was excited about her upcoming shopping adventure with Marilyn. She still wasn't quite sure how her mother would react to Amy spending girl-time with her ex-husband's wife. Amy reminded herself that her mother was also remarried, so it shouldn't be an issue. But then again, her mother could be a little heavy-handed.

Amy consoled herself with the idea that whatever she and Marilyn decided was for Amy's own professional good. Her mother couldn't argue with that. But wait. Yes, she could. Amy pulled a book out of her tote bag and settled in for the three-and-a-half-hour train ride. *She'll get over it.*

When she arrived at Penn Station, she pulled her wheeled suitcase to the New Jersey Transit part of the station and boarded another train for Fair Lawn. The trip would add another forty minutes to her travel time, but so would driving, and she didn't want her father to wrestle with city traffic, especially during the holidays.

Radburn Station was fashioned in the Dutch Colonial Revival style of the 1800s. Throughout many renovations, it maintained its original character. As the train pulled in, Amy spotted her dad and Marilyn, who were standing at the end of the platform. It was a comedic balancing act getting off the train with her big suitcase as she waved wildly at the waiting couple. After exchanging hugs, Marilyn took a good long look at Amy. "Honey. We have some serious work ahead!"

Amy knew it wasn't meant as an affront. Had the comment come from her mother, it would have been. They kept up a lively chatter on the way home, where they immediately left William with the luggage at the front door. "See you in a few!" Marilyn blew him a kiss.

Marilyn put the pedal to the metal, and the two women were off on their shopping caper. True to Marilyn's word, Chico's had racks of interesting pieces Amy could mix and match, but her first request was for that gorgeous red jacket she'd seen on their website. Lucky for her, they had one in stock, and it was her size. Amy thought she had won the lottery! She picked out a long black skirt, black turtleneck, and a black tank top. Marilyn had to talk her out of the red pants. "Black, darling. It goes with everything." Amy also found a zebra-print jacket, a crushed green block tunic, and a black velvet kimono with purple and white floral stitching. "You gotta let me get the purple pants to go with this kimono." Amy feigned a whine.

"Only if you get the matching tee."

"Deal!" Amy felt like a kid. Never, ever had she thought she could be euphoric over clothes, especially something other than her bohemian, mismatched prints. She thought the clothes she wore conveyed her uniqueness. But so did the contents of her shopping bag.

Before they left the upscale mall, Marilyn placed her hand on Amy's arm and stopped her in her euphoric trance.

"What?" Amy turned to her fashion advisor.

Marilyn pointed down at Amy's feet. "Those clogs. Uh, no."

"Heels? Uh, no." Amy mugged.

"Don't be ridiculous. I won't wear them, either."

Amy glanced at Marilyn's shoes. Sure enough, they were short suede ankle boots with low block heels. Marilyn locked arms with Amy and steered her into Nordstrom's. The shoe department was directly inside the entrance. "They know women have a thing for shoes. That's why they display them here. You can't get past the department without walking through a display of Jimmy Choo or Tory Burch." Amy's eyes zeroed in on a pair of lug sole lace-up ankle boots with bronze eyelets.

Amy lifted the bootie from the display table. "They're chic, beautifully made, and versatile."

"I have to agree. And they are just utilitarian enough for your personal taste." Marilyn took the other shoe and walked over to a sales associate. "Do you have these in a size . . ." She looked over at Amy, who held up eight fingers. "Eight?"

"Certainly, madam. Give me one moment." The impeccably dressed young man disappeared into the back.

Amy was still eyeing the other half of the pair of boots.

She gasped at the price tag. $458.00. She quickly walked to where Marilyn was waiting. "Marilyn, these are a little out of my budget. I just blew almost a thousand dollars at Chico's. And then there's the salon thing." She took a deep breath. "Maybe these?" She was holding a pair of platform patent-leather Jon Josef penny loafers.

"Oh, Amy. Consider them your Christmas present from me and your dad."

"Really?" Amy's eyes widened. "I love these!" She held up the boots and the shoes. "And these!"

"Good, because I really don't like shopping for people unless I know exactly what they want or need."

"It's both in this case!" Amy wrestled with her shopping bags as she attempted a hug and kiss.

The sales associate returned carrying the boots. They fit Amy perfectly. "These will go with everything I bought!"

"Yes, they will." Marilyn was glad they'd found the perfect accessory to accommodate Amy's style and personality. She directed her next comment to the sales associate. "And a pair of these in size eight." She placed the loafers on the counter.

"Absolutely, madam." He briskly walked to the back again and returned with the second pair posthaste. They added one more shopping bag to their collection and headed to the mall exit.

From Short Hills, they moved on to a salon, where Amy would begin another makeover. Evian, a highly sought-after hairdresser, took one look at her, snapped his fingers, and frowned. "Sweetheart, that purple thing hanging on your head has got to go. Come with me." He took her hand and pulled her to the dressing area of the salon. Amy had a slight look of terror on her face, but Marilyn waved her on. Two hours later, Amy emerged. Her hair was a rich chestnut brown with golden highlights, and the cut was to her collarbone, with long wispy bangs to slim her round cherub face. Her makeup was subtle, with hints of a golden pink on her cheeks. Amber eyeshadow emphasized her wide hazel eyes, and a light peach lipstick gloss made the most of her pouty mouth. She looked polished, and yet, still adorable. When she saw herself in the mirror, she gasped and then giggled. "Oh, these glasses have got to go!"

There was a one-hour eyewear studio on the way home, and Marilyn stopped there without any direction from Amy. She knew exactly what was needed to finish Amy's new look. A pair of tortoise cat's-eye-shaped glasses. If they hurried, they would just have time to get back to the house, change, and arrive at the restaurant for their dinner reservation.

Amy bolted up the stairs, her shopping bags flailing against the banister. For a moment, she was befuddled as to what to wear and finally decided on the most casual of the items. When she emerged with the crushed green tunic and her new 'do and makeup, her father's eyes misted over.

"Sweetheart. You look beautiful. Sophisticated." He blinked back the tears. "Absolutely smashing."

That was probably the first time her father had ever complimented her on the way she looked. He thought it was better to hold his tongue and let her be kooky and brainy. But now he fully appreciated the woman she had become.

The next unveiling of the new Amy would be when she saw her mother on Christmas Day. A queasy feeling came over her as she rang the doorbell. *What would her mother think? What would she say?* At first, her mother stared at her blankly, as if she didn't recognize who it was. Then the answer came quickly. "Amy! My goodness!" She hugged Amy, then set her at arm's length. "You look marvelous! I am so glad you took my advice after all these years!"

Amy stifled a laugh. Of course her mother would take all the credit. *Duh.*

*    *    *

Nina's parents were up from Florida for the holidays. They were the quintessential "snowbirds" flying south for the winter and north for the summer months, but always returned to New Jersey to celebrate the holidays with friends and relatives. Her mother arranged for a professional decorator to adorn the house with lights, poinsettias, garland, and three Christmas trees. Their social calendar was packed with dinner parties, cocktail parties, luncheons, and whatever other reason anyone had to eat, drink, and be merry. In the past, they would celebrate at the country club, but with most of their time spent in Florida now, the Hunters had given up their club membership and opted for a New Year's celebration at home with approximately fifty-plus guests. It would be catered, with two bartenders and a waitstaff. Nina's mother frequently went over-the-top when it came to entertaining. She, too, had dipped her toe in show business years before Nina was born, but gave it up to be wife to the chief of surgery at a highly accredited hospital. When Nina's father wasn't working, he was noodling around the house, relieving his stress with landscaping. One summer, he roped in Nina and her brother to help lay bricks for a huge outdoor patio that would serve as their summer entertainment space.

Nina thought it was also her father's way of avoiding attending the many social events Nina's mom had on her calendar.

Nina stayed in town and anxiously attended the festivities, dreading the usual cocktail conversation that included questions like, "How are things in Hollywood?" Didn't her parents' friends remember she'd moved back two years ago? Or "How come we don't see your pretty face on TV?" Didn't they remember she had been writing for television? Then there was her favorite, "When are you going to star in your own show?" Her response would be "I prefer being behind the camera. You age better that way." She'd smile and see if the lightbulb went off in their heads, but usually was met with a vacuous stare.

Her face hurt from all the fake smiling, something she had mastered during her tenure in Tinseltown. Even though she imagined her future was a black hole, she embraced her upcoming trip and the opportunity to get out from under the starstruck scrutiny of her parents and their acquaintances. She hadn't told them exactly why she was going to California. "Business." Period.

Rachael was in a foul mood. Her ex-husband Greg had decided to take their son Ryan to Vermont to visit his wife Vicki's parents. Even though the agreement was to alternate visitation during the holidays, she was still annoyed. It seemed as if everything annoyed Rachael right now. Maybe she should go to Lake Tahoe and try to hit the reset button on her life. Maybe being with friends would give her the boost she needed. Maybe Frankie would apologize for being insensitive. Maybe she would give it some serious thought.

She re-read the email she'd received from Nina and Amy, who'd signed Frankie's name. She pursed her lips and shrugged. Maybe she would.

> We're *all* going to Tahoe. Meet up with us on the 28th at La Spa Resort in South Lake Tahoe. Amy, Nina, Frankie

She paced the floor, rearranged books, moved the ottoman from one side of the sofa to the other. Finally she went to her desk, opened her laptop, and typed in *Flights from Newark to Reno*. Newark was the closest to where she lived, but there were no direct flights. She would have to leave out of JFK, a miserable one-hour trip. With no traffic. *As if*. The entire idea was quickly getting on her nerves. She became more perturbed when she discovered the only nonstop flight back was at 7:45 in the evening, arriving at 9:45 the next morning. "Great. The red-eye.

"Okay. So I get to Reno, and then what?" She was speaking to no one as she clicked away on her keyboard. According to Google Maps, it was about a ninety-minute drive from Reno to South Lake Tahoe, which meant taking a jitney or renting a car. She let out a groan. "Why couldn't they find a place in Incline Village? That's only an hour away from Reno. I'll bet Frankie made the arrangements," she grumbled, and her annoyance with Frankie intensified. "Why did she have to make this trip one huge inconvenience?" She growled and slammed the laptop shut. She sat back and folded her arms. "I'll show her!"

Christmas Eve festivities were in full swing at Marco's, where Frankie had reestablished her job from childhood—setting the table. It was configured in a large square surrounded by twelve chairs, three on each side. The setup made it easier for people to converse and also to pass the pasta. Frankie summoned her recently found talent at making artificial flower arrangements and created a centerpiece using a variety of short vases, in different shapes and sizes, clustered together. At the end of the evening, the guests could take home a paper flower as a party favor.

Each year, Marco and Giovanni would debate whether or not they should close the restaurant to the public. Rarely did either of them have an opportunity to enjoy a relaxing dinner with the family. They also reminded each other that a lot of people didn't have family around, and the restaurant was a haven for such folks. In fact, that was how Frankie became part of their "framily." So they compromised.

With the guidance of Frankie, they divided part of the dining room with artificial trees adorned with tiny white lights. It looked like an enchanted forest. The shimmering foliage barrier provided privacy without being confining, creating a mesmerizing atmosphere for everyone, whether they were family, framily, or customers.

Marco's wife, Anita, was in charge of the music. She found three hours of holiday tunes by the New York Jazz Lounge. It was a delightful departure from the typical songs that had been playing everywhere for the past six weeks. By Christmas, people were praying Frosty would finally melt, Rudolph would move to Florida, and Santa Claus Lane would be closed for repaving.

The two brothers promised they would take the evening off, sit with the family, and enjoy their dinner. Unless there was an emergency, no one was allowed to leave the table, except, of course, for a potty break. Even cellphones were to be deposited in a basket set on one of the sideboards. This was family-framily time. All the important people were right here.

Marco and Giovanni asked for volunteers to work Christmas Eve. No one was required to give up their holiday, but whoever agreed would get an extra two hundred dollars. It was no big surprise when more than enough employees stepped forward. One of the hostesses offered to babysit Marco and Anita's children if the rate was the same.

Marco and Giovanni's mother, Michelina, was visiting from Italy. The kids called her "Nona," and she spoiled them rotten. She visited them twice a year and thought it was her right to do whatever they or she wanted. No one was going to argue with Nona. With the usual excitement about Santa's arrival and Nona's doting, the pandemonium was in overdrive. The beleaguered parents wondered if two hundred dollars would be enough; maybe a big tip would be in order. It would depend on how the evening unfolded.

Friends and relatives began arriving at the enchanting dining room, expressing their utter delight. Frankie's mother Julia and her father Anthony took a car service from New

Jersey, while Anita's parents, Leonardo and Maria, drove from Queens with Anita's brother Lorenzo and his wife Sophia. Against the advice of his nephews, Uncle Ralph took the bus in from Jersey City. Even though he'd spent the past fifty years in New Jersey, Uncle Ralph still had not mastered the English language. His buoyant personality, his laugh, and his often-mispronounced English brought guffaws and much laughter.

It took almost a half hour for everyone to finish their *hellos*, well-wishes, and compliments. Anita's calligraphy graced the place cards; she'd taken care to arrange the seating so the noise level would be balanced around the table.

Michelina said grace in Italian, and Uncle Ralph made a toast in broken English. "Health to those I love and wealth to those who love me! Cin-cin!"

Frankie almost spat out her drink. She had never heard that particular salutation before. Not the first half, anyway.

They began with the traditional hot antipasto of clams oreganata, eggplant rollatini, and mussels fra diavolo. The second course of grilled calamari salad followed. A brief interlude of chatting and catching up was necessary to make room for the linguine fruitti de mare and more fish. Another short respite was on the agenda before the main course of lobster topped with seared scallops. One more belly break, and then the waiters brought a parade of assorted desserts, including Anita's olive oil cake, pastries, cappuccino, espresso, sambuca, and anisette. The entire meal took over three hours to consume, which was exactly how it should be. It was a time to share food, laughter, and stories with the people you loved.

Frankie steered clear of any discussions involving the rest of the holidays and was relieved no one asked when she and Giovanni were going to take the next step. It might have been on a few people's minds, but everyone had enough decorum and respect to avoid the matter. She prompted Uncle Ralph to talk about how the family came to America, smuggling their jewelry or what little gold they possessed in the linings of their clothing. He winked at Frankie. "How-a-you suppose I learn to sew?" Even their socks and shoes carried what they could manage. He teased Michelina about not having extra room in her brassiere for anything else except her ample bust. Then she said a few things in Italian that only a few at the table could understand. But by the hysterical reaction, it must have been a doozie. Frankie couldn't help but laugh along with the rest of them, even though she had no clue what had been said. It was in Michelina's delivery, and the subsequent laughter was infectious.

The subject turned to Santa and what he was going to deliver to the kids. When it came to gift-giving, Frankie's family had decided to start a new tradition. Rather than spending money on each other, they made donations to their favorite charities instead. Marco and Giovanni's family also agreed to limit their spending on each other and focus on the children. While Santa usually fulfilled their Christmas Wish List, money from their parents, Nona, and Uncle Ralph was put into a fund for their future. Nona would smile, shrug, and say "*Tradizione!*"

Uncle Ralph had worked as a tailor for fifty years, making custom suits for the Wall Street hucksters. Most of them were thousands upon thousands of dollars. For men at a certain financial level, designer suits were too ordinary. One-of-a-kind, custom made with the finest cloth, was how they rolled. It wasn't necessary for him to have a vast English vocabulary to understand what they wanted. He never married, so he enjoyed sharing his *abbondanza* with the family and always managed to slip an envelope with a few hundred-dollar bills into Marco and Giovanni's pockets. Generosity was a family trait, as was integrity, responsibility, loyalty, and kindness.

A few yawns and stretches were the signal dinner was winding down. Lots of good food, wine, and laughs could be exhausting.

As Frankie surveyed the room, it dawned on her that Giovanni's hesitance—if that's what it was—had something to do with his failed engagement. It had only been two years since the breakup. It took longer for some to bounce back than others. Frankie never wallowed in her disastrous relationships. No, not her. She would move on to the next one as quickly as possible. Then her work took over for a few years until she was able to strike a life balance with Giovanni. Her heart was full. And so was her stomach.

# Chapter Eight

*On the Way to Tahoe*

The day after Christmas, Nina chose a heather-gray casual tracksuit with a hoodie. She applied minimal makeup, wrapped a scarf around her collar, and tucked her signature curls into a hat. No glam for this girl today. Invariably, someone would recognize her and ask for an autograph, but her plan was to masquerade as a tourist. She boarded the flight to Los Angeles with trepidation. She never had anxiety about flying, but this time it was different. She was winging her way into the unknown. Well, some of it was known. She was being fired without actually being fired. She was being canceled. Same thing in her mind.

The plan was to spend two days in LA and then drive to Tahoe to meet up with the girls on the twenty-eighth. Then the three—maybe four, if Rachael showed up—would fly back to the East Coast together on the second of January. She still had no idea what she was going to do after the show ended, so she decided to adopt Frankie's attitude: *What will be will be. The universe will unfold as it should.* They had a deep conversation and debates about positive thinking and letting it be. Could she do both? Throughout her career, it was always one door closing and another opening. She had faith this would be the case again.

The flight was uneventful and landed in LA around noon Pacific time. She followed the crowd to baggage claim, where she waited patiently at the carousel. She recognized a few people but maintained her low profile, staring at the suit-cases popping up and over into the metal merry-go-round. She spotted her bag a couple of yards away but waited until it was directly in front of her. The less commotion, the better. She heaved it off the moving platform and advanced to the car rental area. As she waited for the sluggish line to move, she kept her nose down, pretending to read a magazine.

She thought she heard someone call out her name, but she ignored it. She heard it again but still made no move to ac-knowledge the speaker. Relief filled her mind as she stepped up to the counter. "Hi." Nina slid her driver's license and credit card through the opening in the Plexiglas divider. She hoped that would keep her from having to say her name out loud. The woman on the other side of the protector gave her a knowing look, something she was accustomed to on a daily basis. Not every actor could afford a private jet. Most had to travel with regular folks and go through regular channels.

The rental agent slid the keys through the slot. "The car rental stand is outside to the left." She smiled. "Have a good day."

"You too." Nina smiled. She appreciated the woman's dis-cretion and proceeded to exit the building. They say the sense of smell awakens memory, and now glimmers from the past swept through her mind. It seemed that it was only yesterday when she first landed in Los Angeles, fifteen years ago. It was as if a movie in fast forward was playing in her head as mixed emotions streamed through her psyche. Reality was beginning to set in. Would this be the end, or a new beginning? Once again, she chose to stay positive. It was the only way one could manifest a happy outcome. At least that's what she'd read many times over, and Frankie was constantly whacking her over the head about the same concept. Nina chuckled to herself. *That may be an oxymoron of sorts. Beating spiritual sense into someone? Is that even possible?*

Before she hoisted her suitcase into the back of the SUV, she checked to see if the vehicle had the moonroof she'd requested. One cannot drive into the Sierra Mountains without having a rooftop opening in order to inhale the glorious clean air.

Even though she knew her way around LA, she always used GPS. You never knew when you would have to find your way around traffic, but it turned out to be most of the time. Her agent's office was in Century City, so she'd booked a room at the Fairmont Century Plaza on Avenue of the Stars. It was truly a different world from the rest of civilization. Did the pioneers of film ever envision Hollywood becoming the spectacle it now was? Originality was left to the few, while imitation was bought by the many. Nina was an artist, an actress, and a writer. She had talent, yet it was a roller-coaster ride industry. If you were looking for stability, this was certainly not the place.

Long gone were the days of the studio system, where the producers and distributors signed multiple movie deals with actors and dictated salaries. The studios had argued that the contracts should favor them because they were taking all the risks. But in 1919, in order to take control of their own interests, Charlie Chaplin, D.W. Griffith, Mary Pickford, and Douglas Fairbanks started their own company, United Artists. From that revolt came the now often-used phrase, "The inmates are running the asylum." Over the years, United Artists was bought by MGM, sold, and bought again. It was a volatile industry, with only a handful of people running everything. Not much had changed. It was still only a handful of people. They simply had different faces.

Nina often thought about getting off the hamster wheel of entertainment, but if you were creative, it was difficult to disengage yourself from the capricious business that could give you the opportunity to shine. *Maybe that's why they were called "stars."* She snickered.

She plugged the address into the GPS, which was taking her on the 405, best known for its notorious traffic jams. She checked the time. Just after 1:00. Shouldn't be too bad. Within forty minutes, she was at the hotel. After she checked in, she called room service and ordered lunch. Nina was not ready to run into anyone she knew, not until after her meeting with her agent. Who knew; maybe she would have some good news for Nina.

She called her folks to let them know she'd arrived okay and sent a text to Amy to see if there were any updates from Rachael. So far, nothing. Another question mark in the mix. Nina thought maybe Mercury was in retrograde, causing communication breakdowns. She'd check with Frankie, who stayed on top of such things. Nina considered herself a spiritual person, but all the Astro-babble was over her head. Frankie was good at translating.

After she went through her emails and notes on the final season, it was almost dinnertime. She was still undecided about going out in public. Room service again? Nah. Why should she let her insecurities keep her from dining at Lumiere? She shook off the dreads, changed into something more dinner-appropriate, and braved the world below. On the ride down in the elevator, it occurred to her it was the week between Christmas and New Year's Eve. Very few people would be around. She was relatively sure she could have dinner without being ogled or questioned.

The hostess smiled, as if she recognized Nina. Nina smiled

back. Unless you were a tourist, you knew not to approach anyone who was even slightly famous. Almost every high-profile restaurant had extra security for such encounters. Stars deserved their privacy, even if the public disagreed.

Nina peered from behind her menu and noted there wasn't anyone she knew in the dining room. And if a fan recognized her, they wouldn't be asking her what she was doing in LA. Across the room, a well-dressed, middle-aged male was sitting alone. He gave her a nod, and Nina gave a little finger wave. She held her breath, wondering if he was going to approach her. *Why was she such a hot mess? Because her life was in limbo, that's why.* She sipped her martini slowly and let the alcohol soothe her nerves. One drink was enough if you lingered over it. When she finished dinner, she decided to walk over to the table where the gentleman was sitting. Maybe he knew her; she didn't want to be rude.

"Hello. I'm Nina Hunter." She held out her hand.

"Yes, I thought I recognized you." He had a strong baritone voice. "Michael Powell. Would like to join me for an after-dinner drink?"

Nina was flustered. She couldn't remember the last time a stranger had asked her to have a drink. She thought of Richard. It was only a drink, and she had no place to go. "Yes. Thank you." He stood and pulled out a chair for her.

"What would you like?" he asked.

"Cognac, please."

He gestured for the waiter and ordered two Rémy Martins.

"I would ask what brings you to LA at this time of year, but you are in the business, so that would be the obvious answer."

Nina grinned. "Yes. Yes, it would. So what brings *you* to LA?"

"Visiting family, but I prefer to stay at a hotel. That way I can do things on my own schedule. Don't misunderstand me. I love my grandchildren, but I am not a morning person, and jumping on Grandpa at six a.m. is not my thing."

Nina laughed at his honesty. "How long are you in town?" Small talk with a stranger was refreshing.

"Just a few more days."

"So, Michael Powell, you know what I do for a living. What is your area of expertise?"

"I own several radio stations," he said humbly.

"So you *are* in the biz." Nina gave him a sideways look.

"I guess you could say that. But it's more financial management than talent."

"That's important. Without it, no one would get paid," Nina added.

"Good point." He hesitated for a moment. "I know this may be presumptuous of me, but do you ever do any radio?"

"Radio?" Nina asked. "What kind of radio?"

"Talk radio. I have an open slot, and I am trying to figure out what I can fill it with. I am sure you have a tight schedule, but I need some outside advice."

Nina pursed her lips. "What time does it run?"

"Any time I want it to." He smiled.

"Right. You're the boss." Nina sipped the smooth, mellow libation. "Do you have any particular subject in mind?"

"I do, but it's kind of old-timey."

"They say what was old is new again." Nina felt the warmth of the cognac coursing through her veins.

"I tell you what. I know you are a highly creative individual. You're both an accomplished actress and writer."

Nina flinched. "You're familiar with my writing?"

"I'm in the biz." He smiled and handed her his card. "I'd like to hear some ideas if you're willing to mull it over. And if you have the time. Of course, I'd pay you a consulting fee."

"Sounds interesting." Nina took his card. "I certainly will give it some thought."

They finished their drinks and walked to the elevator together. They said goodnight and shook hands when the car stopped at his floor. "I look forward to hearing from you. Enjoy your stay."

"Yes. Thank you. You do the same." She was relieved there was nothing romantic or sexual about this encounter. A friendly drink with a nice businessman. When the elevator arrived at her floor, she had an illuminating moment. One door closes, another door opens. *Just goes to show you, you never know.*

For the first time in years, Amy was able to spend the holiday with both her father and her mother and their respective spouses. No arguing or competing for her attention, or negative comments about the exes. It was a joyful experience— such a novelty. What was more shocking was the brunch the five of them had together. Perhaps the grown-ups had come to the realization they were happy, and there was no longer a need to complain or be spiteful. Now she understood what Christmas must be like for Frankie. With the exception of the menus, the date and time, the warm feelings of family were the same. Even her mother's sense of humor returned. It was refreshing. A Christmas miracle!

Amy's dad insisted on driving her to Newark Airport, since it was less than an hour away. Because of the limited flights to and from Reno, Amy and Nina had decided to get a car service when they returned to JFK and spare their loved ones the grueling traffic through Queens. Frankie would take a taxi, in spite of Giovanni's insistence on picking her up. Asking someone to take you to or pick you up from Kennedy Airport was akin to asking someone to help you move.

"You ready for this, sweetie?" Amy's dad glanced at his daughter.

"I'm a little nervous."

"About flying?"

"No. Just the whole thing. I already know I'm not going to take the offer. But what if I slip up somehow?"

"What do you mean?"

"I dunno." She shrugged.

"You will be fine. Just listen to what they have to say. Nod and reply with 'that sounds quite interesting.' "

Amy mimicked his advice and nodded. "That sounds rather interesting. *Rather* is a better word for me." She chuckled.

"Atta girl. You know, I am enormously proud of you. I probably don't say it enough."

"Sure you do, Dad. You've always been my greatest advocate. You never pushed me in the wrong direction, like so many other parents do."

"You mean like your mother?" He chuckled.

"I was wondering how long it was going to take for you to besmirch dear Mother," Amy teased.

William laughed. "She's the one who wanted you to become a doctor."

"Well, she can still say 'my daughter, the doctor,' but she won't, because people will ask her where I practice and my area of specialization. Then she has to explain I'm not a *doctor*-doctor."

"Don't kid yourself, kiddo. She is proud of you. There aren't many people who are biochemical engineers, let alone women."

"True, but she never says anything to me about my career. She spends too much time hinting at grandchildren. She talks about her friend's 'grandbabies' as if she was honestly interested in them."

"Does she really use the word *grandbabies*?"

"Yes. It is so annoying." They looked at each other and burst out laughing.

"I promise I will never use that word." He exited the parkway at I-78 East. "And I will never pressure you to have kids. Or get married, either. What makes you happy, makes me happy." He reached over and patted her knee.

"Same here, Dad. I'm happy you met Marilyn. You seem well-suited." She began to blush. "And sorry for stalking the two of you when we were on the cruise." She snickered. "Well, we weren't actually stalking you, personally. We wanted to know who the lothario was who had captivated our new friend."

"Lothario?" He blanched.

"Had I known it was you, dear Daddy, we wouldn't have made a spectacle of ourselves falling over the lounge chairs."

"That was rather funny." William smiled, recalling how they'd discovered they were both on the same ship. Amy and Frankie followed Marilyn to her rendezvous with a mysterious stranger, only to realize it was Amy's dad.

"You could have told me, you know."

"You could have told me, too." He turned his head to look at her. "You know!"

Both chuckled. They were approaching the airport service roads. "This is so confusing," Amy said as she tried to focus on which airline was at which terminal.

"I got it covered." They moved through the traffic and he took her to the departing flights entrance. Cars, vans, people, luggage. It was chaos. It was the day after Christmas. Her father flagged down a skycap and Amy checked her suitcase at the curb. The only thing she carried was a tote bag with her laptop, a book, and a pair of slippers. She liked to take off her shoes when she was on a flight for more than four hours, but she didn't want to be walking around in her socks.

William gave his daughter a hug. "Good luck, sweetheart. See you when you get back."

"Thanks, Pops. I'll call when I land."

When they were making travel plans, Amy realized it would take almost twelve hours to fly from Reno to Boston, because there were no nonstop flights. She decided to fly back with Frankie and Nina instead, spend another day or two with her parents, and then take the train back to Boston. Travel time was about the same when she added it all up, but the thought of being on a plane for that length of time held no appeal. It was too confining.

The airport was a sea of travelers with backpacks, rolling suitcases, duffel bags, strollers, tennis rackets, and golf clubs. She reminded herself it was one of the busiest travel days of the year. *Go with the flow and hope it keeps moving.* The security checkpoint was pandemonium. She had TSA clearance, but it seemed that everyone else did, too. People were fumbling with their shoes, their laptops, and their water bottles, which were not allowed. *Go through the metal detector. Beep! Beep!* Someone forgot to tell the agent they had titanium prosthetics. Back through the metal detector. More beeping. When the agent put the handheld screening device next to the person's hips, he asked, "Sir, have you had hip replacement?"

The passenger sheepishly replied, "Sorry, I've had the prosthesis for ten years and never think about it." Groans echoed through the massive line. The passenger was then sent to the body scanner. More moans and groans as the plastic buckets were jammed with everything people tried to take aboard. One numbskull had a Swiss Army knife; another had a corkscrew.

Amy closed her eyes. *I'm surrounded by idiots,* she thought to herself. She was glad she'd opted to travel in a pair of loafers. It would have taken much longer to unlace and lace her new boots, which could have caused a riot with this particular mob of fidgety, cranky travelers. *What? They didn't get what they wanted from Santa?* She wanted to make an announcement: "Listen, folks, we're all in this together. Sorry if you got coal in your stocking and were forced to have dinner with people you either don't like or don't know. Try to feel some gratitude for what you do have. Suck it up, buttercup." But she thought better of it.

These people didn't look like they were in the mood for anything but getting on the plane, jamming their overpacked luggage into an overhead bin, and climbing over someone to get to their seat. Come to think of it, that's probably why they were in crabby moods. Aside from turbulence, boarding and deplaning was probably the worst part of the flight. In-variably half the passengers would have more baggage than they were allowed and would have to check one of their items at the gate, creating a human traffic jam in the line.

The flight attendants were assisting as much as they could and as quickly as they could. With the thousands of flights in and out of the three metropolitan airports, it was crucial for the plane to be ready when the tower gave them the clearance for takeoff. Amy admired anyone who could manage as a flight attendant the day after Christmas. Stanford was cover-ing the cost of her flight, but she paid for the upgrade to first class. Because she was one of the first to board, she watched the faces of the other passengers as they moved into the rear section of the plane. Some looked back with disdain, while others seemed to think they might spy someone famous.

The flight attendants made an announcement, practically begging people to secure their belongings and find their seat. Amy was wondering when the population became so dense. Not just in size, but in thought. She swore someone was handing out Stupid Pills. Granted, she was a brainiac, but it didn't take an IQ of 160 to figure out how to pack, board, sit, and fasten your seat belt. She might be a space cadet when it came to many things, but these were simple tasks.

Common sense was no longer common. It gave her a new appreciation for her world of academia. She knew she was being a bit of an intellectual snob, but please, people! She laughed, thinking about Nina calling her the absent-minded professor, but at least she knew how to follow directions.

The first-class flight attendant approached her and asked if she would care for something to drink. Amy mulled it over. It was noon, the flight was long, and she was a bit anxious. "Bloody Mary, please." She got a little thrill. Amy wasn't much of a drinker. Sometimes wine with dinner or an occasional cocktail, so this was a rarity for her. And it made her feel special.

She rifled through her tote bag before she had to stow it under her seat and came across the lengthy receipt from Chico's at the bottom of her bag. She squinted and blinked. Then she held it up to the small light above her head when she realized it had been charged to someone else's credit card! Marilyn! She must have slipped it to the cashier while Amy was in the dressing room. Amy was overcome with gratitude. As the flight attendant returned with her cocktail, she noticed Amy's face was flushed.

"Everything all right?"

"Couldn't be better." Amy sniffed and gladly took the drink from the woman's hand. Another Christmas miracle. So far, this holiday was the best ever, and there was so much more ahead.

They were due to take off in a few minutes. She was seated next to the window and wondered if the passenger next to her would arrive. As quickly as that thought crossed her mind, a man who appeared to be in his seventies smiled, removed his coat, placed it on his lap, and settled into the seat. The attendant quickly took it and hung it in a closet next to the aircraft door. When he introduced himself, Amy was elated to be sitting next to a well-known professor at Princeton University. He was astonished Amy knew who he was, and they began a conversation that lasted almost the entire flight.

Just before they landed in San Francisco, they exchanged business cards. You never know when you'll need the advice of a neuroscientist.

Amy waited patiently at the baggage claim. Again she noted the sea of sloppily dressed people. Was it the aftermath of COVID or just that people didn't care anymore? Or maybe they didn't have full-length mirrors at home. She knew her fashion sense was a little funky and often mismatched, but it was a "look," and her clothes weren't stained with who-knows-what-is-on-that-man's-T-shirt? She cringed. She figured if you could afford an airline ticket to San Francisco, you should be able to afford laundry detergent. She then realized she was beginning to sound like her mother! They say that's who we turn into as we get older. She made a mental note to keep herself in check.

She managed to find her way to the car rental and made the thirty-minute drive to Palo Alto, where the committee had made a reservation for her at the Westin Hotel. Like Nina, she found the smell of the air brought back memories. Admittedly, she missed the Northern California landscape and the proximity to some of the most breathtaking sights in the U.S., especially the coastline of Monterey and the Sierra Nevada Mountains, which were within a few hours' drive of the city. Yes, it was absolutely beautiful, but she refused to let the landscape hypnotize her into changing her mind. Besides, she was going to another beautiful spot in two days.

She phoned both her parents to let them know where she was staying and whom she'd met on the plane. Her mother was not impressed. Had it been Clint Eastwood, for sure, but he'd probably travel on a private jet. Conversely, her father was delighted she'd found a like-minded traveler. Truth be told, Amy's father was delighted whenever he could hear the glee in his daughter's voice.

Before her trip, Amy had rung up two former colleagues and arranged to meet them for dinner. She reminded herself to be vague. She didn't want them to know she had already made up her mind about the job. Then it dawned on her that Stanford hadn't exactly offered it to her yet, although at this stage, it appeared to be a fait accompli and just a matter of hammering out the details. At least she wasn't anxious about the interview anymore. Whether they did or didn't offer her the job was of no consequence at this point.

Amy arrived at Evvia Estiatorio, a wonderful Greek restaurant she used to frequent. Dinner was lively with conversations veering from one subject to another, while Amy carefully avoided details about her "interview."

She had pangs of guilt when her friends expressed excitement over the possibility of her returning to the area. She just said sweetly, "We'll see what happens." They wrapped up their meal as the jet lag was descending upon her circadian rhythm. According to her body clock, it was well past midnight. She bade them farewell and promised to update them as soon as she had information. More guilt, but not that much.

The faculty members with whom she was to meet had emailed her itinerary. She was instructed to stop at the Visitor's Center the following morning to get her electronic pass. As with most colleges and universities, security was a priority. Gone were the days when coming and going was as casual as taking a walk. She drove to the Biochemical Genetics Lab, where she was introduced to a small group of professors, adjunct professors, and an associate. The tour of the building and its many departments took over an hour. From there, they took her on a general tour of the campus, including the Arts District and the museums. They wanted her to be enveloped by the atmosphere of Stanford. On that particular day, an exhibit of over one hundred sculptures by Auguste Rodin was on display. It was magnificent. The sculptor's ability to express the many human emotions in bronze was breathtaking and evoked a reaction in anyone who had the opportunity to get up close and personal with his achievements. His most famous work, *The Thinker*, was world-renowned.

Amy's thoughts were teetering. The sheer size of Stanford was astounding compared to MIT. Stanford boasted over 8,000 acres, while MIT was a mere 168, yet MIT produced more Nobel laureates than Stanford. Another proof that size doesn't always matter. By the end of the morning, Amy's head was spinning, which helped seal her decision. Stanford was just too big for her. But she wasn't about to tell them yet. After lunch, they were to meet again to discuss the position they had in mind for her. This morning was just a "getting to know you" tour.

In typical fashion, Rachael stomped around her house as if she were putting out a fire. The entire world was against her. Her friends, her clients, her son, her parents, her romantic partner.

Ryan didn't have to go to Vermont. It was her turn to have him for the holidays. Just because Greg's family had rented a five-bedroom chalet and he'd be with his cousins didn't mean he should have abandoned his mother. And her lover, Henry? What was his problem lately? He hardly ever touched her and was spending long, late hours in Manhattan.

Another thing that was bothering her was why he'd decided not to go on their annual cruise this year. It was the first one in two years, and yet he'd declined. That was not like him. Something was up, and she was going to find out. Maybe a little trip away from Henry would make him jealous. But first, she begrudgingly made her reservations to fly to Reno and arranged for a car service to take her to the airport. She realized there was no one she could depend on to drive her there.

Then there was her clientele, which had trickled down to intermittent drips. The pandemic had wreaked havoc on her dance studio, and she'd been forced to sell the building. At least she made a profit on the property, but she had much too much time on her hands, and it was weighing heavily on her.

On the surface, Rachael was self-centered, but it was her deeply held secret insecurity she was protecting. She truly felt alone and unloved, but then, like a light switch, her mood shifted. She was going to have a face-off with Frankie and drive Henry crazy in the process. Life was looking a little more exciting for the petite, abandoned Rachael.

By the time Amy sat down at a large conference table in a meeting room with two professors, she was more sure than ever of what she would say to them. One handed her a folder with her name printed on the cover:

AMY BLANCHARD, Ph.D.
**PROPOSAL**
PROFESSOR
DEPARTMENT OF BIOCHEMICS
STANFORD UNIVERSITY

Her hands were shaking. Her palms were sweating, and her right knee was bobbing at a rapid pace. It might have registered on the Richter scale. She knew the color was fading from her face. She looked down at the proposal and then looked both of them in the eye. "Would you mind if I had some time alone to peruse this?" It was astonishing she could articulate a complete sentence.

The man and woman sitting in front of her were taken by surprise. Most candidates reached for the papers at the speed of light. They nodded at each other. The woman spoke first and rose from her chair. "Of course. Take your time. We understand it's a big decision."

The gentleman next to her stood. "Half hour enough to review? We can go over all the points one by one later or tomorrow."

Amy looked up. "Half hour should be fine. Thank you." She waited until they were out of the room before she opened it. The first two pages were descriptions of her responsibilities, the number of classes she'd undertake, dissertations, essays, off-campus activities. It was a massive amount of work. When she got to the third page, she saw why. The compensation package was worth over $185,000, over $20,000 more than she was making now. But surely that increase wasn't enough to uproot her life, considering the cost of living in Palo Alto was 185% more than Boston. One needn't be a physicist to understand the ratio was not in her favor: 10% raise to a 185% increase in overhead. These people needed to bone up on their math skills. She was relieved she had already made up her mind before she got on the plane.

But what bargaining chip could she use in her favor at MIT? Telling them she'd been offered a $20,000 increase wouldn't make them blink. They were no dummies. If Stanford was all that and a bag of chips, her superiors would have been on the California train long ago.

Amy started at the beginning. Was there anything in the job description she could dangle in front of MIT? She wasn't required to tell them the salary, but she could mention an increase. Then she spotted a paragraph that would allow her a stipend to pursue research of her own choosing. Amy let out a big huff of air. When the two professors returned, they had big smiles on their faces, anticipating an eager new member of their faculty.

The woman sat across from her. "So, Amy, what do you think of our proposal?"

"It's very comprehensive and very appealing. But to be honest, I can't make a final decision today. There is much to consider, as you well know." Amy was cooking. "If you would allow me a week or so to consider, it would be most appreciated."

The two professors looked at each other; then the woman spoke. "Do you have any questions we can discuss now?"

Amy didn't like her pushiness. "No. As I said, I need time to thoroughly review and will compile my questions accordingly." She smiled what could have been interpreted as a smirk.

"Of course, Amy. You do realize we need to fill this position before the spring semester is over? We must plan class schedules. You understand."

"Of course. I can assure you that you will hear from me by the fifth of January. Is that acceptable?"

They nodded in agreement. The two walked Amy to the main door and shook hands. Amy knew she wasn't going to be seeing them again any time soon.

The Uber driver seemed to be taking every road less traveled to JFK Airport. Rachael kept bombarding him with "Where are you going?" each time he turned onto another road or highway. He tried to explain in an accent Rachael did not understand that he was avoiding traffic and kept pointing to his GPS. Rachael finally gave up being a backseat driver and huffed the remainder of the drive. It was hard to guess who was more relieved when they arrived at the airport. One thing was certain, the driver wasn't giving Rachael four stars. If he could give none, he would. And she felt the same way.

The driver heaved her thirty-plus-pound suitcase from the trunk of his car and set it on the curb. He tried to give Rachael a hand getting out of the vehicle, but she practically smacked it away. "I can get out on my own. I'm not feeble!" She was in a frenzy, all right. The crowd for a skycap was chaotic, so she decided to drag her belongings into the terminal and check in at the counter.

She wheeled her shiny red suitcase through a mob of confused travelers, weaving in and out of heaps of luggage until she could find where the line ended. It snaked around over a dozen times, with airport personnel checking for misguided travelers. She huffed several times until the person in front of her turned, smiled, and looked down. "Don't hyperventilate. If you faint, no one will be able to find you." Rachael finally laughed out loud for the first time in who knows when. The guy had a point.

She removed her coat in the tightly packed line of passengers. *Whose idea was this? Oh yeah, Frankie.* Deep down, she knew her anger at her friend was seriously exaggerated, and probably misplaced. Frankie's biggest sin was calling her out on her voice-mail dump and making a sarcastic remark about needing an appointment. Did that really justify all these negative thoughts? Certainly, the issues with Henry added to her angst. The man in front of her turned around again to see if she was still vertical. "You okay?"

"Just dandy." The kindness of a total stranger tempered her anger. It dawned on her that everyone was feeling the same overburdened, underappreciated mania of the season. The line started to move slowly, and she finally arrived at the counter. The airline representative was pleasant and attempted some small talk as he checked her luggage and handed her the tag.

"Enjoy your trip to Reno," he said.

"Uh, that would be a big no-thank-you. I'm only landing there and then going on to Lake Tahoe."

"Good choice." The young man smiled. "Next in line, please."

Liberated from her bulky suitcase, she was able to wiggle through the crowd and on to security check. When she was in high school and college, Rachael traveled the world. She remembered it wasn't such a hassle back then. Now it was shoes off, bags in buckets, and through the metal detector. Finally, the worst part was over, and she could grab a cup of coffee on her way to the gate.

She couldn't help noticing young lovers hugging and kissing. Funny, you didn't usually see that with people over forty. Not that she was a fan of public displays of affection, but it said something about love and attraction. She wondered how many of her peers still found their spouses or mates desirable. For Rachael, chemistry was vital, and it was obvious Henry no longer found her alluring. And that was the crux of her ire. She did not want to feel unappealing. Her sexuality was an important component of her being. She was not going to let Henry's lack of interest make her feel unwanted. Regardless of what Henry was up to, she was going to enjoy herself. Maybe being with friends could help her shift gears from fury to composure. Well, maybe it wouldn't have *that* drastic an effect, but at the very least, this trip might throw a bucket of water on her fiery feelings. She knew she was spinning out of control. Perhaps it was raging hormones. Frankie once told her she could always tell when Rachael was premenstrual, although it seemed as if that was a permanent state lately. If nothing else, she would do as much skiing as possible.

After she landed in Reno, she took a shuttle to South Lake Tahoe instead of renting a car. Even though the roads were wide, they were winding their way up through the Sierra Nevada Mountains. Going up wasn't as terrifying as going down. The first and last time she drove that route, she thought she would go right off the edge. Driving downhill and navigating all the twists had been so unnerving, she broke out into a sweat. She'd held her phone up to take a photo of the last thing she saw before she died. But she made it all the way without a mishap and vowed never to do it by herself again.

She hadn't told anyone she was going to Lake Tahoe but

booked a small room at the same hotel as her friends. In spite of all the texts and emails asking her what she planned to do, her response was, "Waiting to see what's happening with Ryan—got things to do."

Amy wrote one final note: "Hope you can make it."

Rachael surely was going to make it, and she had a few surprises up her sleeve.

# Chapter Nine

*They're here!*
*December 28th*

Nestled in the Sierra Mountains and considered one of the most spectacular sites in the United States, Lake Tahoe sits 6,225 feet above sea level and straddles the state line between Nevada and California. It boasts some of the purest water in the world, and the crisp mountain air gives it an almost mystical aura. On the eastern side of the lake sits Cave Rock, deemed a sacred site for the Washoe Native Americans. It is said to be charged with spiritual energy and is listed in the National Register of Historic Places.

A cerulean blue sky, majestic mountains, and vast forests serve as the backdrop to "The Jewel of the Sierra." A colorful mix of turquoise and blue waters grace the seventy-two-mile shoreline, giving it the nickname "The Caribbean in the Mountains." Once you've visited Tahoe, its potency will be forever engraved on your soul.

Surprisingly, the lake does not freeze due to its depth, which surpasses the height of the Empire State Building. But that's not to say it isn't cold.

The area is home to both winter sports and summer recreation. With spectacular scenery, Lake Tahoe can be enjoyed any time of the year. The Nevada side is host to many casinos, offering gambling and entertainment for those who choose not to venture outdoors. With so much to do and such beautiful surroundings, Tahoe offers the perfect getaway.

Rachael arrived at the hotel at 1:00 a.m. on the twenty-eighth. She knew the rest of the women wouldn't arrive until late on the twenty-eighth, including Frankie, who wouldn't get there until after midnight. Rachael figured she could get the lay of the land early in the morning. Her trickster personality had resurfaced, and she was in the mood to taunt.

As the shuttle made its final turn into South Lake Tahoe, she saw that fresh green garlands wrapped with sparkling white lights bedecked every building's façade. Trees glimmered and sparkled far and wide. It looked like an enchanted village. Rachael caught her breath in astonishment at the beautifully adorned town.

If that didn't put guests in a festive mood, nothing could. She was feeling better with each passing minute.

As she checked in, Rachael asked about the hotel. How many rooms? Suites? Floors? Spa? Skiing? Shopping? She wanted to know the interior and exterior terrain before sunup. The clerk gladly explained. There were four suites. The Luxury King was on the fourth and top floor, with one each on the other floors. The spa was off to the left of the lobby, with the hot tub facing the lake. "Thank you so much. I am looking forward to enjoying the amenities, but I also need to rent skis." Rachael had opted to leave her gear at home.

"Certainly. The concierge can make arrangements for you and give you your passes. We have a jitney that leaves every half hour, starting at eight o'clock. The last ride from the slopes is at six o'clock, unless they decide to have a night-skiing event. It will depend on the weather. They're saying we may get some snow."

"Isn't that why we're here?" Rachael gave him a wink. "Thanks again." Due to the influx of late arrivals, the lobby was quite busy. She walked over to the concierge desk and gave the man there detailed information as to what type and size skis and poles she wanted. He informed her the skis would be delivered to the bell captain first thing in the morning. One thing was certain—there was no lack of equipment or service in this skier's paradise. She picked up her lift tickets and the brochure outlining the procedures and other pertinent information. Then she asked: "Any chance I can get something to eat?"

"We have sandwiches we can offer."

"Great. Who do I have to annoy to get one?" She chuckled.

"You can annoy me." He smiled. "We have roast beef with cheddar, turkey with Swiss, and mozzarella and tomato."

"Can you send one roast beef and one mozzarella?" Her stomach was growling, and her body clock reminded her it was almost four in the morning.

"Absolutely. Anything else?"

"Herbal tea. Whatever you have will be fine. Thanks."

The bellman escorted her to her room on the main floor in the rear of the building overlooking the lake. It was a bit tight, with the queen bed taking up most of the space, but the view and small patio made up for the otherwise cramped conditions. She pulled the sliding glass door open and stepped outside. Millions of stars glistened in the clear night air. It was breathtaking. *At least Frankie has good taste.* She peered around the corner and discovered she was within a three-minute walk of the hot tub, something she surely would take advantage of. She unpacked her microfiber turban, an important accessory to keep her hair from freezing while relaxing in the hot water. Otherwise, mist rising for the hot tub would settle in her hair, eventually forming ice crystals. In extreme cases, it could cause your hair to break off like an icicle. Rachael learned that the hard way on a trip to Aspen. Now, whenever she traveled, she packed a microfiber turban, which also helped dry her hair faster.

Since the hot tub was so close to her room, she took the very quick stroll to where the subtle garden lights illuminated the foliage surrounding it. Trees and shrubs acted as wind breaks, allowing use of the steamy water regardless of the outside temperature. It was available twenty-four hours a day, as a nearby sign announced. Rachael snickered at the caution notice about time limits and alcohol use: AVOID ALCOHOL WHEN UTILIZING THE TUB. According to Rachael's rules, a glass of champagne was actually required in a hot tub. She sighed. Maybe things would work out with her friends. Maybe her shenanigans would pay off.

Rachael walked back to her room just in time to hear a knock on her door, announcing the arrival of her late-night snacks. She chowed down one sandwich and left the other for the morning. She didn't want to waste time getting breakfast; she needed every minute to scope out the facility and set the rest of her naughtiness in motion. She quickly finished putting her clothes away and shoved the suitcase into the closet. She pulled down the duvet cover, bounced up onto the bed, brushed her hands together. "Let the games begin." She was out like a light as soon as her head hit the pillow.

Giovanni was in a fine mood the morning Frankie left Manhattan. He promised to take exceptionally good care of Bandit and look after her one live plant. Even though Giovanni would miss Frankie for the few days she was gone, her absence would give him more time to spend with his mother before she went back to Italy. He drove Frankie to the airport and dropped her where the throngs of eager, frustrated, and depressed passengers waited to get inside the building.

Frankie was the only one of the friends who departed from
JFK directly to Reno. Or so she thought. But Rachael, plot-
ting her mischief, was one step ahead of them all.

On the morning of the twenty-eighth, Rachael was up
early. She took a few bites of the mozzarella sandwich and a
sip of her room-temperature tea. She'd get some real food
later. First things first—scoping out the hotel. She started on
the top floor where the girls would be staying. Stairwell? To
the right. Check. Count the steps to the elevator. Twenty-
four. Check. Security camera? Not that she was planning to
do anything illegal, but that was how they'd been caught
when they were on the ship. Surveillance: you never knew
who was watching or what they were watching. She peered
down the hall. There was one motion detector facing the elevator doors. It gave her the creeps.

She took the stairs to the main floor. Six minutes if she
walked normally. She giggled. She felt like a character in a
mystery caper. At least her mood had changed. She sashayed
her way through the lobby, smiling and saying "good morning" to passersby.

Once again, she approached the concierge desk. A new
face was smiling at her. "Good morning. How can I assist
you?" a freshly scrubbed young man greeted her.

"Hi. Can you suggest a nearby shop that would sell holiday decorations?"

"Of course." He scribbled two names on a fine cardstock.
He tipped his pen at the name at the top. "High-end." Then
he leaned in and whispered, "Not worth it." He straightened
and spoke in a normal voice. "They curate some of the finest
home accessories." He then pointed to the second name and
lowered his voice again. "If you're looking for chachkas, this
is the place."

She made a note to check his name tag. Rachael had taken
an immediate liking to the young man. Not in a romantic

way. She was sure he played for the other team, but if she didn't reconnect with her friends, she would pounce on Randy as a fun companion for her stay. "Thanks, Randy. I shall check them out. Ta-ta!" She gave him a few eyebrow waves.

Within a few blocks, she spotted a store with a wooden sandwich sign in the front announcing 50% OFF ALL DECO-RATIONS. She scurried inside and bought their remaining mistletoe inventory along with four two-foot-tall elves. She knew she was going to cause a commotion. The smile on her face was happy and devilish.

Rachael was wrestling her way into the lodge with the large overflowing shopping bags when Randy came to her rescue. "Oh, my. What do we have here? Year-end clearance sale?" He gave her a raised-eyebrow sideways look.

Rachael grimaced. "Shush. It's a surprise."

"Ooh. I love surprises."

Rachael found Randy's effusive behavior entertaining rather than audacious. "I might need your assistance, so keep it on the down-low."

"That, my dear, is something I am very experienced at." He raised one eyebrow.

Rachael rolled her eyes. That was enough banter. "Can you ask the bellman to wheel these bags to my room, please."

"As you wish, madame." He gave her a formal bow.

"Oh, and can you please have this box delivered to a late-arriving guest? Her name is Francesca Cappella."

"Of course. It will be my pleasure." He leaned over his desk and typed Frankie's name into the computer. "She's due to arrive on the late jitney. Unfortunately, I won't be here to deliver it myself."

"That's fine." She leaned close to his face and looked him straight in the eye. "And we never had this conversation. Got it?"

He mimed locking his lips with a key. "It's in the vault." He placed the mysterious box on the side of his desk and patted it.

Inside was a sprig of mistletoe. Maybe it was too obvious. What about Amy and Nina? Shouldn't they get mistletoe, as well? No. Just Frankie. They might think it was from Giovanni. He was romantic that way.

Rachael planned for mistletoe to start appearing in random places—first, the doorway to her friends' suite. If they were as sharp as she knew they were, one of them would notice their door was the only one with mistletoe. They'd shrug it off until the next random appearance, this time in the elevator. Now what about the elves? Maybe one near the hot tub. Then outside their room. Rachael wondered how long the charade could go on? Maybe a day. Maybe two. She checked her watch and decided to ponder it during her afternoon ski run. She knew Amy and Nina would be arriving sometime around dinner, so she had to manage to get in and out of the hotel without being seen.

As the bellman unloaded her shopping bags, she asked, "Is there a shortcut to the porte cochere?" She was referring to the covered driveway area at the main entrance.

"I don't know if it's a shortcut, but you can walk through the patio and gardens. There is an entrance to a hallway that leads to the front of the building. When you get to the end, you can make a right into the lobby or go straight to the exit door."

Rachael handed him a tip. "Thanks. You've been extremely helpful."

Nina drove the few blocks to the massive glass and metal building where the top agents in the film industry kept their offices. The revolving doors at the entrance had seen a parade of celebrities. In a wry mood, Nina snickered at the revolving door. *Another metaphor for show business.* She stopped at the security desk and showed her ID.

"Miss Hunter! So nice to see you. It's been a long time." The elderly gentleman had worked in the building since it opened and made it a point to remember people's names, regardless of how big or small they were on screen.

"Hello, Moe. Nice to see you, as well. How's the family?"

"Got a couple more grandkids, so I gotta keep workin'." He smiled as he took her photo. "You know where to go."

"Yes. Thanks!" She confidently walked to the elevator banks. Her attitude had shifted from the day before. It no longer mattered whom she saw or what they asked. Her conversation with Michael Powell had given her a new perspective. *When you take action, it can lead to other things.* She certainly wasn't hanging her hat on an offer from Mr. Powell, but their meeting was a reminder *we should never let fear cripple us.*

When she stepped into the elevator, a familiar face caused her to stop short and catch her breath. "Jane Douglass," she said with little emotion.

"Nina Hunter!" Jane squealed. "What are you doing here?"

"I have a meeting with Lois," Nina replied without sentiment.

"Funny! So do I!" Jane exclaimed. Both women were represented by the same agent, thanks to Nina.

Nina had mixed emotions. She and Jane had a history. Some good, some not terrific.

Jane continued in an animated tone. "So, I heard about the casting for the final season. What's the deal?" She elbowed Nina.

"We are in discussions," Nina said noncommittally. Jane always had an agenda. Even in college.

"I asked Lois to get me an audition for one of the episodes, but she told me they were closed."

Nina waited. She knew Jane was going to ask for a favor and she prepared herself to respond.

"So, girlfriend, do you think you could put in a good word for me with Lois and see if they can write me into a scene?" She gave Nina a coquettish smile. "I mean, I know you *are* the writer and all, but I want to go through proper channels."

Nina took a deep breath and told herself not to say what she really wanted to say. Instead she replied, "I'll see what I can do. I know they're working on the last episode. That's why I'm here."

Jane threw her arms around Nina. "I knew you'd come through for me!"

"I can't promise anything, Jane. I'm only the scriptwriter. The producer and director have the final say."

"Oh, but you have influence, Nina. You have a lot of power," Jane cooed in her disingenuous way.

"Thanks. I'll mention it to Lois." Nina was relieved when the elevator came to a stop. Enough insincere chitchat for the day.

The main door to the agency was locked, because everyone was out for the holidays. Nina picked up the phone next to the door and dialed Lois's office. A few minutes later, Lois appeared, leaned down, and unlocked the glass double doors. "Come in! Happy Holidays!" Lois ushered the two of them into the reception area. "Jane, would you mind waiting here?" She pointed to an array of plush armchairs surrounding a glass cocktail table.

"I know I'm early, but sure. No problem." Jane seemed a bit miffed. Did she really think she would be invited to Nina's meeting?

"Give us a half hour," Lois said.

Jane browsed the magazines, picked up a copy of *Vanity Fair*, and sat in a chair, where she thought she would be able to eavesdrop. No such luck. Lois's office was at the far end of the hall. Around fifteen minutes later, Jane decided to pretend to use the ladies' room. She knew it was on the other side of the reception area, but she feigned losing her way. She was just passing by the agent's office when Lois called out, "Jane?"

Jane sprang into action. "Yes! That's me!"

"Can you give us another fifteen minutes, please?" Lois was firm. She'd worked in this business for over thirty years and had seen it all.

"Of course! Sorry, I was looking for the bathroom. Silly me."

Nina's back was to the door, and she gave Lois an eyeroll.

Instead of going back to the reception area, Jane moved a few feet past Lois's office and flattened herself against the wall so she was within earshot.

Lois made a steeple of her two fingers and pressed them against her lips, then lowered her hands. "The two of you go back a long way."

"College," Nina replied, using every bit of her might to conceal her mixed feelings about her long-ago friend.

"Hmm." Lois could sense a chill from Nina, but decided to let the other woman decide how much she wanted to share. "You know I never would have taken her on as a client if it hadn't been for you."

"I know. What can I say? I am a good friend."

"Yes, you certainly are." Lois nodded.

"Where do we stand on the casting?" Nina asked.

"We have most of it wrapped up. I have two audition videos I need you to look at. We're torn between two actresses."

"Which role?"

"The neighbor who has never been seen on camera."

Nina laughed. "The mysterious cranky voice."

"That's her."

Nina thought for a moment. "Can you let Jane take a shot at it?"

Jane's eyes widened as she overheard Nina pulling for her.

"The director settled on these two." Lois really didn't want to have to go back and ask the director to reconsider.

"I know, but one more may break the tie." Nina realized it might be a bit too much to ask, but what the heck? The show was already canceled. What more could they do to her? Fire her?

"You have a point. I'll call Jamie and let him know to expect one more." She sent a text to the director, hoping she wouldn't upend his holiday plans. "So what are we going to do about you?"

"Me?" Nina was as perplexed as her agent. "I think I'm going to wing it for a while."

"What do you mean, 'wing it'?"

"I need time to think. I'm meeting up with a few friends in Lake Tahoe for some rest and relaxation."

"Now that is a brilliant idea. Where are you staying?"

"La Spa Resort in South Lake Tahoe."

"I've been there. Great place to unwind."

"I am looking forward to it. A few of my high school pals. We did a cruise two years ago and decided it was time to create a rumpus somewhere else." Nina chuckled.

"Sounds like fun."

"Hope you have bail money!" Nina joked.

"I don't think that's in your contract." Lois laughed.

Nina looked thoughtful. "Huh. Thought it was in the rider."

"You are quick-witted, for sure," Lois said reassuringly.

"Maybe someone will appreciate it next year."

"I am sure they will. I'll keep my eye out for you."

"Now *that* is in my contract." Nina got up from her chair.

Jane heard the conversation winding down and raced back to the reception area as quietly as possible.

Lois and Nina walked to where Jane was catching her breath. "You okay?" Lois asked.

"Oh, yes! Just a spate of hiccups," Jane lied.

Nina and Lois hugged and wished each other the usual salutations, and Nina wished Jane luck. She gave her a wink but didn't mention the favor she'd asked Lois. Nina was curious whether or not Jane would acknowledge her kind gesture. *Probably not,* she thought to herself. Especially if she got the part. Jane would want people to believe she landed it on her own.

When Jane entered Lois's office, she faked excitement and surprise at getting a shot at the role. For two years, the character of the neighbor had been only a voice and banging noises from the apartment next door. In the final episode, she would finally be introduced on camera. It wasn't a big scene, but the anticipation of the great reveal would put Jane in the spotlight, even if it were just for two minutes.

Lois turned her computer to face Jane so she could record the audition on the spot. Time was of the essence if she wanted to get it to the director before he left for his vacation. Jane stifled the urge to ask for time to rehearse. Now she had to show how talented she was.

Nina rode the elevator down to the lobby. She was surprised at her feelings of relief. For weeks, she'd dreaded the meeting, thinking she might break down in hysterics. But she didn't. It was odd. Spooky, almost. It was as if an angel had been sitting on her shoulder, whispering in her ear that everything would be all right. When the elevator stopped, she had the same thought as the night before: *Another door opens . . .*

\*   \*   \*

Rachael changed into one of her ski outfits, featuring a white Sterling jacket, a black and turquoise sweater, and black leggings. A white cashmere pom hat and a layered cashmere collar completed the look. She put her ID, some cash, and her room key in one of the zippered pockets. She knew wearing her Smith ChromaPop ski goggles in the hotel might be a little too conspicuous. But with the hat, hood, and collar, she could blend in with the rest of the downhill enthusiasts.

Again, she timed her walk from her room, through the patio, down the hall, and out the door. Ten minutes, tops. She handed her tickets to the driver of the shuttle that would take her to Heavenly Mountain, where she planned a two-hour ski. It had been over two years since she'd skied, and she didn't want to overcommit on her first day. When she arrived, she went to the main shed, where her rental skis were waiting, and located the lift.

She looked around to check if there was anyone she recognized. In her younger years, Rachael had spent a good amount of time on the slopes. She knew she wouldn't see Nina or Amy. She doubted they'd arrived yet, and neither of them were as experienced skiers as she was. If they had their wits about them, they would venture forth on the beginner's trail. Tahoe's mountains were not for the faint of heart. It occurred to her that Frankie didn't ski at all, nor did she have the inclination to try. Maybe she'd do some snowshoeing. Or maybe nothing. Rachael shrugged. *Whatever.*

As Rachael stepped into her skis, her attention moved to the contrast of the white snow against the deep blue sky. It was sublime. Rachael was pumped. Minutes later, she sprang from the chairlift and started smoothly down the slope. As she gained momentum, she was whirring past other skiers. Exhilaration coursed through her entire being. It was liberating. In that moment, she reclaimed her sense of self-determination. She was not going to allow anyone or anything to stand in her way. She might be back to square one, but that's where it always starts. Square One.

The adrenaline rush had slowed to a calm rhythm, and she decided to take one more run before returning to the hotel. When she was satisfied with her performance and newfound revelations, she shuffled her way to the shed, where she was able to rent a locker and leave her skis overnight.

She grabbed a hot chocolate and checked the jitney schedule. Ten minutes. Perfect timing. Then it hit her like a brick. She hadn't given Henry much thought since the day before. She wasn't sure if that was a good thing or a bad thing. But she was in a good mood. And that, for sure, was a good thing.

After leaving Lois's office, Nina had got in her SUV and spent some time checking her email before starting her drive to Tahoe. Now she checked the time and realized she'd better scoot. It was past noon, which meant she wouldn't get to the hotel until after seven o'clock. She hit the speed-dial number for Amy. "Hey, sweetcakes. What time are you heading up to the lake?"

"Already on my way. How about you?"

"Just about to hit the road. ETA is sometime between seven and eight, depending on traffic. So how did it go?"

"Pretty much as expected," Amy answered indifferently. "They had a written proposal with my name on the cover and the words 'Professor Department of Biochemics Stanford University.'"

"Having second thoughts?" Nina asked as she adjusted her rearview mirror. She noticed the revolving door at the office entrance was moving, and she wanted to hotfoot it before Jane left the building. No more chitchat or favors.

"Nah. It's a big job on a big campus."

"And your point is?" Nina asked, wanting more information.

"Even though it's holiday break, there were lots and lots of people on campus."

"Annnd?" Nina stretched out the word.

"I think I might be a little lost there."

"What did they offer, if you don't mind my asking?"

"Twenty thousand more than I am making now."

Nina whistled. "That's not chump change."

"True. But the cost of living is over a hundred and eighty percent higher in Palo Alto, and I am not about to live with three other people again. Cats, yes. People, no. Besides, Blinky and Gimpy would disown me. I don't think they'd appreciate being uprooted again."

Nina smiled. She and her friends always put their pets first. Except for Rachael. She didn't have any. Maybe that was her problem. A thought for another time, another day.

Nina snapped back to their conversation. "Wait, a hundred and eighty percent higher cost of living?"

"It's crazy. A two-bedroom in a two-story garden apartment building is over four thousand dollars a month, unless I want to commute an hour in each direction. The increase in salary wouldn't even cover the difference in what I would have to pay for rent. To say nothing of everything else."

"I totally get it. I'm lucky my parents have basically given me the house, since they spend so little time there." Nina took a breath. "Good thing, too, because I am about to be unemployed."

"Nothing new from your agent?" Amy asked sympathetically.

"No, not yet," Nina answered as she put the car in gear. "But I'm okay. Really. I almost feel relieved. How weird is that?"

"Not so weird, really. All the anxiety you were having before you made the trip is now behind you."

Nina chuckled. "Now I have new anxiety about what's ahead."

"Touché."

"What I *am* looking forward to is our rendezvous in beautiful Tahoe. Speaking of which, I am getting on the highway now, so I am going to buzz off. I gotta keep every one of my senses in high gear driving on these crazy roads."

"Okay, pal. I shall see you some time this evening."

"Be careful out there!" Nina signed off with a *mwah* kiss.

"You, too!"

Nina peered into the side-view mirror. There was a blue Kia that seemed intent on getting behind her. *Why were people in such a hurry?* She finally got through the local traffic on the notorious 405, connected to the CA-14N and then onto 395 North, where she set the speed control. Nina had a lead foot when she drove on long stretches. She didn't want to ruin her vacation with a speeding ticket. The route would take her past the Sequoia National Forest to the west and Death Valley to the east. Farther north, she would pass Yosemite National Park, Sierra National Forest, and then the Eldorado National Forest, which sat at the edge of Lake Tahoe. No matter what people said about California being "the city of smog and glitter," it had some of the most magnificent and diverse landscapes in the country.

A few hours later, Nina stopped at a large gas station complex near Big Pine, the kind with nine pumping stations, a twenty-four-hour quickie grocery store, and a fast-food chain. She noticed a blue Kia pulling in several yards away. Was she imagining it, or was that the same car she'd spotted earlier? The one that was almost on top of her. She got a glimpse of a woman with chin-length blond hair, sunglasses, and an LA Rams baseball cap. The sight gave her an eerie chill. She attributed her unease to the last two days of traveling, meeting with Lois, and running into Jane. That alone was unnerving. She'd thought Jane was a distant memory until she'd seen her at Lois's office.

As she finished filling her tank, the blue Kia pulled away,

giving Nina a sense of relief. *That was strange. But why?* She couldn't put her finger on it. She went inside to use the rest-room and get a pack of gum. She hated chewing it, but she thought it might help relieve the tension she was feeling in her jaw. She got back on the highway and calculated how much time it would take to complete the remainder of her drive. One hundred and ninety miles. A little over three and a half hours. She settled in and turned up the radio. She always liked to listen to the Eagles when she drove, especially in California. "Life in the Fast Lane" came screaming through the speakers, and she sang along at the top of her lungs. She glanced in the rearview mirror and noticed a blue Kia following two cars behind. Listening to the lyrics, she thought perhaps she *was* losing her mind. "Shake it off, Nina," she yelled to herself.

Being a three-point driver, she checked the rearview mirror and the two side mirrors periodically, and she could swear that same blue Kia was always two cars behind her. But the car had left the gas station *before* she did. She let out a big sigh. *Stop being paranoid,* she told herself. There had to be thousands of blue Kias in California, if not more.

By the time she arrived at the hotel, it had been dark for several hours. She was bleary-eyed and road-weary. A bellman helped her with her luggage and the main door. The magical and festive decorations outside flowed seamlessly into the lobby. Sparkling trees of different sizes graced the lobby, and swags of greenery decked the stone fireplace and front desk.

"Good evening, miss. How may I help you?"

Before she gave her name, Nina commented on the decorations. "It's a winter wonderland!" she exclaimed.

"Thank you. We want people to feel it's their home away from home."

Nina chuckled. "You haven't seen *my* home. I have a big

dog." She smiled. "Checking in. Nina Hunter. I'm with the Francesca Cappella party."

"Yes, of course. Miss Blanchard arrived a little over an hour ago." He activated the digital room key and handed it to her. "Patrick will bring your bags up to your room. The spa closes in an hour, but the hot tub is open twenty-four hours."

"Thank you. That sounds divine." Nina took the key and followed the man pushing the cart with her luggage. Just as Nina was about to insert her key, Amy flung the door open and squealed. "Nina! Nina! Nina!" She hugged and danced her around in a circle.

"Amy! Sweetcakes! Wow. Check it out! I'm likin' this new look!"

Amy did a swirl in her matching loungewear of peach cashmere pants, a scoop-neck long-sleeve T-shirt and a pink and peach floral duster. "You are rockin' it, girl!" Nina gushed.

"Marilyn did a makeover." She gave her hair a toss. "Wait until you see my new wardrobe," Amy bubbled.

"Really, Amy, you look terrific. No more fashion police for you!" She gave Amy another hug, while the bellman stood patiently watching the two friends' antics. He cleared his throat.

"So sorry!" Nina burst out laughing. "Reunion."

"Yes." He didn't look impressed.

Nina handed him a twenty-dollar bill, which immediately changed his manner. "Where shall I put this?" he eagerly asked.

Nina looked at Amy as if to ask which room she should take. "All three rooms are alike. I took that one." She pointed to the first one on the right.

"Well, then, I shall claim the one next to yours." The bellman put her suitcase on the luggage rack in the closet.

"Will there be anything else?" he asked.

"No. Thanks very much." Nina walked him to the door. She turned to survey the suite. "Very nice."

"Yep. Frankie worked miracles. Come sit." Amy walked over to the sofa in front of the warm flames in the stone fireplace. "Want something to drink? Eat? The room service menu looks rather good, but they stop serving regular food at nine o'clock. After that, it's sandwiches."

"Did you eat yet?" Nina opened the menu sitting on the cocktail table.

"Nope. I was waiting for you. I didn't know if you wanted room service or to go to the restaurant downstairs. It's open until ten o'clock."

"How about I get the road dust off me, slap on some lipstick, and we'll go downstairs. I'll order something to be sent up for Frankie." Nina scoured the menu. "Hey, they have antipasto. I'm sure she would like that, and it will keep for a couple of hours."

"Good plan." Amy gestured to an alcove, where a small murphy kitchen stood. "We have a fridge and a Nespresso! Frankie will be over the moon!"

"Excellent!" Nina got up from the cozy sofa. "I'll be right back." She hurried to her room to wash her face and "slap on some lipstick." Within a few minutes, she had changed into an outfit similar to Amy's, except hers was gray and black.

"What's this?" she asked, pointing to a box on the sideboard with Frankie's name on it.

"Dunno. It was sitting there when I got here."

"Maybe something from Giovanni."

"Yeah. Probably."

The two went to the main level and entered the dining room. They were seated next to a window that overlooked the garden.

"This is a very pretty place," Nina remarked.

"Wait until you see it in daylight," Amy replied.

"And I am going to get a glimpse of the night sky from our balcony later," Nina said with anticipation.

They each ordered a glass of wine. Since they were technically still in California, it was mandatory they have something from Napa.

Amy recounted the details of her interview and the tour of Stanford. "It is gorgeous. There is so much to do right there on campus. It's no wonder people want to be there. It's like a village."

"You still haven't changed your mind?" Nina peered over her glass of cabernet.

"Nah. It's just too big for me. When I was working as a bioengineer, it was at a large facility, but everyone knew everyone in the building. I mean, pretty much."

"But wouldn't you know everyone working in the building at Stanford?"

"Yeah, but the vibe was totally different. I couldn't help but feel everyone was competing with each other. And that's true on and off campus. Who has the bigger apartment, car, whatever." Amy scanned the menu. "As much as I love Northern California, I wasn't feeling the love at the school."

Nina chuckled. "I get it. Little fish in big pond syndrome?"

"Not exactly, but I know what you're saying. Yes, it's too big for me. And as far as accreditation and accomplishments, MIT has Stanford beat. At least in my area of expertise." Amy set her menu down on the table, and it was if a lightbulb went on. "I think that may be why they wanted me on staff. To round out their faculty." She sat back and folded her arms.

"You're probably right." Nina stopped suddenly. Something caught the corner of her eye. "Hey, have you heard from Rachael? Did she ever get in touch? I haven't heard a thing."

"Last text I got said something like she had to deal with a lot of stuff and wasn't sure if she could get away."

"When was that?"

"Two days before Christmas."

"I wonder what's going on with her. It's not like Rachael to miss out on a party, a trip, causing a commotion. Plus, she loves to ski."

"I know. You heard about the dance studio, right?" Amy asked cautiously. She didn't want to give away private information, if it was really private.

"One afternoon, I was in her neighborhood and drove past the studio and saw it was closed, as in closed-closed. Empty. When I spoke to Frankie, she told me Rachael sold the property. Apparently, she made a nice profit on the building, but she's been radio silent for two months. At least with me," Nina said.

"And then there's the dustup she had with Frankie," Amy added.

Nina looked out the window again.

"What?" Amy asked.

"Nothing. I thought I saw someone who looked like Rachael dashing through the patio."

"If she was here, she would have said something, don't ya think?" Amy's eyes widened.

"I think I need a break. While I was driving up here, I thought I saw a car following me."

"Really?" Amy's eyes grew even wider. "What do you mean?"

"Oh, it's nothing. It seemed like the same blue car was always about two car lengths behind me."

"Did you get a look at the driver?"

"Not the first time, but when I pulled into a gas station, a blue Kia pulled in several yards away. A blonde woman wearing a baseball cap and sunglasses was driving. But then she pulled out before I left."

"So she didn't follow you all the way up here." Amy made it more of a statement than a question.

"That's the creepy part. About an hour along the interstate, I thought I saw her behind me again."

"Wait. What? How did she get behind you if she left before you?"

"Good question. See? That's what I mean. I'm not making any sense." Nina smirked. "I'm hallucinating."

Amy laughed. "Well, you'll be right as rain as soon as you get into that hot tub."

"Are you planning on skiing tomorrow?" Nina asked.

"I'm going to give the baby slopes a try. It's been years since I've been on skis. And I've never skied on mountains this high. I've skied Killington, which is pretty intense, but I'm a little nervous here."

"Probably because you're not familiar with the terrain," Nina said. "Plus, the altitude is higher, so you have less oxygen."

"True. Like I said, 'baby' runs for me. What about you?"

"I don't know if I'm up for all that gear and cold weather. I just might sit by the fire and read a book, something I haven't done since I can't remember."

The waiter took their order, and Nina asked if the restaurant could send something up to their room. They were very obliging and said they would prepare it just before the two finished their meal.

Nina looked outside the window again. "Maybe a hike. That should be enough activity for me. Clear my head."

"Frankie said she wanted to try snowshoeing," Amy said.

"That's something I've never done. It looks grueling, shoving those sticks in the ground and pulling yourself along with those big bear trappy-looking things attached to your feet."

"The sticks are called poles, and you're close about the bear traps. It's another word for snowshoes." Amy laughed.

"I just never got into outdoor winter sports." Nina took a sip of her wine. "I like to be outdoors, but I also like to be doing something less terrifying than whizzing down a mountain at fifty miles per hour."

"But you used to ski," Amy offered.

"Mostly pretended. I'd go down once and then head to the nearest hot chocolate stand."

"Nina Hunter. For someone who hikes almost every day, you never really got into skiing?"

"Hiking is fine. Boots are the only things attached to my feet. I always felt a little out of control with long planks under my boots. I was never a fan of waterskiing, either."

"Ha. You were always so good at it when we went to Lake Hopatcong."

"How many times have you actually seen me water ski?"

Amy thought for a moment. "Maybe twice?" She scrunched up her face.

"Exactly, and both times I was lucky. You never saw me the other half-dozen times I wiped out before I even got up."

"Huh. And all this time, I thought you were a premier athlete."

Nina raised her eyebrows. "I guess I really am a good actress."

"So all those skiing trips you went on were bogus?"

"No. I went on the trips, but I rarely skied. Fireplaces, spas, hot toddies." Nina chuckled as their dinner was being served.

The conversation was light and easy. They ordered dessert and the antipasto for Frankie. Amy charged the dinner to their room, and the waiter said the antipasto would be brought up in about fifteen minutes.

The two women stood and stretched. "Want to take a quick look around?" Amy asked.

"Sure."

As they passed the gift shop, Nina thought she saw the

blonde woman rifling through earmuffs on display. She pulled Amy's sleeve. "I think that's her."

"Who?" Amy looked confused.

"The woman in the car," Nina whispered.

Amy linked arms with Nina. "Come on, my friend. You need to put your feet up and have one of those hot toddies."

The blonde woman moved out of view, leaving Nina wondering if she was being stalked or simply losing her mind. Neither was a good alternative.

When they got back to the room, Amy started the fireplace with a simple click. "Electric. Cool, huh?"

"Very cool. I would never have guessed. They are making lots of things look real."

"And some of it isn't your imagination, either!" Amy joked.

They decided to watch *The Holiday* with Cameron Diaz, Jude Law, Kate Winslet, and Eli Wallach.

"One of my favorite lines is when Eli Wallach tells Kate about being the leading lady in her life," Nina mused. "We often forget and put everything and everybody else ahead of ourselves. Frankie would tell us that's a mistake."

"Well, she is our best bud, so it makes sense she's rubbing off on us." Nina laughed. "You think we'll be able to stay awake until she gets here?"

"I think my body has adjusted a bit to the time difference." Amy pulled one of the toss pillows onto her lap. She frowned.

"What's up?"

"I miss my guys."

"Peter?"

"Oh yeah, him too." Amy giggled, implying she meant her cats.

Nina laughed. "Yeah, I miss my big oaf."

"Richard?"

"Ha!" Nina roared. "Winston, silly girl." She threw the other pillow at Amy.

"Let's see. It's ten-thirty. We've got about two and a half hours. I think we can make it."

"The movie is only an hour and a half," Nina noted.

"Then we can watch one of the late-night shows. There's got to be at least one Jimmy on by then."

In spite of their efforts, both of them dozed off on the sofa. The warmth of the fireplace, their comfy clothes, and the deep plush sofa made it easy to drift into la-la land. Both woke with a start when Frankie opened the door. The beleaguered bellman followed behind. Because of the airline schedules, many guests arrived well past midnight, all eager to get to their rooms.

Nina and Amy jumped from where they were snoozing and ran to give Frankie a hug. "Honey!" Nina cooed. "How was your trip?"

"Flight was fine, but I am glad it's dark outside, because I would have been scared witless if I could have seen the area below the roads." She hugged Nina and then Amy. Again, the bellman waited for the greetings to be over. Frankie dug into her purse and pulled out a twenty-dollar bill. Again, his mood shifted to accommodating rather than brooding.

Frankie's room was on the opposite side of the suite from the other two bedrooms, with the living room separating them. She looked around the suite. "I do good work."

"You certainly do." Nina put her arm around Frankie's shoulders, while Amy hung up her coat.

"We figured you'd probably be hungry, so we had some food brought up for you." Amy scurried over to the murphy kitchen, pulled a dish from the cabinet above the sink, and then placed the awaiting salami, cheese, and prosciutto on the plate.

"You guys are the best!" Frankie exclaimed. "Let me go toss my stuff in the drawers, freshen up, and put on a pair of PJs. Be back in a flash." As she skittered to her room, she called over her shoulder, "Anyone hear from Rachael?"

"Nope," Amy announced. "Last I heard from her was two days before Christmas. Said she had a lot of stuff to do."

Frankie asked Nina, "What about you?"

"Not a word."

"Wow. I must have done some serious damage if she's not even talking to both of you." Frankie's voice flowed from her room.

"She sold the studio." Nina said matter-of-factly. "Do you suppose that's what's bothering her?"

"I wouldn't know. She's not speaking to me, remember?" Frankie said.

Amy and Nina looked at each other. Frankie had a point. But neither of them had a squabble with Rachael.

Frankie appeared from her room. "Maybe there's something else going on."

"She's annoyed at Greg for taking Ryan to Vermont," Amy offered.

"She is always annoyed at Greg," Frankie added. "Oh, that looks yummy." She spotted the platter of charcuterie. "Do we have any wine to go with it?"

Nina opened one of the cabinets. "Not fully stocked, but there is a nice pinot noir or a sauvignon blanc."

"I'll take the pinot." Frankie pulled out one of the chairs at the dining room table. "This looks great. I mean compared to the imitation food they served on the plane." Frankie had a sheepish look on her face. "I know, I know. I am food-spoiled."

"As opposed to spoiled food." Amy giggled.

"You are in the business of food, and your boyfriend is also in the business of food. Which reminds me . . ." Amy walked over to the sideboard, where the box was waiting for Frankie. "This was here when I checked in."

Frankie was in the process of making a sandwich. She wiped the salami oil from her fingertips. "Where did it come from?"

"Dunno. Open it," Amy said anxiously.

Frankie lifted the lid. She furrowed her brow. "No note?"

"Guess not." Amy shrugged.

Frankie lifted the mistletoe from the box and smirked. "Huh."

"Giovanni?" Nina suggested.

"Maybe?" Frankie wasn't sure, either.

"Who else would send you mistletoe?"

"I don't know. But why would he want me kissing anyone else?" She placed the leafy greens back in the box.

"Does he know it's a tradition to kiss under the mistletoe?" Amy asked innocently. "I mean, is it a thing in Italy?"

"He's lived here long enough to know what it's for." Frankie had a strange feeling. Something didn't feel right. Maybe it was jet lag.

"Should we hang it up?" Amy asked naïvely.

"And who might we be kissing?" Nina chimed in.

The three looked at each other and started to laugh.

"I need some shut-eye. You guys have had a little time to adjust to the altitude and the time zone."

"Yes, the altitude!" Amy had a look of wonder. "And the air! Have you ever smelled anything so clean?"

"Before you go to sleep, take a look at the stars." Nina gestured for Frankie to follow her to the balcony. "Check it out." Frankie stared at the starry sky.

"You don't get this in Jersey!" Nina shivered and walked inside.

"What are the plans for tomorrow?" Frankie asked as she let out a big yawn.

"I think I'm going to skip the skiing thing and do some hiking," Nina said. "There are some amazing trails that they keep relatively clear for sissies like me who'd rather walk than get on skis."

"I'm going to try the bunny run," Amy said cheerfully. "It's been a while, and like I told Nina, I've never skied on mountains this high before. What are you going to do, Frankie?"

"I want to visit Cave Rock. It's got a spiritual thing going on, and it's only about a twenty-minute drive away. Could I borrow one of your cars?"

"Sure!" Amy offered.

"Or you can take mine," Nina added.

"Great. Thanks." Frankie gave each of them a hug and meandered to her room. "Sweet dreams."

"Nighty-night," Amy replied.

"Sleep well, girls," Nina added.

# Chapter Ten

*December 29th*
*Every Day is a New Adventure*

Rachael was up at the crack of dawn. She peered out her door. The hallway was empty and quiet. She hustled to the stairwell and climbed up to the fourth floor. She slowly opened the door and glanced for any movement. All quiet there, too. She tiptoed to the door of the girls' suite and deposited one of the elves. She was so giddy she could barely contain herself. She made a swift exit back down the steps, out to the patio, down the hallway, and out to the waiting early jitney. There were only two others willing to brave the mountain at that hour. She pulled out her phone and dialed the hotel.

"Good morning. Can you please connect me with the concierge?"

A much-too-cheerful voice for that time of day answered. "Good morning. This is Randy. How may I assist you today?"

"Randy, this is Rachael Newmark."

"Well, top of the morning mountains to you. What can I do for you?"

"Do you know anywhere I can go dancing tonight?"

"What do you have in mind?"

"Anything, really. I'm a dance instructor, so whatever is happening is okay with me."

"Hmm." Randy paused. "If you don't mind slumming it with one of the employees, a few of my friends and I are going to a club around eight o'clock. I can't stay out late. School night, if you get my drift."

Rachael appreciated his sense of humor and esprit de corps. "Sounds like fun!" She thought about how she could sneak out of the hotel without being seen by any of the other girls. "Er, Randy. Can I tell you something in confidence?"

"Of course. Is this another one of those conversations we never had?"

"Exactly."

"Do tell."

Rachael didn't recognize the couple on the jitney. Apparently, they were staying at another hotel, so she felt free to talk, but in a whisper. "I have some friends staying at the hotel, and they don't know I'm here. I want to surprise them tomorrow."

"How fun!" he gushed.

"Where can I meet you so I can be sure I'm not seen?"

"Easy, peasy. Take the elevator to the main floor. Cross over to the stairs and take them down one flight. There's a huge supply room, lockers, and a slew of other stuff. I'll meet you near the lockers, and we can take the employee exit."

"Randy, you are a genius!" Rachael was tickled pink that she had a new partner in crime.

"I'd like to think of myself as brilliant and talented, but genius will do," he replied stoically.

Rachael cackled. "You are also very amusing."

"I prefer witty. And droll, and sometimes hilarious."

"Well, Mr. Jocularity, I am looking forward to tonight."

"Oh, I like Mr. Jocularity. I shall put that on my business card. Uh, there are some stragglers dragging themselves to my desk. Meet me at ten after eight. Don't be late. Ta-ta!"

Rachael's face hurt from smiling. This trip was turning out to be much more exciting than she'd expected. Maybe Randy would help hang some mistletoe. Her wheels were spinning.

They arrived at the ski slopes twenty minutes later, with Rachael feeling more vibrant than she had in months. And the feeling had nothing to do with Henry. *Interesting*, she thought to herself.

It was eight o'clock in the morning, and only the hardcore skiers were already on the slopes. She decided to put in another two hours and then go into town for lunch, staying far away from the entrance to the hotel. She completed the course twice and then locked up her skis, met the jitney, and went into the village.

There was a small café about a block away where she was sure she wouldn't be seen. She had no idea what Nina, Frankie, or Amy had planned. Amy would probably go to a beginner slope; Frankie didn't ski, so Rachael wasn't sure what she would be up to; and Nina? Nina was ambivalent when it came to skiing. Once they'd gone to the Poconos, and Nina only spent a half day on the slopes. Rachael shrugged, ordered a grilled cheese sandwich with fries, and a cup of tea.

It was a little past ten o'clock when Frankie emerged from her room. She was calculating how many hours' sleep she got. Went to bed at 2:30, woke up a half hour ago. Seven hours. Not bad, considering she was up for twenty hours the day before. Nina was sitting on the balcony, bundled up with a cashmere throw, drinking her coffee. Frankie shuffled to the coffee machine and opened the drawer filled with a variety of capsules. She picked the strongest. Once her cup was full, she worked her way around the sofa, grabbed a throw, and met up with Nina.

"Good morning, sunshine." Nina peeped over the top of her sunglasses. "Gorgeous day!"

"Good morning to you." Frankie stopped abruptly to observe the view. "Oh, my. It's incredible." She spoke in a hush as if she were in a church. "This is categorically God's design."

"Ain't it somethin'?" Nina replied with the same reverence.

Frankie pulled a chair closer to where Nina was sitting and snuggled next to her friend. "How are you, my friend?"

"I'm good," Nina replied.

"Tell me, how did your meeting go?" Frankie didn't want to push Nina if she didn't want to talk about it.

"It was fine. At first, I was totally neurotic about anyone recognizing me and quizzing me as to what I was doing in LA. I practically wore a disguise on the plane."

Frankie chuckled. "You're kidding, right?"

"I am *not* kidding. I suppose I was feeling raw and vulnerable and didn't want to see anyone or answer questions." She took a sip of her coffee and contemplated the view. "Then I realized I was being ridiculous and unnecessarily hard on myself."

"That's my girl." Frankie tapped her friend's arm. "You are an accomplished and creative person. Just because a handful of pinheads in a conference room decide they want to make more money with less work, it's no reflection on your talent. Believe me. I've sat in too many of those mind-draining meetings where I had to kick *myself* under the table to keep from opening up my yap."

"I honestly don't know how you do it." Nina kept her gaze on the crystal-clear lake surrounded by white-capped mountains.

"It ain't easy, I can tell you that much." Frankie reflected on one such discussion. "Like the time they wanted to use cheaper paper for one of my cookbooks. I had to keep from screaming. Then I calmed down and suggested they increase the price of the cookbook by a dollar." She let out a huff. "I went on to explain that cookbooks are not like fiction. People collect them. They refer to them repeatedly. They spill their au jus all over them. They need to be durable."

"Down, girl." Nina snickered. "At least your writers have you in their corner."

"I am sure whoever was in charge of your show fought to keep it alive."

"I know. You're right. But I still have to work at not taking it personally."

"Exactly." Frankie turned her cup to face Nina's, and they clinked. "Here's to not taking things personally."

"I'll drink to that," Nina replied and finished her cup of java.

"What time are you going to Cave Rock?" Nina asked.

"I figured I'd get some breakfast and then drive up there." She checked her cup. Empty.

"Sounds good." Nina got up. "Want another cup?"

"Absolutely!" Frankie handed her cup to Nina and snuggled further into her wrap.

When Nina returned, she asked, "Don't you like winter sports at all?"

"I considered snowshoeing," Frankie replied. "I've done it once before. I just don't like the idea of layering on all those clothes. I feel like a Weeble."

Nina burst out laughing.

"Maybe tomorrow. When in Tahoe, as they say."

Amy walked from her room to the balcony. "Whaddya think?" She was sporting a pink and white ski outfit with a matching cap and gloves.

"Ready to snowboard?" Nina teased.

"Yikes! No!"

"What time are you leaving?" Frankie asked.

"In about a half hour."

"Where are you off to?"

Amy bit her lower lip. "I'm not sure."

"You're not sure?" Nina and Frankie said in unison. Nina elbowed Frankie. "Absent-minded professor."

"I asked for a bunny run, and they gave me the lift tickets."

"How about taking a look at them?" Frankie said.

"Duh." Amy reached in her pockets. "Heavenly Mountain."

"How long are you going to be there?"

"Until I'm pooped." She grinned, then started squirming and fanning her face. "This stuff is hot."

"That's why you wear it outside," Nina said.

"In the snow," Frankie added.

Amy gave them a thumbs-up and winked. "Got it." She spun on her heel. "See you for dinner. Wish me luck!"

Nina almost said "break a leg," but Amy was going skiing, not performing on stage.

"Have fun," Frankie called out.

Amy opened the door and shrieked.

Nina and Frankie jumped up and ran to see what was happening. Amy pointed to an odd-looking thing outside their door.

"An elf?" Nina was baffled.

"It *is* Christmas," Frankie said as she bent down to see if there was a note attached.

"Do you suppose it's for us?" Amy was bewildered.

They looked up and down the hallway. "It appears we are the lone recipients of such a creature," Nina observed.

"Huh. First mysterious mistletoe, and now an elf." Frankie squinted and pursed her lips. "At least it's not a gargoyle."

"Should we bring it inside?" Amy asked.

"It's kind of creepy," Nina responded.

"Let's just leave it out here. Maybe its owner will come by and claim it."

"Good idea," Nina agreed.

"I am outta here." Amy pulled her cap off her head. "Man, I am cooking." Then she waved and headed to the elevator.

Nina and Frankie retreated into the suite. "I have a strange feeling about this," Frankie said.

"Don't get me started on strange," Nina added.

"What do you mean?"

"It's actually two things, but I don't know if they're related."

"Continue, please," Frankie urged.

"When I got to Lois's office, a former friend was also there."

"Former friend?" Frankie asked.

"Someone I was extremely close to in college. She actually lived with us for a while."

"So what happened?" Frankie asked.

"Let's get dressed, and I'll tell you about it over breakfast."

"Alrighty." Frankie went into her room to change, as did Nina.

"Should we bring our coats?" Frankie asked.

"We can come back up for them when we're done."

The two made their way to the restaurant on the main floor. They sat near the window and marveled at the view and the beautiful patio.

Frankie pointed to the hot tub. "I may be spending most of my time in there."

"How about we take a dip after dinner tonight? Which leads me to ask, where shall we go?"

"I'll ask the concierge to recommend something."

"Of course you will," Nina joked.

After the waiter took their order, Frankie prodded Nina about her former friend.

"So tell me, what about this friend?"

"There was a woman, and I say 'woman' because she was in her early twenties, and I was eighteen. Her name was Jane. She was a drama student. She had been married, divorced, had a kid who she lost custody of, so she decided to follow her dream to become an actress. I have to admit, she was incredibly talented. But she was also troubled. She had a devilishly handsome boyfriend who was a compass without a needle."

"You mean a 'bad boy'?" Frankie asked.

"Precisely. Anyway, one day after class, I came home, and my mother had a rather sheepish grin on her face. She looked a little nervous."

"Your mother? Nervous?" Frankie was shocked. That was not the Mrs. Hunter she knew.

"Yes, can you imagine? Jane had that effect on people. Anyway, when I went into my room, there was my friend Jane. And all her stuff. I was baffled. Jane looked up at me with those piercing blue eyes and said, 'Your mother was kind enough to offer up your room. She said you wouldn't mind?'"

"You mean she invited Jane to move into *your* room? Without telling you?"

"Yes, she did." Nina nodded. "She was a real advocate of 'don't ask permission; beg forgiveness,' or however that saying goes." She paused. "I was flabbergasted at my mother's audacity, but honestly? I was mostly thrilled. I had the theatre superstar sharing my room with me."

"How long did that go on?"

"Six months."

"Wow. So what happened?" Frankie was enthralled with the story.

"You know my mother was always trying to be the hero. The one-upmanship stuff. She was going to save Jane from her terrible boyfriend."

"But *your* room?" Frankie was incredulous.

"Yes, *my* room that my dad remodeled with a huge walk-in closet and a long vanity with Broadway lights. It was an honest-to-God dressing room."

Frankie was flabbergasted. "She just moved right in. Like it was no big deal for you."

"As I said, I had the superstar in my house."

"Wow. Chalk it up to youth and naïveté."

"And hero worship."

"What about your brother's room? Couldn't she have stayed there?"

"Remember, Billy dropped out of school. He wasn't going anywhere."

"How come I didn't know this?" Frankie asked.

"You and I were doing our own thing at the time, and I was engrossed in theatre and Jane."

The waiter brought their breakfast, and Nina stopped with her fork in midair. She turned and thought she caught a glimmer of the blonde woman.

"What is it?" Frankie asked.

"That's the other part of 'strange.'" Nina pierced the yolk and dipped her toast in the yellow goo.

"Finish the Jane story and then we'll move on to strange." Frankie followed suit with her over-easy eggs.

"Jane was getting more and more attention. Superlative reviews. Don't get me wrong. She was fabulous in the roles she was performing. They were much more sophisticated than what freshman and sophomores usually get. Then one day, she had an audition for a TV commercial. She asked if she could borrow some of my mother's diamonds. She wanted to look successful."

"They say dress for the role or job you want."

"Well, I said no, and my mother wasn't around to disagree. Good thing, too, because she most likely would have handed them over to Jane and maybe never seen them again."

"Shifty?"

"Crafty," Nina corrected her.

"Did she get the commercial?"

"She did. And then like that"—Nina snapped her fingers—"she announced she was moving to Hollywood. Evidently the commercial got her more exposure, and an agent told her he could find her work, but she had to move to LA."

"So who did she move in with out there?" Frankie gave her a sly look.

"Some guy. But he was also in the biz. I don't know how she met him, but it didn't take long for her to find a bed."

"Did you keep in touch with each other?" Frankie was leaning in.

"As soon as she got her first TV gig, I never heard from her again. Not until I moved to LA and reached out to her."

"Did she get back to you?"

"Only when she got a part and wanted to brag or ask for a favor. Borrow my car, mostly. It was never 'Hey, Nina. Want to go for a coffee?' None of that. But then I ran into her at an audition. She made such a fuss in front of everyone. How I was her best friend from college. Blah. Blah. Blah."

"Did either of you get the job?"

"Yes." Nina had a big smile on her face. "Me!"

"That must have annoyed the pants off her."

"Oh, it got ugly."

"How so?"

"Once I got the part, she wanted to be best buds with me again. I still looked up to her and was still very naïve. She had been in LA almost two years before I got there, so I followed her tips and advice."

"But you were the one who got the part."

"Yes, but it wasn't a recurring role, so there were many auditions ahead. Since she was the 'professional' "—Nina used air quotes—"she convinced me to go to her salon and update my look."

"Okay, and?" Frankie had a feeling she knew where this story was going.

"And she took the stylist, who was one of her pals, into the back and apparently told him I wanted a pixie cut."

"A *what*?" Frankie's voice was loud enough for people to notice. She looked around. "Sorry."

"Can you imagine? I had my back to the mirror and felt this hand at the nape of my neck as he took the first big hunk of hair off!" Nina leaned in closer and brought her voice down to a whisper so as not to annoy the other customers with her animated tone. "I spun the chair around and started screaming every expletive in my vocabulary. I looked like a French poodle who got caught in a Mixmaster!"

Frankie was stunned. "What did you do?"

"I had to let him finish; otherwise, I would have had a reverse mullet. I couldn't stop crying. I came close to hyperventilating." Nina shook her head. "It was one of the worst days of my life. I didn't leave the house for weeks."

"I suppose that's exactly what she wanted." Frankie was getting the picture. Jane was a user. She was jealous and didn't want any competition. "Wow."

"Wow. For sure. By then, she was using the same agent as me. She told Lois that I wasn't well and couldn't go out on calls for several weeks."

"That is one of the worst acts of betrayal I've heard, and believe me, I've heard plenty." Frankie was disgusted.

"Thankfully, Lois called to see how I was feeling. When I told her I was fine, she told me about the call from Jane."

"What did you do?"

Nina sighed. "Nothing."

"Seriously? You did nothing after someone tried to sabotage you?"

"It was Hollywood. You didn't confront people who you thought were more successful. And at that time, Jane had more screen credits than I did."

"Was she ever a regular on a show?"

"No, and that was the real clincher." Nina smiled. "I had three starring roles in a row: *Waitresses, More Company,* and then *Family Blessings.*"

"Did you see each other after the hair debacle?"

"Not for a long time. She was drinking more and working less."

"She sounds like a real piece of work," Frankie said.

"One night we had a cocktail party to bid adieu to *Family Blessings.* Somehow, she found out and tagged along with a few other people I actually invited. Of course, when she walked into the house, she gave her usual disingenuous 'love you so much' greeting. After a couple hours, she'd had plenty to drink and made a snide remark about all the 'nice stuff' I had. 'Guess you're doing great, eh, Nee-Na.'" She let out a long exhale.

"So was the thing at Lois's the first time you had seen her since, Nee-Na?" Frankie emphasized her name in jest.

"Yes. She begged me to get her an audition for the final season of the show. I told her all the parts had been cast. Then she asked me if I could write in something for her."

"Let me guess. You said you would."

"I told her I'd see what I could do."

"And you did," Frankie stated.

"I simply asked Lois if Jane could submit an audition video. Lois said she'd ask the director, so now it's out of my hands."

Frankie reached across the table and grabbed Nina's hand. "You are an amazing person. You always take the high road."

"Isn't that what we're supposed to do?"

"Yes, and that's why we've been friends for as long as we have."

"Oh, that reminds me of one more incident."

"There can't be more."

"There is. Before she made her spiteful remark about me doing well, she asked me what my plans were. I told her I would leave it up to God."

"What did she say to that?"

"She said, 'Cut the God junk. God isn't reality.' "

"Whoa." Frankie blinked several times. "And two years later, you still did her a favor?"

"Well, if she gets the gig, it will be a favor. If not, it's because it's not what God sees for her."

"You are amazing."

"Once I shook off my disappointment, fear, anxiety, and depression about this latest show ending, I remembered: throughout my life, when one door closed, another one opened."

"That's called *faith*, my friend." Frankie and Nina were on similar spiritual paths.

"That's all we really have to go on, isn't it? Faith. Hope. Some people choose to have it, and others don't. I guess it's a good excuse to be negative when something goes wrong. But people don't seem to rejoice or feel thankful when something goes right. For instance, when you just have a normal day. You got everything done, no leaks, no cracks, no bruises. No speeding tickets." She chuckled, then continued her thought. "Counting our blessings isn't always about stuff. Peace of mind. Good friends. No volcanos or earthquakes. People need to show a little more gratitude, if you ask me." Nina waxed philosophical. Then she abruptly jerked her head around to get a better look at the patio.

"What is it?" Frankie twisted to look, too.

"That's the other part of the weirdness."

"What do you mean?"

Nina explained about the blue Kia, the blonde with the baseball cap and sunglasses, and the strange feeling someone was following her.

"Do you think she's the one who left the elf outside our door?" Frankie pondered.

"I have absolutely no idea who she is, even *if* she exists. Maybe she's a figment of my fertile imagination," Nina replied.

"Well, I'll keep an eye out for a strange blonde." Frankie chuckled. She asked for the check, and the two went back to their room to get ready for their outings.

Both of them suited up appropriately. Nina dressed in warm hiking clothes, while Frankie sported a flannel jogging outfit because she didn't anticipate being outside for more than an hour. Nina usually hiked for at least two hours.

They walked to the elevator and noticed mistletoe hanging outside the sliding doors. Nina gave Frankie a sideways look. "If I didn't know better, I'd swear Rachael is here."

"It sure does look like Rachael's handiwork, but she told Amy she had things to do," Frankie replied blankly.

"Makes me wonder exactly what those things are," Nina mused.

"Don't you think she would have told us she was coming?" Frankie asked with a bit of sarcasm.

"That would be the normal and sane thing to do, but we're talking about Rachael, remember?" Nina joked.

"I still can't put my finger on it, but something seems a little strange," Frankie ruminated.

"You and your strangeness, and my stalker. Great combo." Nina gave Frankie a little shove as the elevator opened on the ground floor. Just as they were entering the lobby, Nina gasped. "Did you see her?"

"Who?"

"There was a woman who looked like the one I was describing." Nina raced to see if she could catch up with the mysterious female. But she was no longer in sight.

"You need some fresh air." Frankie held out her hand. "Keys, please."

The women got into Nina's SUV and drove to the hiking trail. "How are you going to get back?"

"Hike?" Nina smirked.

Frankie rolled her eyes and drove the fourteen miles to Cave Rock. She marveled at the views as she crossed the state line into Nevada. It was almost impossible to keep her eyes on the road ahead. But after a few zigs and zags, she clutched the steering wheel and focused on her driving. When she glanced in the rearview mirror, she spotted a blue Kia.

"It can't be," she muttered. It was too dangerous to be distracted, and she couldn't focus on the car behind her, especially with the tunnel ahead. She slowed her speed as she drove through the burrow of the craggy rock formation that rose three hundred feet above the lake. It was the most prominent geological feature along "Big Blue."

Frankie was awestruck, but kept reminding herself to pay attention. She found the entrance to a parking lot and again spotted the blue car behind her. This time, she was able to get a quick look at the driver. Blonde woman. But instead of wearing a baseball cap, she had a black pom beanie covering most of her hair. Dark glasses.

Frankie was tempted to approach her and ask who she was and why she was following her, but Frankie thought better of it. She'd watched too many Investigation Discovery true crime shows where people were abducted and never heard from again. She wasn't about to become a statistic. Frankie looked around for other people she could possibly join. A couple with two children, a boy and a girl. Frankie thought the children were perhaps eight and ten.

As they were getting out of their vehicle, Frankie quickly walked up to them. "Hello! This is my first time here, and the trail is closed. Any suggestions would be much appreciated."

The family nodded and explained the trail was closed due to the ice. "If possible, you should come in the summer months. It's a totally different place. The sunsets are magnificent," the husband said. "They're spectacular all year, but you can enjoy the scenery more when the weather is warm."

Frankie understood as her fingers became tingly from the cold. "I read it's a very spiritual place, and I wanted to get a feel for the atmosphere." She smiled. "I'm a little nutty that way."

The wife spoke. "Being spiritual is not nutty, even though many people may look at you as if you are." The woman had an almost mystical presence about her. She placed her hands on her young daughter's shoulders.

"Oh boy, do I get looks." Frankie snickered. "I'm kinda used to it."

The woman spoke again with reverence. "We come here to remind ourselves of our heritage."

"Washoe?" Frankie asked.

"Yes. My great-grandfather," the woman replied. "Sadly, most were driven out by the gold rush. There are about fifteen hundred registered Washoe now. But we celebrate our culture every year with an event in July at the Tallac Historic Site. It's closed for the season, but we come to visit the rock several times a year. We do not live far."

The little girl spoke. "A coyote led the people here. He told them the plants would provide medicine and nourishment, but the people must care for this sacred place."

Frankie was impressed with the child's knowledge and enunciation. "That is so interesting. Do other animals talk to you? My cat talks to me all the time!"

The little girl laughed and looked up at her mother for permission. "Sometimes they do." She started to blush and buried her head in her mother's coat.

"Do you know sometimes my friends tease me and call me

Doctor Dolittle?" Frankie bent down to bring herself eye level with the little girl as she extracted herself from the folds of her mother's sherpa coat. Her eyes widened. "Really?"

"Yep. But I know they're just teasing me. And sometimes I think they're a little jealous. I have kind of a secret language with animals. You know what I mean?" The little girl nodded her head.

"Every so often, people can be mean, but your real friends will always be good to you and never try to hurt you." Frankie realized she was getting too studious with this young stranger.

"Thank you for saying that. I frequently have to remind her," the mother said as she wrapped her arms around her child.

"As my mother did for me. You have a lovely family. And thank you for sharing the story of the coyote." She wanted to hug the little girl, but thought it would be too intrusive.

The husband finally spoke. "If you would like a better view of the Rock, you should go to the boat ramp. It's a different perspective. Just turn your car around, and you'll see signs."

"Thank you very much. It was nice meeting you. Happy Holidays!" Frankie replied, never losing sight of the blue car during the entire conversation. She quickly got into Nina's rented SUV and drove to the boat ramp, but the blue car didn't follow her. "Strange is right." She got a chill, and not from the weather.

With the suspicious car no longer in sight, Frankie stepped out of her vehicle to view the panorama of the special rock formation. After a few minutes, she decided it was probably in her best interest to go back to the hotel. She didn't know if the blue car was lurking somewhere. Frankie hurried through the parking lot and drove south to the hotel, minding the speed limit, the road, and occasionally glancing in the rear-view mirror. *Am I also getting paranoid?* After several minutes, Frankie acknowledged the blue car wasn't tracking her. Maybe it was because the person realized Nina wasn't driving? She attempted to send her a text, but neither of them was in good cell phone range.

She took a deep breath. "Okay. Girl, what's next? How about snowshoeing?" she mumbled to no one. "Okay, that sounds like a good idea," she mumbled back.

By the time Frankie returned to the hotel, it was almost one o'clock. She walked to the concierge desk and noticed his name tag. "Hello, Randy. I'm Frankie."

"Nice to meet you, Frankie. Are you a guest at our fine establishment?"

"I am indeed."

"Marvelous. How can I help you today?" He sat up tall in his seat.

"Can you tell me if there is an amateur snowshoeing spot I can try?"

"Yes, there's one about ten minutes from here. They have groups that go out every two hours."

"Oh, I don't think I can do two hours' worth." Frankie laughed.

Randy leaned in. "Have you ever done it before?"

"No. I'm not really a snow bunny."

"But you decided to visit Lake Tahoe in the winter?" Randy made a *tsk-tsk* sound. "You should really come in the summer. That's when I like it best. There is *so* much to do."

"Well, Randy, I'm here now, so what *should* I do?" Frankie grinned.

"If you want to try snowshoeing, I can arrange for a lesson. That will only take about an hour. And then if you're comfortable, you can give it a whirl tomorrow. There is a small area near the shed where you can practice." He wrote something down on a card. "You can noodle around and not be attached to a group."

"Thanks. Let's see how I do today." Frankie grinned.

"Excellent. Let me call them and see if someone can give you a lesson." Randy pushed a few buttons on the desk phone. "Hey, Carl. Randy here. Does anyone have time for a snowshoe lesson today?" He listened, then looked up at Frankie. "He can fit you in, but you have to get over there pronto. Shall I reserve a seat on the jitney for you? It leaves in a half hour."

"Sounds good." Frankie's stomach was growling.

He turned his attention back to Carl, who was waiting on the other end of the call. "She'll be on the next jitney. Thanks, Carl."

"Can I grab a quick sandwich to take on the jitney?"

"There's a grab-and-go kiosk outside the gift shop." He looked her up and down. "But you should put on another layer. A heavier jacket. Now skedaddle, or you'll miss the bus." He handed her the complimentary card for the ride and a pamphlet about the lodge where she was heading.

Frankie placed the card in her pocket and realized Randy was right. She hadn't packed the most appropriate attire for the trip. Outdoor sports weren't her thing. She was more focused on the spa part of the trip. She remembered seeing clothing in the gift shop, dashed inside, and quickly went through the rack of jackets. Luckily, there was one in her size. It was white with a hood. She picked up a pair of earmuffs and an extra pair of gloves. She charged everything to the room, grabbed a sandwich, and hurried to the jitney stand. On her way out, she thought she noticed the blonde woman again. Was she seeing things, too? Between the shadowy blue car, the blonde, the mistletoe, and the creepy elf, Frankie wondered if coming to Tahoe was a good idea.

With Amy skiing and Nina hiking, it really hadn't turned out to be a reunion. Not yet. Tonight they planned to have dinner, spend time in the hot tub, and sit in front of the massive fireplace in the lobby. There were large club chairs and cocktail service. It would be a nice way to wind down.

Frankie read the brochure on the way to Lake View Ski Lodge. *The Best Place for Beginners*. That was a relief. At least she wouldn't be the only novice in the snow.

As promised, the jitney arrived in ten minutes. Frankie brushed the crumbs from her mouth and jacket into her hands and placed them in her brown bag. As she exited the jitney, she gave the driver a petrified look. "Wish me luck."

One thing was certain—Lake Tahoe folks knew how to clean up snow. Every sidewalk was pristine. Fewer falls, fewer lawsuits. Frankie walked to the welcome booth. "Hi, I have a lesson with Carl. My name is Frankie. Randy called from La Spa Resort."

"Nice to meet you, Frankie. Have you ever snowshoed before?"

"No, I have not."

"Skied?"

"No, again. Well, I tried it once and fell right over before I got on the lift. That was as far as I went."

"No worries, Frankie. We'll have you bear clawing in the white fluffy straightaway." Carl had a hint of a New Zealand accent. "We'll start ye out with flat terrain shoes. About how much do you weigh?"

"Excuse me?" Frankie balked.

Carl laughed. "Need to know the bearing load on the shoes. I'd take you for about sixty kilos."

"Just don't tell me what that means in pounds."

Carl laughed. "I can't tell you how many horrible comments I get."

"And don't ask me my age, either." Frankie laughed.

"No worries. We're done with the personal stuff. If you just sign this waiver, we'll get goin'."

"Excellent. I am here with some friends, and I am the only one who isn't an outdoorsy person. At least not in the winter."

"I'd say you came to the right place, but maybe some

other time of the year?" Carl plunked a pair of snowshoes on the counter.

"You're the third person who has said that to me in the past three hours." Frankie laughed.

"Maybe that's a big hint from above." Carl edged his way past the counter. "Foller me."

The two walked to a bench, where Carl instructed her to slide her boots into the snowshoe. "Get it up as far as you can where the first strap comes across the top of your toes. Tight enough?"

"I guess. Is it supposed to cut off my circulation?" she joked.

"Nah. But if it does, the blood will freeze first before your toes fall off."

"Oh, that's very reassuring."

Carl tightened the heel strap, which had a ratchet fastener. "Good?"

"Perhaps?" she asked mockingly.

Then he tightened the instep. "Howz it feelin'?"

"I think it's okay."

"Don't feel like they're gonna fly off your tootsies?"

"Nope." Frankie grabbed onto his arm to stand. He handed her two poles.

"Sweet. Now watch me." He showed her the simple step. "It's really quite intuitive."

Frankie made a few cautious moves.

"Good on ya." Carl urged her on. "Let's see how far ya can go. Foller me."

Carl set out with a slow and steady pace while Frankie mimicked his every move.

He kept looking over his shoulder. "Er doin' awesome. Now I'll get behind you." He came around and instructed her to keep moving forward, synchronizing her steps.

They were well into the woods when Frankie noticed smoke in the distance. "Is there a fire?"

"Nah. Just some bloke who lives in a cabin up there."

"It's truly beautiful out here." Frankie began to understand why people enjoyed the snow. There were few sounds
except for the calls of a couple hungry birds. There was a
serenity about the winter woods that made the world seem
like a much calmer place. "I think you may have changed my
mind about winter sports activities," she called over her
shoulder.

"Glad to hear it," Carl replied. "Yer done fer now."

Frankie was bordering on disappointment that her lesson
was over. "Do you think I can come back tomorrow?"

"We'll check the schedule when we get back. You may not
need another lesson, from what I've seen."

"Thank you!" Frankie's face was pleasantly chilled, but
tomorrow she'd be sure to dress more appropriately. Good
thing she was only outside for an hour.

When they returned to the shed, Carl helped her unbuckle
her shoes. "Ye did great, Frankie." He held out his hand to
help her up. "Come on." He gestured her to follow him to
where they kept the schedule. "I don't have time for a lesson,
but you can join a group we have going out around two
o'clock."

"How long does the group usually take?"

"Two hours. Three tops."

"That's a bit too much of a commitment for me."

"Tell ya what. You come by in the afternoon, and I'll let
you go back along the trail we took today. It's close enough
to be a short trip, but far enough so you can enjoy the peace
of the forest."

"That sounds like a super plan. Thank you, Carl." Frankie
put her hand out to shake Carl's.

"And we can thank my boy Randy. He's a pip, all right."

"Sure seems to be."

"Good lad. Likes to go to the casinos in Nevada and the
clubs."

"Why am I not surprised?" Frankie kidded. "I have a feeling there's a wild thing under his buttoned-up uniform."

"You have no idea."

"I'm from New York. I have plenty of ideas." Frankie chortled, and Carl echoed her.

The jitney was pulling up with some late-afternoon skiers. Frankie waved to Carl. "See you tomorrow. Thanks again."

When she got onboard, she noticed Amy sitting in the rear. "Amy!"

"Hey, Frankie. What are you doing here?"

"I had my first snowshoeing lesson."

"How did you like it?"

"I have to admit, I did." Frankie looked around. "So this jitney hits a bunch of ski resorts?"

"Uh-huh." Amy had a distant look on her face.

"What?" Frankie knew that look meant Amy was calculating something in her brainiac head.

"What do you think of the idea that Rachael may be here?" Amy speculated.

"The thought occurred to both me and Nina, but why wouldn't she tell us?" Frankie had another thought. "Mistletoe in a box. An elf outside our door, and then when Nina and I got in the elevator, there was mistletoe hanging in the car."

"If I were Hercule Poirot, I would surmise someone is toying with us."

"Do you think she paid someone?"

"It is a possibility," Amy replied. "But there is also the possibility she is here and is waiting to surprise us."

"But we're only going to be here for three more days. If she wanted to spend time with us, wouldn't the joke be over by now?"

Amy shrugged. "Despite all my calculations, Rachael is one puzzle I have yet to solve."

"Some detective you are." Frankie gave her a friendly tap on the arm.

"So how was your skiing?" Frankie asked.

"I only wiped out once," Amy said proudly.

"Another reason I don't ski. I'd never be able to get up. I'd be making snow angels until the first thaw."

"There are people who can help."

"I'd rather avoid the situation entirely."

As the jitney pulled in front of the main entrance, Frankie thought she spotted the blonde. She jumped out of her seat and pressed her face against the window.

"What are you doing?" Amy asked.

"I'll tell you later." Frankie watched the woman retreat into the hotel lobby.

At the same time, Amy gasped.

"What is it?" Frankie asked.

"Rachael wears a white jacket, doesn't she?"

Frankie pointed to her own. "As do I." She hoisted Amy out of her seat. "I think we all have a case of brain freeze."

The two linked arms as they entered the hotel lobby. "Where are we going for dinner?" Amy asked.

"Oh, geez, I forgot to ask Randy the concierge for a recommendation."

"You? Miss Bossy Pants, party planner?"

"Brain freeze." Frankie pointed to her head.

The two strolled up to Randy, who was sitting pertly at his desk.

"And how did my lovely guests do today? Miss Frankie? I see you are not in a body cast, so the snowshoeing must have gone well."

"It did. Thank you very much. I plan on going back again tomorrow. I had no idea how serene it is out there."

He cocked his head. "Told you so. And you, Miss Amy?"

"The beginner slopes were good. I'm glad I opted for them. Tahoe's idea of beginner and mine are slightly different."

"It's the altitude," Randy remarked.

"Could be," Amy ruminated. "But I only wiped out once!"

He clapped his hands. "Brava! We'll turn you two into snow bunnies before you leave."

"Let's not get carried away," Frankie warned with a big grin. "So, Randy, where do you recommend we have dinner?"

"What are you in the mood for? There's a fabulous Italian place a few miles from here."

Frankie looked at Amy, who replied, "Frankie is a little pastaed out." She leaned over and whispered, "Her boyfriend owns an Italian restaurant in New York City."

"Oh, fancy." Randy batted his eyes.

"No, not really, but I do eat a lot of Italian food at home."

"Too bad. Four of our top five restaurants are Italian. We have a few restaurateur transplants here. They come here on vacation, and before you know it, they've opened a restaurant."

"So what else would you recommend?"

"Either Evans or The Lake House. Both are five-star restaurants, American cuisine, whatever that means."

Frankie was about to give him a lesson in gastronomy, but thought better of it. Lots of restaurants referred to themselves as "American." It was a catchall for whatever the chef felt like making that wasn't dominated by any particular country. The words *nuevo* and *nouvelle* had been badly overused during the past two decades.

"The Lake House is a bit cozier."

"Can you see if they can fit us in?"

"I am sure they can. I am Randy, your concierge." He did a little toss of his head. "What time?"

Frankie looked at Amy. "Want to do the hot tub before or after?"

"After? This way we can crawl to our rooms and not have to think about getting dressed."

"Capital idea. Say seven-ish?" he suggested.

"Great! Thanks!"

"Last name, please?" he asked.

"Cappella."

Randy stopped abruptly. Then he remembered he was not supposed to discuss the box the woman named Rachael had left with him. "Is that with one *p* or two?" Quick recovery.

"Two *p*s and two *l*s."

"How many will you be?"

"Three."

He picked up the phone and dialed The Lake House. "Hello, Josephine. Randy here. Yes, I am!"

Frankie could only imagine what was said on the other end of the call. It was probably a funny tease.

"Can you fit three of my lovely guests around seven, seven-ish?"

"Marvelous. Name is Cappella. Mm-hmm. Thank you. Have a swell evening."

Randy hung up. "You're all set."

"Can you order a car for us, too? None of us are familiar with the roads, and we may have a glass or two of wine."

"Certainly. I'll call your room when he arrives. Should be around six forty-five."

"Thanks so much, Randy. You have been so accommodating," Frankie said.

"We aim to please."

"And you have," Amy said as she pulled off her cap.

When they got to the elevator, they halted as the doors opened. Another creepy elf was waiting inside.

"Okay, puzzle-woman, what are you thinking now?"

"I think we have a prankster in our midst."

"But where is she?" Frankie asked.

"Good question. You know we never checked with reception to see if she's registered."

"You're right. We'll do it later. I need to get out of these clothes and into a hot shower," Frankie urged.

When they got back to the suite, Nina was reading a text she'd received from Lois. "Hey, girls. How was your day?"

Both started talking at the same time until Nina held up her hand. "Wait. Frankie, did you say someone in a blue car followed you to Cave Rock?"

"What blue car?" Amy asked.

"That's a story for dinner," Nina said. "Frankie, did you get a good look at the person?"

"Not a good look, but it was definitely a she, and she had blond hair. But she was wearing a pom beret instead of a baseball cap."

"So what happened?" Nina asked curiously, sounding concerned.

"I stopped in a parking lot at the base of the Rock. I didn't realize the trail was closed and wasn't sure what to do. There was no one else around, and I didn't want to get out of the car. Abduction phobia? Anyway, a family pulled up, and I walked over to talk to them, and they suggested I go to the boat launch. When I got back in my car, the woman took off."

"She didn't follow you to the boat ramp?"

"No. Which leads me to think she was looking for *you*. Once she realized it wasn't you driving the car, she left."

"This is becoming one big puzzlement," Amy said as she informed Nina of the second elf in the elevator.

"Don't forget the mistletoe in the elevator," Frankie pointed out.

"Sure has the makings of Rachael naughtiness," Amy said thoughtfully.

"Yes, it does," Frankie agreed. "I am going to check with the front desk." But before she had a chance to pick up the house phone, her cell buzzed. It was Giovanni. Frankie realized they hadn't spoken since she left. Yes, she'd sent him a text when she arrived, but because of his schedule and the time difference, there didn't seem to be a convenient moment when they could talk. She took the call into her room while the other two dispersed to get ready for dinner.

"Gio! How are you doing, my love?" Frankie was happy to hear from him.

"*Cara*. I am well. But I miss your *bellissima* face."

Frankie actually blushed. "You are sweet. All good in the Big Apple?"

"*Molto bene*. I am taking *mia madre* to the airport tomorrow. She had a very much good time with her children and grandchildren."

"That's wonderful. I'm sorry I didn't have much time with her." Frankie was feeling guilty about abandoning Giovanni during the holidays. The trip could have waited. But then again, the spur of the moment seemed to work when it came to herding people together. No time for excuses.

"Don't worry, Francesca. The children kept her busy. I told her maybe you and I will take a trip to Italy next year."

"I would love that!" Frankie's excitement was genuine. It would be wonderful to travel with someone who knew the country and the people.

"Yes? You like the idea?"

"Of course! It would be *fabuloso*!" she exclaimed. "As soon as I get back, we will make a plan."

"*Va bene*. We shall do this." Giovanni's smile could be felt across the continent. "Tell me, what have you been doing all day without me?" he teased.

"I went to Cave Rock, but the trail was closed because of the ice. Even so, it was impressive. I met a family whose heritage is Washoe Native American. Did you know a coyote told their people to move there? And that it would bring plants and animals to them."

"A coyote?" Giovanni snickered. "Sorry. I know. You like to talk to the animals."

"And they talk back, Mr. Smarty Pants."

Giovanni laughed. "Frankie, you are a joy."

"Yes. I know," she said assuredly. Then she giggled. "And then I had my very first snowshoe lesson."

"My Frankie? But you do not like the cold."

"Yeah, but it is absolutely gorgeous here, and it would be sinful to miss having at least one outdoor experience."

"Did you like?"

"It wasn't difficult, but tiring. Snow is heavy, and you gotta pull yourself across it. The best part was the tranquility. The trees, the birds, and nothing else. No police sirens, fire trucks, garbage trucks, people screaming, horns honking. At first, I thought I had gone deaf."

"You are funny. I know what it is like. I skied when I was young. But too young to appreciate the splendor. We were too busy racing against each other down the hills." Giovanni reminisced about his youth.

"Youth is wasted on the young, so they say."

"What are your plans for the rest of the trip? More snow-shoes?"

"Maybe for an hour. Today we really didn't spend much time together, which was the whole purpose of the trip. Tonight we're going to dinner, and then tomorrow we'll do whatever in the morning and then meet for lunch and browse through the village. There are some wonderful shops and art galleries."

"Perfecto!" Giovanni sounded very encouraging. Frankie was happy they'd got past that rough spot about her making plans without him.

"I'd better get a move on. I have to shower and be ready in an hour."

"*Cara*, you need more time than that!" he kidded.

"Don't be fresh!"

"*Fresco*?"

"Don't pretend you don't know what I meant."

"Yes. Tease. I am not to tease you."

"You can tease me, but not right now. I can't pinch you from here."

Giovanni let out a guffaw. "You enjoy your friends and the *tranquillita*. The noise has not gone away here."

"Will do. Love you!"

"*Ti amo, mi amore.*"

Frankie made a loud kissing sound and then ended the call. It dawned on her that she and Giovanni never ended their calls with "Love you." It was always *Ciao*. Or *Ciao bella*. She decided not to put too much thought into it. The last time she tried to read into his gestures and comments, she got neurotic.

An hour later, the three women met up in the living room, each wearing a very stylish and weather-appropriate outfit. Nina was in a deep wine-colored jumpsuit. Her hair was tied in a matching bandanna. She wore a long multi-strand chunky necklace, with similar pieces of bronze dangling from the knot in the bandanna at the nape of her neck.

Frankie was in her regular tunic and leggings "uniform," as she liked to call it. But this was more elevated than usual, a black cashmere boat-neck sweater and matching leggings. She pulled a cashmere scarf of cobalt blue with black swirls around her neck. Her long black hair was tied back in a loose ponytail.

Amy surprised both of them when she glided into the room wearing the red rose soutache and black duster jacket over a black tank and black pants. Her Tory Burch boots finished the look.

"Amy Blanchard!" Nina exclaimed. "You look like you just came from a fashion photo shoot!"

"Aw, gee. Let's not get carried away," Amy said modestly.

"You look spectacular!" Frankie joined in.

"If you ask me, I think all of us look mighty spectacular!" Nina announced as they moved in for a group hug.

The phone rang. It was Randy. "Good evening. Your chariot awaits."

The girls got a big kick out of Randy. "He's a pip," Nina remarked.

"He sure is. Too bad Rachael isn't here. She would be best buds with him by now," Frankie added.

Amy picked up her purse and coat. "Shall we?"

Nina slung her open-front ruana poncho over her shoulder, and Frankie slipped into her Gobi Mongolian double-breasted black coat and stuffed her gloves in her pocket.

When they opened their door, they noticed there was not one, but two elves staring at them.

"Geez!" Amy jumped. "What in the heck is going on?"

"Blonde lady?" Frankie turned to Nina.

"Not her style."

They walked down the hall to the elevator and discovered another batch of mistletoe hanging from a ceiling fixture. "How much more of this stuff do you think we're going to find?" Amy asked rhetorically.

"How much more can there be?" Nina asked.

"I guess we'll find out," Frankie said as they exited the car and entered the lobby.

Nina saw someone dart out the side door. She was sure of it this time. She grabbed Frankie's arm. "Go out the front and see if you see her."

"Rachael?" Amy asked innocently.

"No, the blonde," Nina said as Frankie raced to the entrance.

But before Frankie could get a good look, the woman sped away in a blue car. "That was her," Frankie said when she met up with them in front of Randy's desk. "I am sure of it."

"Well, at least I know I am not losing my mind." Nina sighed. "Now I only have to worry about being stalked. Fun times."

"Is everything all right?" Randy seemed genuinely concerned.

"Oh, just a stalker and some creepy elves," Frankie replied.

Randy tried to hide his expression. He had noticed elf heads popping out of the bags after Rachael's shopping spree. He had no idea what was going on between these women, but he'd promised he wouldn't say anything. Maybe he'd try to pry it out of Rachael later when they were on the way to the casino and club.

"I'm sorry, did you say, 'creepy elves'?"

"Yes. There was one earlier today, and now there are two." Amy huffed. "And they are staring at our door."

"Would you like me to have them removed?" Randy asked. This would be juicy info to tell Rachael.

Nina was the first one to respond. "I think we should leave them. Amy? Frankie?"

"They kinda give me the willies." Amy frowned.

"But if we have them removed, then the person who is trying to psyche us out wins," Frankie pointed out.

"How about I turn them around to face away from your door? I get off work shortly, and I'll handle it personally. How does that sound?"

"Perfect. Thanks, Randy," Frankie replied. "Oh, before I forget, could you arrange for me to take the jitney back to the snowshoe place in the morning?"

"Oh, so you enjoyed yourself?" Randy folded his arms as if to say, *I told you so.*

"It was almost surreal. I'm not ready for a long trail, but Carl said I could come back and practice some more."

"You bet. I'll slide the jitney pass under your door when I reposition the elves." He looked at Nina and Amy. "Either of you need a ride tomorrow?"

Amy said she'd like to go early, and Nina was planning to hike a different trail.

"Splendid. I'll put both your passes under the door. Have a pleasant evening. Enjoy your dinner."

The three women exited the hotel, looking in all directions for the phantom blonde. She was nowhere in sight. Nina let out a big breath of air. "Maybe she's finished with her stalking."

"This is baffling. Do you think maybe she is in on the elf thing? Or maybe she *is* the elf thing?"

"Time will tell. I hope. And I hope soon, because this has been a bit bizarre."

"Okay, girls, let's put these apparitions and ugly elves away for now. Time to unwind and enjoy a good dinner. I, for one, had a grab-and-go sandwich, so I am ready to sink my teeth into deliciousness," Frankie announced as she noticed her name in the window of a town car.

The three piled in, said their hellos to the driver, and nestled together for the fifteen-minute ride. Before they proceeded, the driver handed Frankie his card. "I figure you'll be there for about two hours. Give me a fifteen-minute heads-up." Frankie took the card and put it in her purse.

"I've heard this is a very good restaurant," Amy chimed in.

"One of the best. If you are a meat eater, I strongly recommend their short ribs. Meat falls right off the bone."

"Please stop. I am so hungry!" Frankie groaned.

Amy leaned forward. "You have to excuse her. She's a 'foodie' and had to settle for a premade sandwich she ate on the jitney."

The driver looked in his rearview mirror. "We'll be there shortly." He looked in his side-view mirror and noticed the same blue car that had pulled out a block from the resort. He dismissed it. *It's a small town.*

Frankie noticed the changed expression on the driver's face. She turned to look out the rear window. There was a car following very closely, its lights shining directly in her face. She turned back and asked, "Do people always drive this close?"

"Probably a tourist. They get intimidated on these roads, especially at night. They like to follow the car ahead of them. Makes them feel safer. Beats me. The lead car can go off the road, too."

"That's reassuring," Nina said sardonically.

"Not to worry. I grew up here. I could drive with my eyes closed." He paused for effect. "But I won't."

"What a relief," Frankie added. The three women exchanged curious glances. *Was this guy trying to be a comedian?*

A few short minutes later, they arrived at The Lake House, and the following car continued on past them. It was blue. Once again, the women looked at each other skeptically. "Do you think we should tell someone?"

"Who? And what would we tell them?" Nina asked with resignation.

"All right, ladies. The car moved on, and so should we." Frankie yanked their sleeves, dragging them toward the front door. "Let's not let whoever is messing with us ruin our evening."

"Or our trip, for that matter." Amy gently stomped her foot. Oh, how she loved her boots.

From the outside, the place looked like a cabin, perhaps a shed. The interior had a completely different vibe. It sported light woodwork and paneling with ambient, diffused lighting, creating a warm and inviting atmosphere. Mountain Modern.

The host welcomed them. "Good evening. Frankie Cappella party?" he asked confidently.

"Yes. Good evening." Frankie removed her coat. Amy followed suit, while Nina unwrapped herself from her ruana. They were quite a stunning trio. Each with her own personal flair.

As they followed the host to a comfortable booth, Frankie kept a keen eye as they passed other diners. The presentation of the food was artful and looked delicious. Comments of gastronomical delight mixed with the aroma of the food, heightening her anticipation.

"Good choice, Randy," Nina said as she took her seat.

"He really has been super helpful," Amy commented. "He found the perfect beginner's slope for me."

"And my new adventure in snowshoes."

"Yes. Quite accommodating. He gave me several brochures for hiking. I realize it's his job, but he does it with such aplomb."

"Makes you feel special." Amy nodded.

"And we are!" Frankie said as she nodded to the waiter. "May I see a wine list, please, or is there something you recommend? I prefer a Chianti or pinot noir; my friend Amy likes a dry white; and Nina, a cabernet."

"Let me get a few tastings for you." He nodded, handed them menus, and receded into the beautiful, modern, pale wooden walls.

Frankie couldn't stop expressing her excitement over the items on the menu. "Beef tartare. Yum. Crabcakes. Double Yum. Oh, New Zealand lamb chops."

"We can read." Amy crinkled her nose.

"Sorry. This menu is very impressive. Not a huge selection, which means the dishes are no doubt impeccable."

"Is she always like this?" Amy squinted through her glasses.

"Always. Such a bore." Nina snorted as the waiter returned with several tasting glasses.

He placed three white wines in front of Amy. "Rather than tell you what it is, I'll let your palate decide what it likes."

"Then will you tell me?" She pretended to give him a suspicious look.

"But of course." He placed three other glasses in front of Nina, and then four in front of Frankie. "I'm afraid we have only two Chiantis this evening."

Another server brought some thin crackers to serve as a palate cleanser between tastings.

They each did the requisite swirl, sniff, and sip; eat a cracker; repeat until they decided on which of the wines they preferred with their dinner.

"Such fun!" Amy gushed. "We really need to get together more often!"

"We're only a train ride away," Frankie said. Then she fixed her stare on Amy. "Right?"

"Right. No movin' for this girl."

Their waiter gave the wine order to the other server as he explained the specials. Frankie rolled her eyes. "Yer killing me!" she burst out.

"They make the absolute best lamb chops on this side of Lake Tahoe." He smiled proudly.

"I normally don't eat lamb chops. I like them, but not as my main course."

The waiter suggested they try an order as an appetizer and share it. Amy was all atwitter. Boston had good restaurants, but she rarely went to one unless Peter was in town, and they usually stayed close to her apartment. This was a real treat for her.

Nina decided on the steelhead trout, and Frankie the filet mignon. "Heard of extreme sports? I'm going extreme carnivore tonight." Frankie chuckled.

As they finally began to relax, they took turns recapping their day. The conversation was light, sprinkled with humor. They even made fun of the elves.

As dinner was winding down, they decided to order dessert to take back to the hotel. "We can eat it while we're in the hot tub," Nina said with a twinkle.

"Are we allowed?" Amy asked.

"How about we just bring it back to the room, and we can have it after the hot tub," Frankie suggested.

"Deal," Nina said.

Frankie pulled out her cell phone to call the car service, but she had no bars. "Dang. Cell service is tough up here." When the waiter returned with their to-go Death by Chocolate, Frankie asked if she could use the restaurant landline. He escorted her to the phone, and she reached the driver. "We should be ready in about fifteen minutes. Does that work for you?" Frankie nodded as she listened. "Excellent. Thanks."

She made her way back to the table, where they split the check and gave the waiter a generous thirty-percent tip.

"Not to sound like a snob, but this is the kind of food you expect in New York."

"You are right. You are a snob, and you expect it in New York," Nina ribbed her.

When they returned to the hotel, another shuttle from the airport was arriving. "Busy place. We were lucky we were able to get that room," Frankie said.

"You are a miracle worker, my friend." Nina put her arm around Frankie's shoulders. "So what did Giovanni have to say, except how much he misses you?"

"We are going to plan a trip to Italy next May. We'll visit his mother and cousins and then go to Florence and Rome for a couple of days."

"Let me take a wild guess. You already have it plotted out," Amy said with certainty.

"Have you met me?" Frankie laughed. "I've been trying to plan a trip to Italy for years. At least in my head. Now I can put those ideas into action."

"Brava!" Nina said. "Let's bring this deadly dessert to the room and get suited up for the hot tub."

"*Perfecto*!" Frankie said.

"*Buon giorno*!" Amy answered, not realizing she was saying "good morning."

Frankie and Nina howled all the way to the elevators. "Hey, did you guys bring bathing suits?" Amy asked innocently.

"Well, yeah. Hot tub. No naked ladies allowed," Nina replied.

"Shoot. I didn't bring one." She grimaced. "Do you think they might have some in the gift shop?"

"Why don't you just wear your underwear?"

Amy's face brightened. "Excellent idea! I have granny panties and a full-coverage bra."

"No one is going to notice, and I doubt there will be a lot of people around. It's almost ten o'clock."

"*Buon giorno*!" Amy said again.

"Honey, that means 'good morning,'" Frankie said, gently trying to stifle a laugh.

"Oh. I thought it meant something like 'good deal.'"

"Are you sure you're a professor?" Nina asked.

"Bioengineering, smarty pants. I speak biomechanics and cybernetics." She stomped her foot on the floor. Yes, she *really* loved those boots.

"You can say *molto bene* or *eccellente*." Frankie patted Amy on the shoulder. "There. Your first Italian lesson."

"I'm bilingual." Amy batted her eyelashes.

Nina raised her eyebrows and shook her head. "Ya gotta love Amy!"

When they reached their room, they noticed the creepy elves were at an angle facing away from the door. "You gotta love Randy."

The girls covered their scantily clad bodies with the thick Turkish robes the hotel provided, then proceeded to the mistletoe-laden elevator. No one said a word. It was becoming commonplace. They got off on the second floor, and walked down one flight to the door nearest the hot tub. It was the most private access from the building.

As expected, no one was around. They had the warm, bubbly water all to themselves. Their chatter slowed as they wound down from the delicious food, excellent wine, and good company. As well as their vigorous day of outdoor activities.

While they were discussing their plans for the next day, a shadowy figure was creeping behind the windbreak of foliage. This time, she wore a black cap and had tucked all of her blond hair underneath. The black leotard made her look like a ninja. She eased closer to listen in on the conversation. She could hear everything loud and clear. The problem was, they weren't talking about her. Nina never mentioned Jane, nor did they discuss the stalker. They'd agreed to leave the "strange" and "weird" outside the restaurant, and the subjects never came up again. As far as Jane was concerned, she had gone unnoticed since she'd started tailing Nina back in LA.

"I think I'm poached," Nina said. "I'm heading back to the room. You guys coming?"

The three carefully climbed out and quickly grabbed their robes. "Yikes, it's cold!" Amy cried, dancing around and rubbing her arms and legs.

"Wish I had my phone. Professor Amy Blanchard discovers new cybertechniques in her own likeness."

"Oh, stop," Amy whined. "Don't tell me you're not cold!"

"I won't, because I can't." Frankie pulled the robe tightly around her, and the three high-tailed back inside.

While the women were at dinner, Rachael sneaked down to the lower level and met Randy at their rendezvous spot. Rachael was surprised at his attire. He looked like something from the 1980s. "Disco fever?" she asked.

He reached his arm above his head and snapped his fingers. "You ain't seen nothin' yet."

"Am I appropriately dressed?" Rachael opened her coat to reveal one of her dance costumes. The tight red-sequined dress clung to her body as if it had been painted on.

"Whoa, girlfriend! Where did you get that dress?"

"It's one of the costumes from my dance studio."

"And you brought it to Tahoe because you were going to do what?" Randy eyed her up and down.

"Find someone to go dancing with." She pinched his cheek. "Now let's blow this popsicle stand. I've got my dancing shoes on!"

They walked through the employee parking area below the hotel. A blonde woman was getting out of a Kia. Randy looked over at her. "Huh. I've never seen her before. Must be new." He made a crook in his arm. "Shall we?" They walked a few car lengths down and got into his Jeep. "It's not a Ferrari, but it gets me places no Ferrari can dare go."

Rachael was beginning to appreciate her new companion. "Where are we headed?"

"We're crossing the state border," Randy whispered, as if they were committing a crime.

"Oh. Sounds exciting," Rachael whispered back.

"There's a casino that has disco night once a month, and tonight you are in luck." Randy grinned from ear to ear. "We're hooking up with a few of my friends."

"The more the merrier." Rachael snickered.

They arrived at the State Line Casino about half an hour later. As expected, there were flashing neon lights, and the noise of slot machines and bells was deafening. It was an alternate universe to the pristine slopes. Rachael blinked and blanched at the cacophony of noise and stimulation. She had been to many casinos in her life, but the contrast between her afternoon and this circus atmosphere was staggering.

She thought perhaps it wasn't such a good idea after all.

Randy could sense Rachael's unease. "Not to worry, darling. I know this place is an assault on one's senses. Come with me." He grabbed her hand and pulled her past the rows of dinging machines and cursing and/or shrieking customers.

They came up to a large ballroom decorated with disco balls and posters of movies and bands from the 1980s. They were a little early, and the DJ was setting up the sound system. "Never Gonna Give You Up" by Rick Astley was playing in the empty room. Randy took her coat and flung it on a chair. Then he grabbed her hand and dragged her onto the empty dance floor. "Okay, dearie. Let's see what you've got."

They spun, slid, and jiggled around each other, dancing The Running Man, Kris Kross Jumping, and The Snake Dance. Rachael was in her best form, and Randy had no trouble keeping up. By the time the song was over, a crowd had gathered and broke into enthusiastic applause. "That song never goes out of style."

"It's happy. People really want to be happy, even if they think happiness is out of reach." Randy waxed philosophical.

Rachael looked at him with different eyes now. He was kind. And fun.

One of the spectators asked, "Is there a competition tonight?"

"Not that I am aware of," Randy replied.

"Well, there should be," Rachael added with raised eyebrows. "Maybe we should ask the DJ to have one." She grabbed Randy's hand and trotted him across the floor.

"You know it's going to be rigged." Randy gave her a rascal look.

"Exactly." She approached the DJ.

He looked up from the sound bar. "Nice footwork out there."

"Thanks. Any chance there's a contest tonight?" she asked coyly.

"Would you like one?" He grinned. "I'm the one in charge, so I may be able to arrange it."

"That would be fantastic."

"The only catch is, you two have to win."

"We'll do our best." Rachael blew him a kiss. "Thanks!"

Randy's friends started trickling in, welcoming each other with the European kiss on each cheek. He introduced his new friend Rachael to his pack. She couldn't tell if some of them were gay or straight, but it didn't matter. They seemed nice and gave her a warm welcome, offering to get her drinks, a chair, everything a refined person would do. All the attention she was getting was an unexpected bonus.

Randy was generous enough to allow a few of his friends to dance with Rachael. Feelings of buoyancy filled the room with songs by The Pointer Sisters, Kool & the Gang, Rick James, and Earth, Wind & Fire. The hours skipped past until the DJ announced they would end the evening with a contest. "If anyone has any steam left." His voice boomed against the walls.

Randy took one look at Rachael, and they pranced into the center of the room. Hoots and catcalls were shouted over "Flashdance . . . What a Feeling." Randy and Rachael owned the floor. Everyone else stepped back and let the two of them govern with their moves. No doubt they were the winners. Questions were shouted at them. "How long have you been dancing together?" "Are you professionals?" "Are you on tour?"

One of Randy's friends handed Rachael a towel. She wiped her face. "Never. Yes. No."

Confusion flowed over the faces. "Never?"

"Nope. This was our first night out," Rachael said with an air of confidence. "But, yes, I am a professional dancer. And no, we're not on tour."

"Well, you should be," someone in the crowd shouted.

Rachael took a bow. "Thank you so much." She turned to Randy. "And here's to my wonderful partner, Randy." He also took a bow and kissed her hand.

The larger group began to disperse, leaving Rachael and Randy with three of his friends. The guy named Jimmy spoke. "We've never seen Randy this Randy before."

"Oh, stop. You've seen me dance."

"Not with a girl!" Jimmy teased. "And it was spec-tac-u-lar!"

"Maybe if you were as good as Rachael, I'd dance with you more often," Randy bantered.

Rachael was elated, and not just from the attention. It was also from the rush she got from dancing. And her heart appreciated the camaraderie these friends felt for each other. She realized how much she missed her friends. She vowed she would make amends.

After the excitement waned, Randy and Rachael gathered their belongings. "Hey, wait. Don't we get a prize?" Randy asked half-jokingly.

"The prize was in the moment. And it was a golden moment." She gave Randy a peck on the cheek.

"I have to admit, I haven't had this much fun with a girl since I was eight years old, and my friend and I pushed ourselves down a hill in a wagon."

Rachael laughed. "Don't worry, I won't try to turn you."

Randy came back with, "What a relief."

On the drive back, Rachael asked, "So tell me, Randy, where did you learn to dance like that? Don't tell me clubs."

"You got me. I took a lot of dance classes when I was in high school. It was my dream."

Rachael did a double take. "Seriously?"

"Yes."

"I am sure you're tired of people asking, but I must. What are you doing with your talent now?"

"You saw it."

"Stop. You gave up dancing?"

"It gave up on me. I did a few stints with some entertainers who offered residencies. But when the you-know-what hit, all live shows were canceled. When they started bringing back entertainment, it seemed like they only wanted drag queens, and that's not my jam. Not that there's anything wrong with it. But I'm not into dressing up in women's clothes, high heels, and makeup. I'd rather be a background dancer. With a troupe." He sighed. "Then life gets away from you."

"I know how that goes. And it gets away from you fast. Have you ever thought about moving?"

"To where?"

"I just sold my dance studio, but I get calls to do ballroom dancing."

"Someone like *you* must have a partner. No?"

Rachael thought about how she should answer that question. "Yes. And No."

"Explain, missy."

"Two years ago, I met a famous dance instructor. We got into a relationship and worked together. He has a special program for people who are physically challenged. Mostly kids. But same thing. The 'you-know-what' shut his program down for over a year. And then I had to close my studio because of the 'you-know-what' and eventually sold the building."

"We dare not say the name. Wearing a mask totally messed up my complexion," Randy said earnestly.

Rachael threw her head back and laughed out loud.

"Why do I feel like you haven't given me all the juicy details?" Randy gave her a sideways look and raised one eyebrow.

Rachael huffed. "He kept his studio in the city, where he's been spending more time each and every day." She stared straight ahead. "I feel like things are slipping away." She stared out the passenger window, watching the holiday lights and trimmings go by.

"I'm sorry to hear that, dearie." Randy reached over to pat her hand. "Have you talked to him about it?"

"He never seems to have the time." Rachael pursed her lips. "I think he's having an affair."

Randy snapped his head in her direction. "Oh, that is not good."

"No. It is not." Rachael was relieved she felt no need to cry. She'd finally arrived at the acceptance stage.

"What are you going to do?" he asked in earnest.

"Ask him to meet me for dinner when I'll let him off the hook."

"You can't be serious! Let him off the hook?" Randy was aghast.

"What are my options? We're not married. We have no financial or property arrangements. The only thing to do is to move on. Kaput."

"You are one strong woman. I would be beating the bejeezus out of him."

"And ruin my manicure? Surely you jest." Rachael laughed again.

"Well then, what are you doing to stay out of trouble?" he asked lightly.

"Hanging around with you. Leaving ugly elves outside my friends' suite."

"A-ha. I had my suspicions. So what's the deal?"

Rachael explained her tiff with Frankie and how the girls had planned this trip and she was being stubborn. She wanted to punish Frankie, but realized the only person she was punishing was herself.

Rachael sighed. "Frankie is a fierce and loyal friend. I have to tell you this hilarious story about one night when we were out dancing and my boyfriend at the time was with us." She went on to describe how Fierce Frankie scared a woman straight out of a club. "What's funny is Frankie doesn't have a violent bone in her body. Unless you mess with someone she loves, or an animal."

Randy howled with delight. "Oh, sister, you positively need a friend like that in your back pocket. Front pocket. Wherever. Don't you dare continue your silly charade. You need to kiss and make up."

"You're right. I'll call first thing in the morning." She took in another big breath of air. "Thanks, Randy. I needed an impartial ear."

"Okay. I am going to hold you to it."

"I am sure you will." She paused and gave him a peck on the cheek. "Thanks again. You've been a real pal."

"Thank you. I had a blast. Tonight was awesome."

"Yes, it was." Rachael leaned into her seat. Tomorrow would be the day to reconcile.

# Chapter Eleven

*December 30th*
*Reconciliation Day?*

Amy, Nina, and Frankie were up early. They sat on their balcony wrapped in blankets and sipped their coffee as they watched the sky change to the colors of dawn.

"This is mind-blowing," Amy said softly. "It's so, so beautiful. Makes me want to never leave."

"We have three more days. Let's try to stretch it out spending more time together."

"We have plans today to meet for lunch and go shop-hopping," Amy said.

"Shop-hopping?" Nina asked.

"I don't like to call it shopping exactly. That implies I am going to purchase something."

"And shop-hopping doesn't?" Frankie scoffed.

"Semantics." Amy giggled.

"Tomorrow night is New Year's Eve. There's a party in the lobby, and then there are fireworks on the lake. Randy said you can see them from all over."

"Sounds good to me. I wonder where we should have dinner?"

"Why don't we go out again tonight and stay here tomorrow? The food at the restaurant is particularly good, and I imagine a lot of places are already booked," Frankie said, and quickly got up to use the house phone. "I should call now." She called the front desk and asked to be connected to the restaurant. She was told they could accommodate her party at the nine o'clock seating. "Perfect. Thank you." She walked back to the balcony and gave the girls the info.

Room service knocked at the designated eight o'clock hour stipulated on the card they'd left hanging on the doorknob the night before. After they finished breakfast, they went down the elevator and boarded the jitney that would drop off each for her morning activity. They agreed to meet back at the hotel at noon, change their clothes, go to lunch, and then meander the streets of the town.

Nina decided to try a different trail where the jitney made a routine stop. She didn't notice the blue car following them. As she got off the small bus, she thought she saw a glimmer of blue but brushed it off. Even though they hadn't figured out who might be following her or why, the three had agreed to ignore their phantasms, and of course, the ugly, creepy elves. Several people got off the jitney at the same place, which made it easier for Nina to ignore the intrusion. If it really was an intrusion. She decided she would stick close to the two couples ahead of her, but far enough away so she wouldn't be considered an intrusion herself. As long as they were within sight, she was okay.

Just before she entered the park, her phone buzzed. There was a text from Lois saying: *Meant to tell you. Busy packing. Jane did not get the role and the director doesn't want any changes to the script.*

Nina wrote back: *Thanks. Enjoy your trip.* Nina sighed. At least she'd done her best, even if Jane didn't deserve it. Nina always took the high road.

It was a clear sunny day with the temperature hovering around fifty degrees. There had been talk about snow, but it surely didn't feel like it. As she walked farther into the woods, she heard a twig snap behind her. It startled her. She really didn't want to look over her shoulder, then decided it would be in her best interest if she did. She slowly turned her head as she moved forward. It was a young deer. Behind it were two more. She marveled at this glorious part of Mother Earth. She then moved swiftly to get closer to the couples in front of her. Her Fitbit buzzed, telling her it was time to turn around and start back. But she would have to do it alone. She checked her pockets. "Good girl," she said to herself as she pulled out the small container of pepper spray. She always carried it when she went hiking, but wanted to double-check. Being alone in the woods never bothered her, probably because Winston, her Bernese mountain dog, always went with her. Today she was on her own.

She reached the bench within ten minutes of the jitney's arrival and took a seat. Again she heard a twig snap. She had her hand on the trigger of the pepper spray and turned to look in the direction of the noise. A woman in a tracksuit with a hoodie was running in the opposite direction. She couldn't see her face or hair. "Take it easy," she reminded herself. She decided it was better to stand and wait. She didn't want to be a sitting duck.

Much to her relief, the jitney was in sight and came to a stop in front of her. She was glad she'd decided to go on a trail that had service to and from the hotel. Despite all her resolve, she admitted she was a little jumpy and wasn't up to walking back on her own. They passed houses and shops decorated in holiday gear. It gave her mixed feelings about leaving Richard behind for New Year's Eve, even though they'd agreed there were 365 days and nights in a year. They could pick any one of them to celebrate.

\* \* \*

Amy's skiing had slightly improved from the day before. Only one little fall, and she made a quick recovery. It was an unusually warm day for winter in Tahoe, but she welcomed it. She decided winter outdoor activities should be limited to snowball fights once a year.

She'd given up ice skating years ago. Too cold. Too icy! When she was eight years old, she'd begged for ice skates for Christmas. Her friend Chrissy had a pair and went skating on a pond near their house as often as she could. Her mother wasn't keen on the idea, but her father thought it would help Amy with her social skills. He worried she spent too much time with her nose in books and was missing out on normal childhood fun. Before her mother agreed, they took her to an indoor rink so she could practice. She seemed confident and managed to get halfway around the rink before she tumbled over. She didn't cry or whine. She simply asserted that she needed more practice, and having her own skates would enable her to do so.

Amy's father was often surprised by the mature logic of his child. Neither of her parents could disagree, and they bought her a pair of girl's DBX skates for Christmas. Amy was elated and couldn't wait to go to the pond and put them on. Her parents wouldn't allow her to go alone and phoned Chrissy's parents. Everyone had finished opening the rest of their gifts and agreed to meet at the pond.

When they arrived, there were a dozen people ranging in age from kids to adults. Amy pulled on her new skates and was ready to go. Her mother thought an adult should go out on the ice with her, but Amy wanted to show her independence. Unfortunately, she also showed her inelegance, as both her feet flew out from under her. She must have skidded several yards, flailing and spinning until she hit the ice with her face. The sting from the impact was excruciating. People were scrambling to get to her, some wearing only their boots. It was pandemonium. People were slipping and sliding in all directions. Luckily no one was seriously injured. A few bruises, and a couple of sore butts, and total humiliation for Amy. She may have survived the embarrassment of falling, but causing all that commotion was mortifying. When the kids returned to school after the holiday break, they teased her with names like *Blanchard the Bungler* and *Awkward Amy*. She never showed any emotion, even though it really hurt deep down inside. She never put on a pair of skates again.

Today was going to be her last hurrah down the snow-capped mountains. It was a thrill for sure. To be honest, it was the kind of thrill you can't wait to be over, like being on the biggest Ferris wheel, or some crazy roller-coaster ride where you end up screaming all the way. One and done. Okay. Maybe two, but this was it.

Frankie borrowed Nina's car and returned to the Lake View Ski Lodge. She wasn't going to stay long and didn't want to be at the mercy of the jitney schedule. "Hey, Carl. Mind if I noodle around a little out back?"

"Noodle all you want. I'll be here." He handed her the shoes and the poles. "Need some help?"

"Thanks. Let me try it on my own. Not that I plan on doing this again any time soon, but I'd like to think I could if the occasion should arise."

"Atta girl." He watched as Frankie slid her toes in and tightened the strap. Then the back. Then the instep. "You're a good learner," he called over to her.

"You're a good teacher." She stood, dug the poles in, and ventured toward the back of the lodge and into the woods.

Frankie was getting the hang of it now as she glided over the snow, going deeper and deeper into the woods. The quietude was alluring. She thought about Giovanni and how well-suited they were to each other. Maybe she would get up the nerve to broach the subject of taking their relationship to the next level. She snickered, thinking about how many times people told her she was intimidating. She certainly didn't intend to be. She was outgoing. Warm. Friendly. Then she remembered her friend Ken telling her, "That's the problem. You are right there in front of them being *you*." She made a face. Who else was she supposed to be? She knew Giovanni didn't think she was intimidating. He thought she was delightful.

She reached into her pocket and pulled out her phone. If she had service, she would send Nina a text to tell her she was running late, and then send Giovanni a text to let him know she was thinking about him. She figured her gloves would not work on the keypad. When she attempted to remove one, her phone slipped out of her hand and landed about two feet away in the snow. As she tried to reach for it, the snowshoes didn't pivot as easily as her body. She jabbed a pole in the snow to keep from toppling over, but that just made the situation worse. She tumbled sideways over a small hill and into the snow. She held her breath for a moment to regroup, but the throbbing in her ankle made her cry out in pain. She started yelling, "Help! Somebody help me!" She listened. Nothing. She tried to move. It hurt too much. She didn't think she'd broken her ankle. She *hoped* she hadn't, as she continued to call for help. She looked in the direction of the ski shack. It was much farther away than she'd thought. She didn't realize how much terrain she'd covered. She tried to get up. No such luck. She called out again. Still nothing. Just the silence and the echoes of her cries.

Rachael sat on her bed and stared at the house phone. Fifteen minutes had gone by. What should she say? "Hey, guess who? I'm he-ere!" She finally got the courage to lift the receiver and asked to be put through to the room registered to

Francesca Cappella. Rachael started to shake as the phone continued to ring with no answer. When the voice-mail prompt invited her to leave a message, she hung up. Her announcement was nothing to leave on a recording. It had to be done in person. At least a conversation. She decided she'd try again around lunch, then put her things together for a morning run down the slopes. She made a point to stop at Randy's desk to thank him for the great night.

"It was a total pleasure, madame. My friends were impressed with your fancy footwork."

"As am I with yours. We need to talk about that some more."

"Speaking of talking, did you call your friends?"

"I did, but there was no answer. I'll try again around lunch. If I don't reach them, I'll keep skiing through the afternoon and then try to catch them around dinnertime."

"No message?" Randy queried.

"This has to be done in person, or at least a real-time phone call."

"You have a point. Enjoy the day."

"Thanks. See ya." Rachael gave him a wave as she trotted to the door. The jitney line was queued and ready to board, and people were stowing their skis in the baggage compartment below. She was thankful she'd left hers in a locker at the slope. She thought, *Too much baggage. Literally and figuratively.* It was time she took an honest assessment of her life and relationships. She was always too quick to become enamored with men who paid attention to her. She thought sex meant love until she discovered it was not really a prerequisite. Then after the oxytocin wore off, she began to see the person for who he really was. Most of them were losers or users. For years, she'd traveled a bumpy road of heartbreaks until she realized her relationships always moved too fast.

But what about Henry? He seemed genuine. He was

benevolent. Charitable. Kind. But did he love her? Equally important, did she love him? Idolized? For sure, but that wasn't love. She appreciated his talent and generosity, but that did not make their relationship any stronger. He was generous with his time instructing handicapped children, which was admirable. But he hadn't been spending any time with her for the past few months. When she was in the crisis of shutting down her studio and selling the property, he just kept telling her she was being dramatic. Of course she was. That's how she handled most things. Then she almost laughed out loud. She realized she was much more of a drama queen than Nina. In fact, Nina was the opposite of drama queen. Despite her fame, Nina was one of the most down-to-earth people Rachael had ever met.

The jitney arrived at the slopes while Rachael was still musing about her relationships. She would give the subject more thought when she pushed off. The lift reached the top, and Rachael began her descent.

She thought about Amy, the brainiac. She was as loyal as a Labrador. The girl didn't have a mean bone in her body. She could be a bit of a space cadet, but every move she made was without malice.

And Frankie? Frankie had many moving parts. She was successful, generous, and kind. And full of surprises. Rachael recalled the time they were at a club and a woman was flirting with Rachael's boyfriend du jour. Frankie followed the woman into the ladies' room and blocked the door with her arm. She looked straight at the floozy and said, "You hurt my friend and I will rip your face off." Rachael snickered. How Frankie had pulled off that without laughing, she'd never know. The woman had shriveled and left the club. When she was sure the bimbo had vanished, Frankie turned to Rachael: "You do realize he's not worth it. And I'm glad it didn't have to come to hair-pulling and such. I really wasn't in the mood for a fistfight. Or worse."

Rachael hugged her friend. "Thanks, pal. Good thing, because I don't have bail money!" They both laughed as onlookers watched, dumbfounded. Rachael imagined some were disappointed. *Fun and crazy memories*, she thought to herself.

She dug in her poles and once again whipped past other skiers, reaching the bottom of the slope even faster than before. She thought it might be a record for her. More importantly, she'd cleared her head of misconceptions. She would get square with Frankie. She had no beef with Amy or Nina. Then there was the subject of Henry. She would also have a sit-down with him. She finally admitted to herself they weren't making it as a couple. She would survive as a single woman again. She corrected herself. She would survive as a single woman once and for all. Let the chips fall where they may. She would pick up the pieces and start again.

Nina and Amy arrived at the hotel just before noon. When they got to their room, Frankie was nowhere in sight.

"Maybe she missed the jitney coming back?" Amy suggested.

"I'll try her cell. Service is a bit wonky, but maybe I can get through." The call went straight to voice mail. "Yo, Frankie. Babycakes, you on your way? Amy and I are famished."

A half hour passed. Amy and Nina changed into less wintery clothes, but still no word from Frankie. "Do you think we should call the snowshoe place?"

"I don't know where she went, but Randy might." She dialed the concierge.

"Good afternoon. This is Randy; how may I be of assistance?"

"Hi, Randy. This is Nina Hunter. We've been waiting for our friend Frankie, but she is MIA."

"She went snowshoeing this morning," Randy replied.

"Yes, we know. Can you please give me the number so I can call and see where she might be?"

"I'll call Carl right now. Stand by."

Randy dialed the number, and it rang several times before someone picked up. "Hi, it's Randy from La Spa. Do you know if our guest Frankie Cappella is still there?"

"I just got here, and Carl is on a lunch break. Hang on, let me check." The person looked at the tour board, but her name wasn't on it. "She's not signed up with any group."

"Maybe she went out back to practice?" Randy suggested.

"I'm the only one here, so I can't check right now. Carl should be back in a half hour. I'll let him know."

Randy didn't like what he was hearing, but had no choice but to wait. He phoned Nina, saying no news is good news, but Nina wasn't having any of it.

He suggested Frankie had already left and was on her way back. It hadn't occurred to him to ask if Frankie had turned in her snowshoes. He dialed the number again, and the person who answered said he was in the middle of signing people in and couldn't check. He'd have to wait until Carl got back. Randy heaved a big sigh. It wouldn't take more than a couple of minutes to check. *People. Ugh.*

Randy phoned Nina and told her they couldn't get any information until Carl returned. Nina said she would go to the Lake View Ski Lodge herself. She and Amy headed down to the lobby and walked over to Randy's desk.

"This is not good," Nina said. "Frankie is never late; she is not answering her cell." Nina was trying to remain calm.

Randy gave them directions to Carl's. As soon as they walked out, he sent a text to Rachael, hoping it would go through. *URGENT. FRANKIE SEEMS TO BE MISSING.*

Rachael was unlatching her skis when her phone vibrated in her pocket. She gasped at the message and sent a reply. *EXPLAIN PLEASE.*

Randy typed out what little information he had: *SHE*

*DIDN'T RETURN IN TIME FOR LUNCH DATE AND ISN'T ANSWERING HER PHONE.* Rachael bundled her skis under her arm and moved to the jitney stand. She was huffing and puffing, waiting for all the slowpokes to move along. She practically threw her skis in the bin and grabbed the nearest seat. It would be at least a half hour before she got back to the hotel. She sent Nina a text:

**I'm in Tahoe. Heard Frankie is missing. Will be back at the hotel in half hour.**

Nina commandeered Amy's vehicle. She wanted to be in charge of the wheels. She was just about to drive off when her phone dinged. She was stunned.

**You're where? Here? In Tahoe? Going to look for her.**

Rachael typed back.

**Wait for me. I have my skis.**

"Can you believe this?" Nina was astounded. "Rachael is in town. She is on her way back to help us look for Frankie. She has her skis."

"Wait. What? She's here? Why didn't she tell us?"

"I think she was telling us with all that mistletoe and your little elf friends."

"Fiends, you mean." Amy was about to explain the background of elves when Nina interrupted her.

"Whatever." Nina took a few deep breaths. "Well, one mystery is solved. The next one is where is Frankie?"

"You're forgetting your stalker," Amy reminded her.

"She is the last thing on my mind right now. But I can tell you one thing, if I see her, I am going to tackle her to the ground." Nina was pumped. And scared. Heaven forbid something had happened to Frankie.

As the two women sat in the SUV waiting, Nina's phone buzzed again. It wasn't a text. It was a call. Nina looked at Amy. "It's Giovanni. What should I tell him?"

"Let's see what he can tell us first. Maybe he's heard from her," Amy said. "Try to remain calm."

Nina took another deep breath. "Gio! What's going on?"

"Nina. *Come stai?*"

"I'm good. How are you? Where are you? There's a lot of noise in the background." The Bluetooth from her phone automatically connected to the interior speakers in the car, and Amy could hear the conversation.

"I am dropping Nona at the airport." He waited for another plane to pass overhead. "I have been trying to reach Frankie all morning. Her phone is going to voice mail, and she does not reply to my texts."

Nina looked at Amy and mouthed, "What do I say?"

Amy mouthed back, "Tell him." She flapped both hands at her.

"Gio. Listen. We were supposed to meet Frankie for lunch, but she's late."

"How late?" Giovanni demanded with some concern.

"It's going on almost an hour now." Nina cringed, waiting for his response.

"This is not like Frankie. And she does not call you?"

"No. We got the same thing: voice mail and no response to texts."

"Where was she?" Giovanni was holding back his panic.

"Snowshoeing."

"*Madonna Mia.*" Giovanni was now obviously concerned. "What are you doing to find her?"

"We're waiting for Rachael to go to the Lake View Lodge. The snowshoe place. Rachael has skis, so she can get through the woods more quickly than the rest of us."

"What about the people at the ski shoe place?" He was getting his English words mixed up.

"The guy is out to lunch, and there's no record of her going out on a trail with a group."

"No search party?"

"It's too soon, so we're going to start our own."

"Okay. Okay. I am going to fly out there. Just text me the address of the hotel and the shoe place."

"But the flights from New York don't get in until after midnight," Nina said.

"I am going to see if I can find a charter jet."

"That will cost you over ten thousand dollars!" Nina exclaimed.

"What does it matter? It's Frankie. There is no price too high for her. I will let you know. *Ciao*."

Nina looked at Amy. "We should probably tell Peter and Richard."

As Nina sent a text to Richard, Amy sent one to Peter. Once the men acknowledged what was going on, they sent a text to Giovanni:

**Is there anything we can do?**

He responded.

**Not yet. I will let you know as soon as I can find a jet.**

# Chapter Twelve

Frankie had closed her eyes to cope with the pain, but as she opened them, she was faced with the sight of a wolf, dangerously close. She let out a bloodcurdling scream that was instantly muffled by the snow-laden trees. The animal tilted his head, and Frankie realized it was an Alaskan malamute, not a wild creature. And he was gorgeous.

She decided to try her Doctor Dolittle voice. "Hey, fella. Do you have a home? Where's your mommy and daddy?" The dog continued to look at her curiously, turning his head back and forth as if he understood what she was saying. Or was trying to understand what she was saying. "You're a good boy. You are a boy? If not, I apologize."

Frankie realized that talking to the dog helped ease her pain and fear. Someone would surely be looking for this magnificent animal sooner or later. But what if he decided to go home and leave her there? That particularly frightening thought left as quickly as it had come. She had something new to fear.

It was a man whom she imagined was over six feet tall. He had a full head of bushy hair and a face that reminded Frankie of Grizzly Adams. She didn't know whether she was going to pee in her pants, scream, or cry.

The man moved closer and called to the dog. "Duke. Come here, boy."

Frankie was relieved she hadn't mistaken the dog's gender, but who was *this* guy?

"Hello, Miss." He had a metropolitan accent. She guessed he wasn't some wild mountain man. "You look like you need some help."

"Boy, do I ever." Frankie tried to wiggle, but she was jolted by pain with every move she made. She pointed to her ankle.

"Mind if I take a look? Make sure it's not broken." He gingerly lifted her leg from the snow and pressed lightly on her snow pants.

"Ye-ouch!" Frankie blurted out.

"That's a good sign."

"What is?"

"You didn't shriek." He made a mound of snow and elevated her foot. "I'll go back and get my snowmobile. Duke will keep you company. Should take less than ten minutes. Don't go anywhere." He gave her a big smile.

"I'll try not to."

Duke came over and sat next to Frankie. "Gonna keep me warm?" She put her arm around the dog, and he rubbed the back of his neck against it. "You are a good boy." She rested her head on his back. A few minutes later, she heard the sound of a snowmobile getting closer. Duke sat up as his master got off the machine in front of her.

"The name is Troy. Sorry I didn't introduce myself before."

"Nice to meet you, Troy. I'm Francesca, but everyone calls me Frankie."

He bobbed his head. "Good to meet you, Frankie. How did you manage this?" He slowly lifted her from the ground. "Lean on me."

Frankie noticed a type of sledge was hitched to the snow-mobile. "Oh, I figured I'd get myself lost, drop my phone in the snow, twist my ankle, and wait for someone to rescue me."

"Where did you come from?" He looked up and saw her trail marks started much farther back, in the direction of the Lake View Lodge. "Carl's?" he asked.

"Yes. Carl's."

"How long have you been out here?"

"Not sure. Maybe two hours." She squirmed to prop herself up higher. "I mean, I haven't been sitting here that long. Probably a little less than an hour. I was enjoying the tranquility and lost track of the time. So. I was going to text my friends to tell them I was running late."

"Let me guess, you took off your gloves and dropped the phone."

"There was a lot to juggle. Poles, gloves, phone. Not so easy."

"Come on. I'll take you back to my cabin so we can get a better look at that ankle."

"Shouldn't I go to the hospital or something?"

"You could, but you might be out here another hour before an ambulance can get to you. Plus, I have heat. Once we assess the damage, we can decide the best course of action."

"Okay. I'm sold." Frankie had a good feeling about this guy named Troy. There was nothing sinister about him in spite of the way he looked. Plus, he had a beautiful dog.

Troy placed her gently on the sledge, tucked her poles next to her, and drove the snowmobile slowly toward his cabin; all the while, Duke loped through the snow to keep up with them.

When the snowmobile came to a stop, Troy unhitched the sledge and dragged it onto the porch and then into the small wooden house. A cast-iron stove was throwing off welcome heat. Frankie looked around and noticed fishing rods and photos hanging on the walls. "I saw some smoke yesterday. Was it coming from here?"

"Probably. I'm the only one crazy enough to live way out here in the woods." He helped Frankie out of her jacket and wrapped a warm blanket around her shoulders. "This place used to belong to my grandfather."

Another hint that he wasn't a hillbilly; otherwise, he would have said *grand-daddy.* Either way, she was grateful he'd saved her from turning into a popsicle. She shivered at the thought. "Here, let me get you closer to the stove." He pushed the sledge farther into the room. "I think it's time we take a look at this thing." He unbuckled the shoes and gently removed the boot from her injured foot. Next came her sock. She was wearing the ones with the cat faces.

"We'd better not let Duke see those." Troy chuckled.

"Doesn't he like cats?" Frankie winced.

"I'm kidding. Duke likes just about anybody and anything, unless they try to lay a hand on me. Luckily, that doesn't happen often."

Frankie also noticed his diction. He spoke like a person who was *not* raised by wolves. "Where are you from originally?"

"I grew up in Bakersfield, moved to LA, and now I'm here." He examined her foot and ankle. "I don't think it's broken, but I am not a doctor. What I can tell you is you're going to have some bruising here." He pressed lightly on the discoloration that was already forming. "We should get you back from whence you came, madame."

"I'm staying at La Spa Resort."

"Ah. Nice. I am going to have to put some gas in the snowmobile. I'll just be a few minutes."

Frankie looked around the cabin again. The photos showed a younger version of Troy with an older man. Probably him and his grandfather. There were photos from when he was a little boy until he was probably in his twenties. She recognized his eyes. Good-looking man without that coat of fur on his face. As she gazed across the room, she spotted an acoustic guitar propped against a low table. On top of the table was an album. She stretched her neck to see what band it was. You could tell a lot about a man by the music he listened to. *The Troy-Man*. "Huh. Troy. Guitar. Troy-Man," she mumbled.

He came back inside, holding two small planks. He unwrapped the blanket around her, used the planks as splints, and tied them to her leg with some cord. As he was tending to her, she motioned to the guitar. "Do you play?"

"I used to. But not anymore. At least not out in public."

"Are you the 'Troy' in The Troy-Man?"

"Guilty." He placed his hand on his heart. "One album. One-hit wonder."

"I remember that song. It was one of my favorites. Five years ago, maybe? 'Janie-Jennine.' Wow. So nice to meet you."

"Nice to meet someone who actually remembers it and liked it." He wrapped a blanket around Frankie's foot since she wasn't going to be able to put her boot back on, and then made some tea for the two of them.

"Do you live here permanently now?" Frankie asked. She noticed the cabin was well-kept with recent furnishings.

"For now. My grandfather passed away two years ago and left it to me. I was so over LA and the music scene."

"But you guys were really good. Your harmonies were pristine."

"You know what they say about Hollywood? Nobody knows anything. We were told there was already a Crosby, Stills & Nash sound. The world didn't need to revisit it, or some such nonsense. My argument was that people *like* that kind of music. People still listen to 'Suite: Judy Blue Eyes'."

"I know exactly what you're talking about," Frankie said with authority. "I, too, was an aspiring singer. Went the whole route. Demos, pressed my own record, paid for radio promos. My strength is ballads. And I was told that people don't listen to ballads anymore."

"It's like the time Linda Ronstadt wanted to do standards and her record label wouldn't agree. They said the music was outdated," Troy added.

"Yep," Frankie broke in. "She hired Nelson Riddle and paid his fee herself, from what I've been told. Or at least made some arrangements so the record label wouldn't lose money. It went on to sell over three million copies, and she won a Grammy."

Troy shook his head. "If you want to do something new or different, no one wants to sign you until someone else is successful doing it. It's so aggravating. And frustrating. And demoralizing." He heaved a big sigh. "Sorry. I get on my soapbox once in a while. Especially when I have an audience other than Duke." The dog raised his head and made a little yapping sound.

"Please don't apologize. After music gave up on me, I went to work in book publishing. It's the same. No one wants to do something new or revisit something until someone else does, and then the market gets flooded with similar stuff."

"Television and movies, too. Like I said, nobody knows anything." He snickered. "Right after my record deal ended, I went through a bad breakup. She had her own agenda. An actress. She didn't want to be with someone who, in her estimation, was a nobody. That was the last straw, and I decided to escape and spend some time here." He handed Frankie a cup of herbal tea.

"Thank you." She wrapped her fingers around the warm mug. "She sounds like a real piece of work. Better you're out of that relationship. At least you have this place." She scanned it again. "It's a lovely cabin, and the surrounding property is glorious."

"It is. I used to spend almost every summer here when I

was a kid. Then when I got into the music thing in LA, I spent fewer summers. I kinda regret it now."

"Looks like you have a lot of memories." She pointed her cup toward the photos on the shelf.

"The thing is, if I don't live here, the town can take away the land."

"What do you mean?" She looked at him quizzically.

"Several years ago, it was zoned for commercial use, and this particular plot can only remain residential if someone actually occupies the space." He took a swig of his tea. "The family's owned this modest ten-acre plot for almost a century. And now it sits smack in the middle of a resort whose owners want to expand, and I am in their way." He rested his elbows on his knees. "The whole thing is a bit hinky. I was told the caveat in the new zoning was that my grandfather had to live here. But since he's passed on, I've been fighting the locals."

"They can't simply take it away from you, can they?"

"They'll declare the place condemned and then sell it off." He looked around the room as if for an answer. "At least that's what I've been told."

"But what about your rights to the property?"

"The laws are extremely complicated. They say the land is only deeded to my grandfather, so they're trying to get me out. I need a top-notch lawyer, but I can't afford one right now."

The wheels in Frankie's mind were already spinning. She knew a slew of attorneys in New York who worked in real estate law.

"That really stinks."

"Yes, it does." He leaned over and held out his arms. He took her mug and set it down on the table. "Let's see if you can stand up. Don't put too much pressure on your foot."

Frankie climbed up and rested her weight on her uninjured foot.

"Okay. Now slowly put your other foot down."

"Ouch. Ouch. Ouchy. Ouchy." She whimpered.

"At least you're not wailing." He set her back on the sledge.

"Do you have a phone, by any chance? I know people are probably worried about me right about now."

"You are not the only one with cell-phone issues. My battery is dead, and I can't find the charger."

"Maybe you dropped it in the snow," Frankie teased.

Troy closed one eye and scrutinized her. "As I said, I am no doctor, but by the sound of your sassiness, you're going to be just fine."

"Thanks to you."

"I'll bring you back to La Spa, where they can call an ambulance or have someone bring you to the hospital so you can get that x-rayed."

"That sounds like a good, but crummy plan."

"Why?"

"I don't want to go to the hospital." Frankie pouted, and her eyes got wide.

"Listen, missy, you will be seen by an exceptional ortho guy. We have plenty of them around here because of all the skiers, and the yahoos."

"Right. Good point." Frankie nodded. She wanted another cup of tea, but she was in dire need of the bathroom. "Troy?" she said sweetly.

"Yes?" he replied kindly.

"I have to use the bathroom," she said sheepishly.

"Oh boy. How are we going to manage this?" He looked around the cabin and then moved the furniture out of the path of the bathroom. He pushed the sledge close to the doorframe. "If I help you, do you think you can stand up?"

"Probably, but in case you haven't noticed, I have different equipment from you, and I need to sit."

Troy chuckled. "Yes, I noticed. If you can, lean both arms

on the door jamb, then hop over to the, er, commode. Can you make it in there?"

"Yes." She was able to turn herself around, then realized she couldn't shut the door. "And?"

"Oh, right. Sorry. I'll be outside. Give a holler when you're done."


Rachael, Nina, and Amy were all talking at the same time. "Ladies! Please. Everyone take a deep breath. First things first." Nina turned to Rachael and bellowed, "What on God's green earth are you doing here?"

"I was invited. Remember?" Rachael was stoic.

"No kidding," Nina barked back. "Why didn't you say something? For heaven's sake, Rachael. What kind of game are you playing?" Nina was fuming. There were too many things going sideways.

Amy rested her hand on Nina's arm. "How about that breath you just suggested?"

Nina realized she had been holding hers for way too long. She let out a big whoosh of air. "Sorry, Rach. This has been one heck of a day."

Amy tried to lighten the mood. "Rachael, where did you find those hideous elves?" She giggled.

"They really are revolting, aren't they?" Rachael chortled.

"I thought elves were supposed to be cute," Nina put in.

"On the contrary. We have been misled. According to Norse mythology, elves are evil by nature. There are dark elves known as Dökkálfar who live in a place called Niflheim, the cold, dark, misty world of the dead. They steal children, curse humans, or drive them mad," Amy informed her friends. "I told you they were fiends." She sat back and folded her arms as if to say, *I told you so.*

"Now, isn't that special?" Nina grumbled. "I shall never look at an elf again without making the sign of the cross or dangling garlic in front of it."

"My, how we have been led astray," Rachael commented. "Makes me wonder what other fables have been misrepresented?"

"Please, let's not bring Santa into the conversation. I am sure he has a very reasonable explanation as to why he employs elves," Amy snickered.

"Or maybe they're doing community service." Nina also laughed.

Rachael was looking at the address and then the GPS. "It's the next turn." She rolled down the window and pointed.

Nina blew into the parking lot like she was going to put out a fire. The three clambered out of the vehicle, while Rachael yanked her skis out of the back.

Nina was the first at the shed. "Hi, anyone named Carl here?"

A man got up from one of the benches. "That would be me, Miss. What can I do fer ya?"

"Frankie Cappella. Have you seen her?"

"Only this morning when she came up and strapped on her snowshoes."

"Where did she go?" Rachael looked off into the distance.

"Probably out back. That's where she was practicing yesterday."

"Wait a second. Didn't you speak to Randy?" Nina asked.

"No. Not today."

"He said he called. Someone else answered and said you were at lunch, and he was too busy to check if she'd turned in her snowshoes."

"Well, doggone it. Nobody told me anything." He turned and yelled to the back. "Bart? Get out here."

The sound of shuffling footsteps got louder. "Yeah, Uncle Carl?" The kid must have been in his teens, his teeth already stained from tobacco.

"Randy called earlier looking for a woman named Frankie."

Bart rubbed his chin. "Oh yeah. He wanted me to see if she checked her shoes back in."

"And did you?" Carl was starting to fume.

"I was busy putting a roster together." Bart looked apathetic. "You know. Taking care of business."

"Well, I know she didn't turn them in when I was here." He felt his temperature rise as he looked over the sign-in sheet. Just as he feared, Frankie hadn't turned her shoes in, and she'd been out there almost three hours by now. He wanted to slap the stupid grin off his nephew's face.

"All right. Let's get moving before we lose the light," Carl said. "I'll get my skis. I can cover more ground faster." He looked over at Rachael. "I see you brought yours."

"Yes, sir. I'm Rachael."

Nina and Amy introduced themselves. "Sorry for the lack of manners."

"No problem." Carl was strapping on his skis.

"How should we handle this? Amy can ski, but she doesn't have any. I kinda stink at it."

"How are you on snowshoes?" Carl asked.

"Never tried." Nina tightened her lips.

"I don't suggest you try to learn right now." Carl took charge. This wasn't the first time someone had wandered off.

"The good news is we can follow her trail."

Nina didn't want to say it, but the bad news was they didn't know what condition Frankie would be in when they found her.

"There's a red phone on the wall." He pointed to a space on the wall with several first-aid supplies on display. "It's for Mountain Rescue. One of you call them while Rachael and I get going. Just tell them you're at Carl's. They'll know where to go."

Rachael and Carl started the trek, following the marks in the snow made by Frankie's snowshoes. Nina stayed on the phone with the rescue team and described Frankie. But Nina didn't know about Frankie's new white jacket and described the clothes she'd last seen her friend wearing.

Giovanni had wracked his brains for anyone he knew who might be willing to let him use their private plane or who subscribed to a charter service. Such services required a minimum number of flight hours over the course of the year, and the price was slightly discounted, if you could call fifteen hundred dollars an hour a discount. It didn't matter. He would pay for the fuel and the pilot and any other fees.

Surprisingly, his first thought was Mateo. He used the service when his crew traveled to areas that didn't have commercial airports. But how could Giovanni get in touch? Then it dawned on him to call Frankie's assistant. She would have the information. Giovanni knew it was a big ask, but it was Frankie. *Their* Frankie.

Giovanni was relieved when Dottie answered. He was one inch from panic. He'd explained the situation which, in turn, put Dottie on edge. She'd told Giovanni to hold while she called Mateo. His first sigh of relief came when Mateo answered. On the three-way call, Dottie gave him a short explanation, but Giovanni interrupted, added a few more details and asking if he could use Mateo's jet service to fly to Tahoe.

The second sigh of relief came at Mateo's willingness to help and his offer to go along. Giovanni thanked him profusely, but said they had little to go on at the moment. If they were lucky, Frankie would be found safe and sound by the time he got to Tahoe.

Mateo explained it was a very stripped-down version of a private jet. No frills, no big-screen TV, no sofa. Just seats, a lavatory, a pilot, copilot, cabin attendant, and a phone-charging station. Giovanni thanked him repeatedly in English and Italian. Mateo told him he would call the service and have them get the jet ready. He would text him the location and the name of the person he should speak to.

While Giovanni was waiting for Mateo's instructions, Richard and Peter sent a group text offering to go with him. The only problem was location. Peter was in Harrisburg, and Richard was in Philadelphia. Once Giovanni got the information from Mateo, he asked if the jet could stop in Denver to pick up two more passengers. Mateo told him it wouldn't be a problem, and the stop would give the pilot an opportunity to refuel and stretch his legs. Then he sent Giovanni the name of the jetport in Denver where Peter and Richard could catch up with him.

Mateo sent Giovanni a text:

**Wheels up in one hour.**

Giovanni sent a group text to Richard and Peter:

**Meet me in Denver. At Villiers Jet hangar. Then two more hours to South Lake Tahoe. Should land by 9:30.**

Richard and Peter scrambled to find flights that would coincide with Giovanni's plans. It was fairly easy for Richard, but Peter had to fly on a very obscure airline. One he had never heard of. He hoped the pilot was qualified; if there was a chimpanzee in the cockpit, he would not be fastening his seat belt. *Giovanni would understand.* Peter nervously laughed to himself.

Richard's and Peter's flights were due to arrive between eight and eight-thirty in Denver. If everything ran on time, they would be in South Lake Tahoe by nine-thirty Pacific Time.

Giovanni had sent Nina the details, including the posse formed by Peter and Richard. He hoped and prayed Frankie would be waiting for him at the hotel, safe and sound.

Now, as Giovanni boarded the jet, it dawned on him he hadn't contacted his brother. He'd been so busy making arrangements. He smacked himself on the forehead. "Stupido." He instantly sent a text to Marco before he had to turn his phone to airplane mode.

**Frankie è scomparso. Sulla strada per il lago Tahoe.**

He was too flummoxed to write in English: *Frankie is missing. I am going to Lake Tahoe.*

Marco decided to phone Giovanni. This was much too important for a text. The two brothers spoke half in English, half in Italian. Once Marco understood the situation, he wished his brother "*Buona fortuna. Dio ti benedicta.*" *Good luck. God bless you.*

As much as he hated doing it, Giovanni turned his phone to airplane mode. It was unnerving to be out of touch with the woman he loved and the people who loved her.

He finally had a chance to inspect the interior of the Embraer jet. Mateo was correct. It wasn't fancy, but it sure beat a city bus. The wide comfortable seats were arranged in two quads so four people could face each other and discuss business, with a pull-out table on each side. A narrow center aisle ran from the cockpit to the rear of the plane.

The captain and copilot were the only two in the cockpit, with one cabin attendant. The cabin attendant asked if there was anything he needed before takeoff. "We have alcoholic beverages, soda, coffee, and snacks. Nothing fancy." She smiled.

Giovanni checked his watch. It was past five o'clock. He could use a cocktail right about now. "Please, vodka and soda."

"Certainly." The plane did not have a typical galley. It was just one cabinet above a small refrigerator, similar to the minibar in a hotel room. She returned with a mini bottle of Tito's, a can of seltzer, and a plastic cup. "We're sorta the budget airline of private jets." She cracked a smile.

Giovanni managed to smile back. "*Grazie.* I mean, thank you. It's been a stressful afternoon."

"Enjoy your beverage and try to relax. Those are the only two things you can do right now."

He nodded in agreement. A feeling of guilt washed over him. He had been jealous of Mateo. His talent, his good looks, his cookbook, his relationship with Frankie, and his altruism. It was Mateo's altruism that had enabled Giovanni to be here. He felt as if he owed Mateo an apology, but Mateo didn't know Giovanni had felt that way. *Had.* That was the operative word. Giovanni no longer felt resentful. He understood why Frankie admired Mateo as much as she did. Giovanni promised he would find some way to thank Mateo once this nightmare was over.

Troy inched his way to the edge of the hotel property, where there was enough snow to accommodate his craft. "Duke, you stay with Frankie. I'm going to get help."

Duke responded with an "absolutely" woof. Troy dashed to the lobby, alarming a few guests with his wild looks and expression. "I need an ambulance."

Randy was standing with the manager at that point. "What seems to be the problem?"

"I have one of your guests outside. Frankie Cappella. She fell while she was snowshoeing, and my dog found her."

"Is she all right?" Randy and the manager asked in unison.

"I think it's just a sprain, but she should really have it x-rayed."

An associate phoned EMS. Randy and the hotel manager followed Troy out to the beleaguered Frankie, who was sitting up in the sledge leaning against Duke, and vice versa. He was guarding his precious cargo. She wiggled her fingers. "Hey, guys."

Randy and the manager ran over to her, firing questions:

"Are you all right?"

"What happened?"

"Are you in a lot of pain?"

"Do you want to go to the hospital?"

As quickly as they launched their requests for information, Frankie shot back her answers.

"Yes. I fell. Not too much. Not really." She definitely seemed perky for someone who'd had a harrowing experience. "Thanks to Duke and Troy, I've been well cared for." She pointed to the makeshift splint.

Troy interrupted. "She needs to get that looked at."

The manager and Randy agreed.

"I'll go with you," Troy offered.

"You have done enough. Please. I don't want to ruin the rest of your day." Frankie's appreciation was heartfelt.

"I insist. You're a fan. I can't let you go without knowing you're okay."

"Thanks, Troy. I really appreciate it." The sound of an ambulance could be heard in the distance.

"Where are Nina and Amy?" Their absence was conspicuously obvious to Frankie, even as the shock of her ordeal was setting in.

"They went to Carl's to look for you," Randy said. "I'll call and let them know you're okay. Well, sort of okay, and that you are on the way to the hospital to get an x-ray."

The EMS team lifted Frankie into a stretcher and then into the truck. Troy walked over to Randy. "Mind keeping an eye on Duke 'til I get back?"

"He's gorgeous. Of course, but I can't promise either of us will be here when you do." Randy gave him an impish grin as Troy jumped into the truck.

"Boy, have I created a mess of things," Frankie groaned, just before they placed an oxygen mask over her face. Her blood pressure was down slightly, a common occurrence during shock.

"It could have happened to anyone," Troy said kindly. "I promise I won't tell them it was because you were trying to use your phone."

"Thanks. I appreciate that," she muttered through the clear plastic cup-like thing covering her nose and mouth. "I am going to get such a scolding from Nina just for being lost."

"Sounds like you and your friends are really . . ." He stopped abruptly and peered out the back window.

"What is it?" Frankie asked.

Troy cocked his head. "I thought I recognized someone." When he turned to look again, the person was gone.

"This has been one big bizarro trip." Frankie settled into the heated blanket. "People think they're being followed, seeing things, real or imagined. And now this." She rolled her eyes.

"Followed? As in stalking?"

The EMS attendant subtly motioned him to stop the chatter. Give the oxygen a chance to work, get the patient's pressure and pulse back to normal.

Troy got the message. He patted her hand. "Try to take it easy. You can tell me all about it later." He looked one more time at the entrance to the hotel as the ambulance made its final turn onto the road.

The captain announced they were beginning their descent into the Denver area. "We should be on the ground in twenty minutes." Giovanni was stirred from his lucid dream. Was he dreaming he was on a plane? His eyes flickered several times as he adjusted his frame of mind. It was a very odd feeling, but he was truly on a plane. He mentally checked things off his list: *Landing in Denver. On his way to Lake Tahoe. Need to find Frankie.* His palms began to sweat. It wasn't a dream. It was a nightmare.

The cabin attendant brought him a warm moist towel. "To freshen up."

"Thank you," Giovanni said. He appreciated her consideration. He could not think of the last time he'd felt so helpless.

His stomach was pitching about. Not from turbulence, but from fear of losing Frankie. Then a strange sensation came over him. He *felt* she was all right. Wishful thinking? Why not? They say we create our own reality, and Giovanni chose to create a healthy and happy Frankie.

When the plane landed, he unbuckled his seat belt and stood. His head almost touched the ceiling. He had been so immersed in thought during the flight, he hadn't noticed the close proximity of the interior of the small ten-passenger craft. He moved down the short flight of steps to the tarmac and stretched his arms and legs. The pilot followed and told Giovanni they would have to take off in twenty minutes, with or without his friends.

Giovanni paced back and forth, visualizing Peter and Richard arriving on time. He smiled to himself; *Frankie's spiritual approach to life had been rubbing off on him.*

As she once said, "Giovanni, you do not have the luxury of a negative thought." When he first heard her say it, he didn't understand the overall concept. He thought he'd lost something in translation. But she went on to explain about time and how you want to spend it. Time is fleeting, and it cannot be replaced. Why spend it being negative when you can spend it being positive? And then her philosophy began to make sense.

He sent Nina a text and waited desperately for a response. Still no word from anyone. It was 7:30 in Tahoe. It would be dark. And cold. He shivered just thinking about it.

The roar of jets and the beeping of baggage carts was deafening. It was no wonder everyone wore noise-canceling headsets, and he wished he had a pair right then and there. He checked his watch. Fifteen more minutes, and they would have to take off.

He thought he saw a speck of something in the distance. As it moved closer, it became more visible. It was a passenger cart pushing its speed to capacity. Someone was waving, but he couldn't tell who it was. Then he saw two sets of arms flapping. He frantically waved back. The cart came to a screeching halt, and the men jumped out, each with only a small carry-on. Neither of them had had time to pack anything more than a toothbrush, a few pairs of socks, and clean underwear, which was more than Giovanni had. It was just the clothes on his back, his phone, his wallet, and his keys. And of course, a handkerchief.

Giovanni hurried over and gave Richard a hug and kiss on each cheek. "*Molto bene*! Thank you so much for coming all this way."

"Are you kidding?" Richard replied, as they hurried to the plane. "Anything for Frankie."

"Ditto!" Peter was still not used to the European greeting, but extended his hand and gave Giovanni a big pat on the back.

Giovanni ushered them up the short steps as the cabin attendant greeted them. She opened the small cargo space at the rear of the cabin so they could stow their few belongings.

Giovanni looked at them. "I have none. I was dropping my mother at the airport and left immediately." He made light of it. "I'll think of something." He looked at the two men with roguish expressions on their faces. "Oh, no. I will not wear ladies' underwear." The joke put everyone at ease as they buckled their seat belts.

The captain stepped into the cabin. "Good evening. Glad to see everyone made it. We should have wheels up shortly. If you need to make any phone calls or use the lavatory, please do that now. Anything you need, please let Georgia know before we take off. We have some reported turbulence over the Rockies, but I'll do my best to skirt around it with the help of air traffic control."

Giovanni took a nervous breath. "Georgia? May I please have another vodka and soda?"

Richard was the second to pipe up. "Make that two."

"Count me in," Peter called from his seat.

Giovanni punched out a text to Nina:

**Leaving Denver now with Richard and Peter. Should land around 9:30.**

He hoped Nina would send something. Anything. But after another minute, he had to turn off his phone and wait. And wait. And wait.

Georgia hustled down the aisle with their drinks. The engines started to rev, and the small plane slowly moved from the apron to the taxiway, waiting for clearance. Shortly thereafter, the roar became louder, and the plane began to pick up speed. It made a sharp turn onto the runway and started its ascent. Because of its size, you could feel the power and velocity as it climbed into the dark sky.

Silence filled the cabin until the pilot made the announcement that they had reached a cruising altitude of forty thousand feet; most commercial jets flew at thirty-five thousand feet. He went on to explain the higher altitude would most likely give them the advantage of circumventing turbulence. There was a chorus of sighs of relief. Giovanni was comforted knowing he wasn't the only nervous person on the plane. The idea of turbulence only added to his angst.

"Our flight time is approximately two hours and thirteen minutes, arriving in South Lake Tahoe at nine-thirty. Yes, this is a time-zone machine. We gain two hours. Sit back, relax, and enjoy the ride."

*Easier said than done.*

Rachael and Carl had followed the tracks they assumed were Frankie's. They were led deep into the woods as darkness descended around them. In the dead of winter, daylight only lasts for about nine hours. Now Carl sidled up next to Rachael and handed her a headlamp. "Here. Put this on." A few hundred yards ahead was a small hill, where Frankie's tracks ended. It looked like there had been a wrestling match in the snow. There were pawprints from either a wolf or a dog. Carl pointed one of his poles at the snowmobile tracks.

"Looks like someone took her."

Rachael started to shriek. "Took her? You mean abducted her?"

"Now calm down, little lady. That's not what I meant." He then pointed his pole again. "A sledge was hooked to the snowmobile. See the smooth tracks?"

Rachael leaned over and looked. "What do you think it means?"

"It means somebody pulled her out of the snow. I'm thinking it was probably Troy Manchester. He has a cabin up a little ways from here. In the direction of the tracks. Some people call him a squatter, but his great-grandaddy bought that parcel nearly a hundred years ago." They edged closer to the cabin. "He don't bother me none, but the resort developers want him out." He snorted. "They'd like to see me out, too."

There was no light coming from the cabin. No dog. No snowmobile. Nobody. "From the looks of the tracks, he brought her inside, and then took her somewhere else." He pointed to the ruts and skids going in the opposite direction from the cabin.

"Do you think he took her back to the hotel?"

"Possibly." With that, a crackle from his walkie-talkie pierced the air.

"This is home base. Carl, can you hear me?"

"Copy that," Carl replied. "We're up at the Manchester place. Looks like she may have been up here. Over."

More static and then, "Troy found her. She's at the hospital now getting an x-ray. Over."

"She all right? Over."

"Far as we can tell. Over."

"Well, that sure is good news. Heading back. Over."

"Copy that."

Rachael was practically jumping out of her skis. "She's

okay! She's okay! Oh my gosh! Oh my gosh!" She tried to get close to Carl to give him a hug, but their skis got tangled, and they both fell into the snow.

Carl heaved himself up and brushed off the snow. "You city folk," he joked, and helped her up.

They barreled back to the shed, where Nina and Amy were waiting, both crying from relief.

"You best cut that out or your faces are gonna freeze," Carl kidded.

Mountain Rescue had been called off. Frankie was safe. The dark pall of night had been lifted by the illumination of the full moon. The women embraced each other and performed a happy dance in front of Carl and the two remaining Mountain Rescue team members. They thanked the men for their assistance and invited them to be their guests at the hotel's New Year's Eve party.

Then Nina got the address of the hospital and jumped into her car, hoping Frankie had left the keys tucked in the visor. "Good girl!" Nina grinned and turned to Amy and Rachael. "You guys follow me. It's about ten minutes from here."

"Cool beans!" Amy shouted. Their elation was palpable. A true reunion was underway.

Troy helped Frankie fill out the paperwork, giving the hospital permission to x-ray her leg. The orthopedist gave her a quick once-over and was confident it was just a sprain, but an x-ray was necessary to be absolutely certain. They rolled Frankie down the corridor, while Troy sat in the waiting room of the E.R. Two police officers entered, asking the receptionist about Francesca Cappella. Troy immediately stood.

"Can I help you?"

"Do you know Ms. Cappella?" one of the burly officers asked.

"I found her, or should I say my dog Duke found her, in the snow a few hundred yards from my place."

"Why didn't you call for help?"

"I don't understand." Troy was perplexed. "She lost her phone, and my battery was dead. I brought her to the hotel, and they called EMS."

The bigger of the two cops gave Troy a suspicious look. "You sure about that?"

"Absolutely. What is this all about?"

"Aren't you that squatter up near Carl's place?"

"What does that have to do with anything?" Troy stood up. "Besides, I am not a squatter."

One of the nurses heard the volume of their conversation start to rise. "Excuse me, gentlemen. Can you please keep your voices down?"

"We're going to want to interview Ms. Cappella when she gets back."

"Have at it. I have nothing to hide. If anything, I probably saved her life." Troy had had enough of the constant harassment of the local authorities. *And now? Here? After he provided the best care he could offer to a stranger who could have died of hypothermia?* He counted to ten silently in his head. He knew the police favored the resort developers. They were big donors to the force. "Listen, I have not broken any laws, and your line of questioning could be considered harassment."

The bigger cop snickered. "If you say so, Mountain Man. Take a seat."

"No thanks. I'd rather stand." Troy would have given almost anything to punch the guy in his big fat cheeks.

Several minutes later, a smiling Frankie was being wheeled back to a curtained area of the E.R. The two police officers followed. "Ms. Cappella? We would like to have a word with you."

"Of course, officers. What can I do for you?"

"Did Mr. Troy Manchester abduct you?"

"Abduct me?" Frankie squawked. "You have got to be kidding. He saved me. He *and* his dog." If she had been able, she would have jumped off the gurney and poked her finger in the cop's chest. "You listen to me. I don't know who said what, but I do not see any purpose in your being here."

The nurse stepped in and pulled the curtain behind her. She scolded through tight lips, "This woman has been through an ordeal. Unless you have police business, I suggest you leave and give her the opportunity to regain some equilibrium." She stared them down. The nurse couldn't have been more forceful if she'd had a yardstick to beat them with.

They sheepishly apologized and exited as fast as their feet would allow, blowing past Troy without saying a word.

Frankie looked at the nurse. "Nice work. You from New York, by any chance?" Then she laughed.

"Brooklyn, honey." She winked and pulled the curtain open, allowing Troy to enter.

"How are you feeling?" he asked.

"Better than I did a couple of hours ago."

"Did they give you any pain meds?"

"They offered, but I declined. Extra-strength Tylenol is good enough. I don't know how people tolerate that stuff. It just makes you stupid."

Troy laughed. "You *are* feeling better."

The doctor came into the small space. "As predicted, it's a sprain. We're going to wrap you up and send you home. Do not put any weight on it for a couple of days. Ice, then heat. Repeat. Got it?"

"Got it." Frankie gave him a thumbs-up. "Thanks, doctor!"

"You were starting to tell me a story about a stalker when we got into the ambulance," Troy said. "Care to share? Simply curious." He looked around, but there weren't any chairs near the beds. The area was too small, so he folded his arms and leaned against the wall.

"Sure. If you've got nothing better to do."

"Not until they spring you from this joint." He grinned.

"Okay. I don't know if you could call it stalking, but my friend Nina thought she was being followed all the way from LA. Then she kept getting a glimpse of someone, but could never get a good look at her." Frankie rearranged her pillow. "So when you said you thought you saw someone, it sounded like everyone was delusional." She paused and pursed her lips. "Maybe it's the altitude."

Troy chuckled. "That might have something to do with it."

The two stopped talking when they heard several women's voices begging the stern nurse to let them see their friend. "That sounds very familiar." Frankie cocked her head to listen as the voices approached the curtain.

Rachael was the first face she saw. "Rachael! You naughty girl! I *knew* you were the one planting that mistletoe. And those elves."

Amy and Nina were right behind her. "Don't talk about elves," Amy ordered as she leaned over to give Frankie a kiss. Nina wiggled her way in to do the same.

"You gave us such a scare!" Nina blurted.

"We were so worried!" Amy cried. "And Rachael went out in the woods to look for you!"

Troy stood back to watch the friends gush and fuss over Frankie. Finally, when the tears and laughs subsided, Frankie introduced him.

"Ladies, meet my knight in shining armor, Troy."

He held out his hand. "Troy Manchester."

Nina stopped suddenly. "As in The Troy-Man?"

He looked at her. "Nina Hunter?"

"That would be me." She shook his hand while looking at him curiously. "Didn't you used to date . . ."

He broke in before she could say the name. "If you are talking about who I think you are talking about, then yes."

"So what are you doing up here?" Nina asked. "And with that fur? On your face?" she teased. "I would not have recognized you."

"It's a long story. I'd rather not get into it now. It looks like you ladies have a lot of catching up to do, and I have more fur waiting for me at the hotel."

"Troy, if you don't have anything on your calendar, please be our guests at the hotel New Year's Eve party tomorrow night." Frankie reached out for his hand.

"I think my schedule is pretty open." He gave them a big smile.

"And please bring Duke. He was part of the rescue, after all," Frankie urged.

"Do they allow dogs in the hotel?" Troy asked.

"They will now!" Nina chuckled.

"How are you going to get back to the hotel?" Frankie asked.

Nina jumped in right away. "I'll take you and then come back and get Frankie when she's released."

"Sounds good," Frankie said.

As Troy and Nina passed the stern nurse, Nina offered the woman a quick apology. "Sorry to have made such a fuss, but we were terrified something had happened to Frankie."

"No worries. I'd much rather see people laughing than crying." She gave them a wink. "Happy New Year!"

Troy and Nina walked through the parking lot to Nina's vehicle. She hit the key fob to unlock the doors. Troy could barely fit his legs in without moving the seat back. "You are a tall drink of water," Nina observed.

"And some beer," Troy added.

Nina started the SUV, plugged in the GPS to the hotel. "No need. I can tell you as we go."

"So you live here?" Nina asked.

"Sort of. My grandfather owned a cabin and ten acres of land. I used to spend summers here. When my grandfather passed away, he left me the cabin and the property. Turn left at the next intersection," he directed.

Nina put on the directional signal. "Sounds lovely. Having a place to escape to."

"Well, that's just it. Yes, I did escape the LA scene, but the deed to the property is complicated. When it was handed down to my grandfather, resort developers were buying up land like candy. My grandfather didn't want to sell. The place had been in the family for years. So developers put on the pressure, or should I say contributed to a few local political campaigns, and the entire swath was rezoned for commercial use."

"And you are smack dab in the middle."

"Yep. My grandfather deeded it to me, but now the authorities say it was literally a grandfather clause, and only he could live there. Once he died, the property zoning became commercial."

"And they'd have to buy it at commercial property rates, no?"

"That's the hitch. Because of the age of the building, they can condemn it and declare eminent domain. Plus, they say I have no real claim to the property because of the way it was zoned, my grandfather's deed and all the caveats contained therein."

"You sound like a lawyer," Nina replied.

"Only because I've read the words 'contained therein' a dozen times. Which brings me to my latest challenge, finding a lawyer who can sift through all the documents to see if I am entitled to anything. I'd hate to lose the place, but it's an exhausting battle. I am constantly being badgered. The only guy who isn't against me is Carl."

"I don't envy you." Nina wondered if Richard would have some insight. She made a mental note to ask him.

It finally occurred to her she hadn't checked her phone or let Giovanni know Frankie was safe. "I am such an idiot!" she cried out. "I never got back to Giovanni to tell him Frankie was safe! I am such a bozo! I was so excited to see her. Oh man, he is going to kill me." Nina pulled over to the side of the road so she could dig out the phone from her pocket. She immediately dialed Giovanni's number. This news couldn't be delivered by text. The call went immediately to voice mail. "Shoot. Airplane mode." But she continued with a message. "Gio! Frankie is okay. She sprained her ankle, and I am going to take her back to the hotel in about an hour. Call me."

"Boyfriend? Significant other?" Troy asked.

"Yes, Frankie's. He and my boyfriend and Amy's boyfriend are on a private plane that's supposed to arrive in a couple of hours. Nine-thirty, I think."

"This was quite an elaborate vacation reunion," Troy said.

"It's more convoluted than elaborate. Two years ago, the four of us went on a cruise. This year, we decided to make a plan to get together, but I had a meeting in LA, and Amy had one in Palo Alto. We figured Tahoe would be a good spot to connect with each other."

"Sounds reasonable." Troy nodded. "Turn right at the next intersection."

Nina clicked the indicator. "But then Rachael would not confirm. She kept sending texts that she was busy doing whatever."

"I take it she surprised you?" he surmised.

"She kept leaving mistletoe hints and then put a couple of creepy elves outside our suite door." She made the turn when she spotted the hotel and a snowmobile at the end of the property.

"When she found out that Frankie was missing, she joined the search party."

"Mystery solved." Troy slapped his knee.

"Well, at least one of them," Nina said as she pulled in front of the main entrance.

"And the other?" Troy asked.

"I thought I was being followed from LA. A blue Kia kept showing up behind me on the highway, even after it pulled out ahead of me at a gas station. At one point, I got a glimpse of a blonde woman wearing a baseball cap and big dark sunglasses. I didn't recognize her, and she was so fast, I couldn't get a good look. Then I thought I kept seeing her out of the corner of my eye. At the gift shop. On the patio. It was starting to wig me out a bit."

"I can understand that."

"Then yesterday, Frankie borrowed my car. This one. And sure enough, a blue Kia followed her to Cave Rock. Frankie still couldn't make out who it was, but this time, the woman was wearing a pom hat with most of her hair tucked inside."

"So what happened?"

"According to Frankie, once the woman realized it was someone other than me driving, she took off."

"Do you have any idea who it might be?" Troy asked.

"I have my suspicions." She put the car in park. "You want to talk about Jane?"

Troy blanched at the question. "Not really. It was over a year ago. I've moved on."

"You know, she tended to be quite secretive about her boyfriends."

"Which is probably why you and I never spent any time together. How often did you and I actually see each other? Twice? Maybe three times? And there were always a lot of other people around," Troy ruminated. "I knew you were doing well, but it was only because I was reading the trades and saw you on TV. One time, when I asked her how you were doing, she said she thought you just got lucky."

"Boy, does that sound like her." Nina clicked her tongue. "I guess you could say we were both used and burned by her."

"I would not disagree. But I'm over it. Her. LA. Time for me to figure out my life, starting with the cabin situation." He hopped out of the vehicle.

Randy walked outside to greet them, Duke following right behind. "See? He likes me better," Randy teased.

"Come here, pal." Troy squatted down to hug his pooch. "Was he a good boy?"

"He behaved better than most humans," Randy replied.

"I was asking Duke if *you* were a good boy." Troy laughed. "To be continued," he said to Nina. And then, back to Randy, "What time does the New Year's Eve party start?"

"The dining room has a prix fixe menu. Last seating is at nine. Champagne and music in the lobby start at ten."

Nina wrote down her cell number. "If you ever get your phone charged, here's mine."

"Thanks. Come on, boy." Troy and Duke headed back in the direction of the snowmobile, but this time, Duke was the passenger in the sledge.

Randy bounced over to the driver's window. "How is Francesca doing?"

"Just a sprain. But she's lucky. If Duke hadn't found her, she could have frozen to death."

"I called and spoke to Bart. He was supposed to check if Frankie turned in her shoes." Randy closed his eyes, shook his head, and let out a deep sigh. "I am so sorry. I shouldn't have trusted him to follow up."

"Not your fault. You did what you were supposed to do."

"Yes, but."

"No buts, buster. Now back to work. You have a party to host tomorrow. Get busy." She chuckled and pulled away. Then she hit the brakes. "Dang." She'd just got another glimpse of the mystery woman walking quickly toward the side entrance, but once again, the figure disappeared too quickly for Nina to get a second look. "I am going to hunt her down, so help me, or my name isn't Nina Hunter!" As she pulled out of the driveway, she realized she no longer had a copilot giving her instructions. She punched the hospital into the GPS and accelerated.

As she drove, Nina replayed the events of the past couple of days. *Convoluted* was right. Such a strange journey so far. By the time she made it back to the hospital, Amy and Rachael stood behind Frankie, who was sitting in a wheelchair. "Oh no!" Nina shouted. "A wheelchair?"

"Protocol," Frankie answered. "Heaven forbid I fall before I get in the car." She turned to Amy.

"Right. They do it at every hospital," Nina replied.

"Even if you have an earache," Rachael quipped.

"Show them my latest accessory," Frankie said with a smirk.

Amy produced a pair of crutches and a cane.

"Whoa. I thought it was just a sprain."

"Yes, it is, but the doc wants me to use these to keep me stable when I move around, although he recommended against undertaking much activity."

"Ha." Nina laughed. "It didn't take him long to figure you out."

"Bingo," Amy said. "I'll put these in the back seat. "Rachael's skis are in mine."

Rachael wheeled Frankie to the passenger side of the vehicle, and all three struggled to help her get into the SUV. "Off! Everybody off me!" she said playfully. "I'll grab the thingy handle and pull myself in."

"As you wish." Nina took a step back and bowed.

Once Frankie was settled and buckled, the others followed suit—Amy and Rachael in Amy's car, Nina and Frankie in hers.

"Whoof. Talk about excitement," Nina muttered. "You okay there, girlie?"

"I am now. This was surreal," Frankie said in a hushed voice.

"You can scream if you want. It might let out some of the stress."

"I'm all screamed out." Frankie snorted. "You should have heard me when I first got a look at Duke! I thought he was a wolf, and I was going to be dinner!" She paused. "And then this rugged-looking guy comes ambling up, and I thought I was going to be his prisoner. Hostage. Playtoy. I was totally freaked out."

"I can only imagine."

"But he was soft-spoken and seemed rather kind. He went back to get his snowmobile and brought me to his cabin on some kind of sled. I was still a little dubious as to what he would do next, but he made me a cup of tea, looked at my 'injury' "—she used air quotes—"made a splint, and hauled me back to the hotel." She paused. "Oh, and when I saw the guitar and the album cover, I asked if he played, and then I did the math. Troy plus guitar plus The Troy-Man album. He told me he was fed up with the music business, had a bad breakup, and moved up to the cabin."

Nina raised her eyebrows. "Take a wild guess who the breakup was with." Nina had a mischievous grin on her face. "Come on. Who has been the subject of my latest stories?"

Frankie furrowed her brow. Then it hit her. "Holy smoke! He lightly touched on the subject. Said she was an actress. Jane!"

"Precisely."

"I am nonplused. Stupefied. Baffled," Frankie responded, her mouth agape.

"You forgot bothered and bewildered."

"What are the odds?" Frankie asked.

"Perhaps Amy could figure it out." Nina laughed.

"This is so crazy." Frankie was shaking her head in disbelief. "Troy was Jane's boyfriend. Wow."

"She scorched him, too," Nina said. "She doesn't burn bridges; she blows them up. That's what she does."

Nina checked the time. It was going on seven-thirty. "Giovanni, Peter, and Richard should be here in a couple of hours."

Frankie let out a roar. "Say what?"

Nina gulped. "In all the excitement and anxiety, I forgot to mention it."

"That's a big forget."

"Things were moving so quickly, I honestly thought I said it at some point during all the drama."

"Well, you didn't. Not that I'm mad or anything. Just a little shocked. Surprised. Bowled over. Stunned."

"You forgot 'flabbergasted.'" Nina glanced at her friend. "Sweetcakes, I am so sorry. I didn't mean to spring it on you. I just thought somehow you knew. Amy maybe? Oh, I am such a ninny."

"You forgot nincompoop, nitwit, and featherbrain," Frankie taunted.

"Let's start with you being late for lunch. Then missing. Then our discovering Rachael was here. Then the search party. Lots of balls in the air. Amy and I were heading to the lodge when Giovanni called me. He hadn't heard from you, and he was getting worried. Amy and I thought it was best to tell him right away."

"But there wasn't anything he could do about it. Flights don't get in until midnight. Then it takes another hour to get here." Frankie huffed.

"Listen. I don't know if I would have told him immediately. But he happened to call when Amy and I were just about to go looking for you. Then he said he was coming. Period. End of story. Well, actually not the end of the story. Come on, Frankie, he's your boyfriend. You know how hard it is to tell him not to do something when he has made up his mind to go on a mission."

Frankie nodded in agreement.

"Here's one of the best parts."

"This better be good," Frankie mocked.

"Of course, Amy told Peter . . ."

"And you told Richard. Okay. Continue."

"During Giovanni's frenzy to find a plane, it occurred to him to—are you ready for this?"

"Will you please stop tormenting me? Get on with it already or I am going to reach over the seat, grab the cane, and give you a smack on the head. Pretend it's a monologue. Keep talking."

"Giovanni called Dottie, who called Mateo." Nina paused when Frankie gave her that *don't make me hurt you* look.

"Mateo made arrangements for Giovanni to borrow his time-share-plane-thing. Richard and Peter got on flights and are supposed to meet him in Denver."

Frankie was staring at her. She looked like a "big-eyed girl" painting. "When is all of this supposed to be happening?" She was completely bewildered. Maybe she'd actually hurt her head during the fall, and this was part of a fugue state she was experiencing.

"We keep missing each other, but they are on their way from Denver. He's probably on airplane mode, because when I called, it went straight to voice mail."

Frankie was slowly taking in the information. "Let me know if I've got this right. Giovanni is using Mateo's plane, with Richard and Peter, and they are arriving within the next couple of hours."

"Correct."

"And the guy who rescued me is the ex of this sorta ex-friend of yours?"

"Yes. Troy and Jane."

"Six degrees of separation. You know, the idea that everyone knows everyone if you make six connections."

"Honey, I lived in LA. They turned it into a game. *Six Degrees of Kevin Bacon*."

"Yes, I know. I'm thinking out loud." Frankie pursed her lips. "Let's see if I have this right. I am connected to Troy, who is connected to Jane, who is connected to you. Wait, that's only three."

Nina laughed. "I am sure we'll come up with a few more before this adventure is over."

"How about this?" Frankie was trying to put Giovanni and Mateo into the mix. "We add Mateo and Giovanni, and Peter, and Richard."

"You're losing me, honey. Your brain has been through enough today. Give it a rest."

"Oh, wait! I think I have it now. Mateo is connected to Giovanni, who is connected to me, who is connected to Troy, who is connected to Jane, who is connected to you." She huffed. "Only five."

"Please stop. You're making my hair bleed." Nina begged.

"You're right." Frankie tried to suppress a yawn and went back to the subject of Jane. "So, when was the last time you heard from Jane?"

"At Lois's office. I told her I'd do what I could and left."

"Does she know that you know she didn't get the part?" Frankie asked.

"I can't say. I assume that *she* would assume I know because, like it or lump it, I'm still the head writer of the show."

"Would Jane have called you?" Frankie asked. "To complain, or whatever she does to make you feel guilty."

"*Tsk-tsk*. I am done. I won't be mean, but I will no longer do anything for her. Except maybe pull her off the railroad tracks if there was an oncoming train."

"Oh, and I am sure she would do the same for you," Frankie said with a touch of sarcasm.

"She would probably throw a brick on me so I couldn't move."

Frankie was laughing out loud now. "She can't be *that* bad."

"Okay. Maybe not *that* bad."

The GPS indicated they had one more turn before the hotel. Within minutes, they were pulling up in front and no worse for the wear. Maybe a little. After the day they'd had, anything that went right was a blessing. "If I could kiss the ground, I would," Frankie said with sincere gratitude.

"But didn't you do that once already?" Nina hopped out, moved to the passenger side, and opened both doors. "And look where it got you."

Randy emerged from the front door and sidled up to the SUV. "Let me help with those." He pulled out the crutches and the cane. "Oh, these could be fun." He lent them a mischievous look.

"Stop it." Nina gave him a playful slap.

Nina helped Frankie get out of her seat and balance on the crutches.

"Do I really need these?" She had a look of chagrin on her face.

"Only if you don't want me to beat you with them instead," Nina replied.

"Okay. Okay. You're so bossy."

"Ack! Look who's talking, Miss Bossy Pants!" Nina barked.

"Now ladies, behave," Randy chided. "Follow me."

The valet was quick to open the doors for the small parade.

When they entered the lobby, guests and staff began fawning over Frankie, expressing relief and good wishes.

"I don't know if I should feel embarrassed or special." Frankie was blushing.

"Pick special, sweetcakes," Nina assured her.

Frankie acknowledged all the remarks with thanks and smiles. Randy took over and began to sweep his arm back and forth as they moved through the two dozen or so onlookers.

"Please step aside. Give her some room. Thank you. Please. Yes. Thank you. Someone get the elevator, please?" He was over the top and quite hilarious, giving her the celebrity treatment.

Frankie was about to burst. "All of this over a sprained ankle. Imagine if I really did something extraordinary?"

Nina jumped on the opportunity to remind her, "Let's not forget the catalyst. You fell because of your phone."

Randy turned and put a finger to his lips. "Shush. Grab it while you can, sugar."

He escorted them to the elevator, where someone was kind enough to hold the door. "Tootles. Thanks for an exciting afternoon!"

Frankie leaned against the wall of the elevator car. "I am famished."

"Didn't they feed you at Chez Troy?" Nina teased.

"Tea. And no, no watercress finger sandwiches, either."

"If I were you, I would give him a one-star rating on Yelp."

Frankie snorted. "What a day this has been."

The elevator door opened on the second floor, but there was no one there. Nina thought she heard a door close down at the end of the hallway before the elevator continued to the fourth floor.

"I just got another eerie feeling," Nina said.

"It's Jane-o-phobia. She's haunting you."

When the elevator doors opened, Nina caught a peek of someone exiting down the stairs. "If you weren't on crutches, I swear I would have followed whoever that was."

"Well, now we know it's not Rachael." Frankie adjusted her crutches, and they made their way to the suite.

Once they were inside, Frankie hobbled and hopped to the sofa. "Do you suppose it could be Jane?"

"The mysterious stalker?" Nina asked. "I don't think she would have the guts, or the gas money to follow me up here."

"Maybe she paid someone to spook you."

"She doesn't have the money."

"From what you've told me, she is quite the manipulator. Maybe she told someone if they got near you, she would help them get a part in a show."

"That sounds much more like Jane. But I think she is too lazy to go through all this trouble to freak me out."

"Let's call the front desk and see if she's registered here."

"Right. We were going to do that for Rachael, but got sidetracked." Nina picked up the house phone. "Good evening. Can you please tell me if Jane Douglass has arrived?" She listened. "No, I am not sure when she is expected." More listening. She could hear the click of the keyboard from the front desk. "I see. Thank you." She turned to Frankie. "No Jane Douglass on the premises."

"In the past, she could have used an alias, but with all the security now, she would have to show her ID. Could she be staying somewhere nearby?"

Nina sat across from Frankie. "How about this: we forget about whoever it is. Maybe it's just random coincidence."

"Oh, wait! Maybe it's a fan, and she's too shy to approach you."

Nina let out a huge sigh. "Ha. That thought had never occurred to me!" She slapped her forehead for the second time that day. "It's been two years since I was on air, and no one in New York bothers people they recognize. Well, most people don't." Nina's face relaxed. "Thank you for saying that."

"What are friends for?" Frankie yawned again. "Can we please get something to eat? Rachael and Amy should be here any minute."

Sure enough, they could hear squeals, laughs, and chattering coming toward the room. "And get those things outta here!" Amy ordered, pointing to the elves.

"And they're back," Nina said dryly.

Nina took charge. "First things first. We have to get Frankie something to eat."

"And drink." Frankie looked at the other women's faces. "I am not on pain meds. Even the doctor said a glass of cabernet sauvignon would be better than anything he could prescribe."

Amy spoke next. "Rachael has a room on the first floor off the patio. I vote she moves in here with us."

"I second that!" Frankie held up her hand.

"Third!" Nina shouted.

"Super!" Amy cried out.

"But after we eat. Please?" Frankie thought she might pass out from hunger rather than pain or discomfort.

"Right!" Rachael responded. "I'm gonna go back to my *old* room and change my clothes. Meet you in the restaurant in ten!" She charged out the door. Amy ran after her. "And take these fiends with you!" She pointed to the evil twins resting in the hallway. Rachael scooted back and scooped up the dreadful figures in her arms.

"You make quite a trio!" Nina chimed in and shut the door.

Amy clapped her hands. "I am so happy we're going to be together for New Year's Eve!"

"And in one piece," Nina added.

"For sure!" Amy bubbled and did a little geek shuffle to her room. "I'll be right back."

"Speaking of changing clothes, I need to do the same." Frankie squirmed her way onto her good foot and grabbed her crutches.

"You're getting the hang of it," Nina praised her.

Frankie turned and gave her a snarky look. "Don't get used to seeing me like this."

"Only until you're healed," Nina called out as Frankie hobbled to her room. "Let me know if you need any help!"

Frankie sat on her bed in stillness. It was a lot to process. Getting lost, then getting rescued—on a sledge, no less. Seeing Rachael. Giovanni reaching out to Mateo. Richard and Peter reaching out to Giovanni. She snickered. It's that *six-degrees-of-separation* thing again. Like a flash of light, it struck her: it was the power of friendship, and kindness. Tears started to roll down her face. "I am a lucky, lucky girl," she whispered to herself with the utmost gratitude. "Hey, Nina?" she called out.

A few beats later, Nina poked her head in. "You rang?"

"Can you help me with my clothes, please?" She snuffled.

"Absolutely, babycakes. Just tell me what you need."

Frankie pointed to a navy-blue terrycloth tracksuit. "Too caj?" she asked, abbreviating casual.

"You are, after all, a recently discharged mental—I mean hospital—patient." Nina cracked herself up.

Frankie caught a glimpse of herself in the mirror. "Who is that?" she said in mock horror. "I look like I went through the spin cycle of the washing machine. Look at my hair! My face! Yikes!"

Nina used her best hillbilly accent. "Don't you worry your pretty little head there, sugar plum. We'll get y'all cleaned up in a jiffy."

Amy changed into one of her new cashmere outfits and joined them. "What can I do to help?"

"Washcloth. Blowtorch." Frankie groaned.

Amy returned with said washcloth and a can of dry shampoo. "This was the best I could do."

Amy and Nina continued to help Frankie primp a bit. After fifteen minutes, she looked pulled together, with a fresh glow on her face, and her hair tied in a low ponytail with a navy and white scarf.

Amy looked at Frankie with a straight face. "Shoe?"

That put all of them over the top in hysterics. When they

SANTA & COMPANY   213

recovered, Frankie pointed to a pair of flats she wore when she was inside. "Left one, please."

"Ready?" Nina asked sprightly.

"Ready!" Frankie hoisted herself onto the crutches, and they made their way to the restaurant.

People shouted and applauded when they entered the dining room.

"Okay. This is getting a little ridiculous," Frankie said with clenched teeth.

"Just keep smiling and nodding. This is your fifteen minutes of fame," Nina said encouragingly.

Rachael was waiting for them at a table near the fireplace. "I took the liberty of ordering a bottle of wine. One for each of us," she joked.

"Ahh, brilliant." Frankie sat in the first chair she came upon. "And cozy."

Nina checked the time. Almost eight o'clock. "So do you gals want to go for a dip in the hot tub after dinner? Before the guys get here?"

"Guys? What guys?" Rachael wore a serious look of concern and surprise.

Nina gulped. "Richard, Giovanni, and Peter are arriving later."

"What?" Rachael's mood soured. "I thought it was just us!"

"It was until Frankie decided to lose her phone." Nina stuck her face within inches of Frankie's.

"What are you talking about?" Rachael asked with a furrowed brow.

"Frankie? Our friend? She went missing today."

"Well, duh," Rachael spat.

"Giovanni was concerned because he hadn't heard from Frankie, so he called me. I didn't want to lie to him, so I told him Frankie was missing, and he went into hyper-action mode. He borrowed some of Mateo's flight time and took his jet. Richard and Peter met up with him in Denver. The plane is due to land at nine-thirty, and they should be arriving here, at the hotel, around ten."

Rachael was crestfallen. She'd thought she would be spending the next two days with the girls. Now she would be the seventh wheel.

Frankie reached over to grab her hand. "Listen, you can still stay in the suite if you don't mind sharing the living room. I mean, you'll have it to yourself to sleep, but we'll be all over the place."

"No. It's okay. I'll keep my room." She choked back tears. How quickly the mood had changed.

"Rachael, please come and stay with us," Frankie urged.

"You won't have any privacy with me there."

"Do you think *anyone* is going to have any privacy with seven people in that suite?" Nina noted.

"You'll be skiing during the day. We'll meet for dinner, have some after-dinner drinks in the lounge by the fireplace. Then go back to the room and crash," Frankie added.

Rachael's mood shifted. "You're right. No one is going to have any privacy. Including me!" She laughed out loud. "Thank you for the invitation, but I think I shall keep my own room."

"Oh, Rachael, please?" Amy crooned.

"No. Seriously. I'm good with this arrangement. We can have our meals together, and then hang out at the end of the day." She paused. "And I can run around in my underwear." Everyone laughed and exhaled sighs of relief.

"Speaking of underwear." Amy nodded in the direction of the hot tub.

"Right. Some of us do not have bathing suits," Nina said.

"Then we should all go in the hot tub in our underwear!" Amy suggested.

"No one else will be out there," Nina urged, in case Frankie had an opposing opinion.

"What about robes?" Frankie asked.

"Hmm. Good point," Nina replied.

"I have an idea." Rachael got up and left the dining room. A few minutes later, she returned with a conspiratorial grin. "I know someone who knows someone who will take care of that situation for us."

They all leaned in at the same time. "Randy."

After an hour and a half of conversation that rambled from one subject to another, they were ready to be poached. Nina gave Frankie a hand, and the four marched single file out the door, across the patio to the private area where the hot tub and four very fluffy robes waited. As predicted, there was no one else in sight.

They began to remove their clothes, shrieking expletives about the cold air. Nina looked up at the sky. "They say it might snow tomorrow."

"Really? It's kinda warm for this time of year, isn't it?" Rachael asked.

"That's when storms happen. When the weather patterns shift dramatically. It's like an atmospheric wrestling match. Who is going to win? The Nordic air? The heat? The humidity? The wind?" Amy was attempting to explain her limited understanding of meteorology.

"We get the idea, Einstein," Rachael quipped.

Amy, Nina, and Rachael dunked themselves into the bubbly water, while Frankie thought it would be in her and everyone else's best interest if she sat on the edge and let her leg get a little water therapy. Getting in and out of the tub could be tricky.

When they finally settled in, they resumed the various conversations that had begun over dinner.

"Rachael, you have been rather mute about Henry. I don't think you mentioned him once except for when we asked how he was doing."

Rachael puckered her lips. "I think it's over."

The *what*s, *what happened*s, and *what are you talking about*s bubbled up as fast as the water.

Rachael began. "It's been a few months since he's touched me in bed."

"I don't suppose you've talked to him about it?" Nina asked kindly.

"That's part of the problem. We don't seem to be in the same room long enough to have a conversation. He spends more time in the city than with me. Much more. I think he might be having an affair."

Silence replaced the blurted questions.

"Oh, my," Amy said in a hushed tone. "And he's twenty years older than you."

Everyone's head snapped toward Amy. "What does that have to do with it?" Nina asked.

"Well, older men. You know. That's why they invented the little blue pill."

"Exactly. And that's why older men take them," Rachael reminded her.

"Are you all right?" Frankie asked. She surmised this was the reason Rachael had been out of touch and out of sorts.

"I'm better now. Since Henry wouldn't talk to me, I decided to talk to myself, on the way down the slopes yesterday. I forgave myself for being foolish and needy. Yes, needy. I needed attention. I needed to feel like someone loved me. Sure enough, whoever paid attention to me got *my* attention. Too bad I wasn't paying attention to what was really going on in those so-called relationships. You know the rest of the story. Heck, you guys know all of the story. I admit I was infatuated with Henry. He was an icon in the dance world. I was flattered and excited that he thought I had talent. Things were good in the beginning, but then came the pressure of the lockdowns, canceling classes; I was losing money, he was unfulfilled. Funny thing about it, I'm not heartbroken. I'm almost relieved."

"That's a big step in self-actualization, Rachael," Frankie complimented her.

"I guess you could say I had an epiphany. Being out on the slopes, in the silence, among the trees. It was illuminating. I am okay."

Nina stared at her friend. "And I am impressed. I knew there was a you under all that smoke and mirrors."

"Don't get me wrong. That is no indication I will behave myself. Just a little differently." She turned to Frankie. "I want to apologize for blowing you off. Instead of blowing you off, I should have told you what was going on. But at the time, I didn't want to admit I'd made another mistake."

"Sounds like it was more of a lesson than a mistake," Frankie said gently.

"I really love you guys. I don't know what I would do without your friendship." Sloppy hugs in dripping underwear created more hilarity.

"Speaking of friendship. Nina, tell them about your encounter with Jane."

"You guys may remember I was friends with Jane Douglass in my freshman year?"

"Vaguely. Didn't she do some dish soap commercials or something?" Amy asked.

"That's the one," Nina replied, and recounted the story she had told Frankie about the brilliant actress who'd barreled into her life. The moving in, the hair, and everything in between. Yes, the ups and downs of her friendship with Jane. It was mostly downs.

In the shadows, a figure was leaning into the hedge to better eavesdrop on the discussion that was taking place in the hot tub. The rustling created a short pause in the conversation. Then Nina continued.

"When I went to my meeting with Lois, I ran into her in the lobby. She begged me to get her a part in the final episode. I told her I'd do what I could."

"After all those years of taking advantage of you?" Amy was shocked.

"And lying to Lois about your being sick, so she could steal your auditions?" Rachael was aghast. "You still tried to help her? You are a true friend."

"What happened? Did you talk to Lois?" Amy asked.

"Yes, and she said she would call the director. She gave the script to Jane to look over and shot a quick video on the spot."

"Well, did she get the part?" Rachael demanded to know.

"No. In spite of all the things she did, she's a hugely talented actress. If a part for her would be good for the show, why not? Unfortunately, the director said he didn't want any more changes. They were too close to shooting." She sighed. "But I tried."

The rustling in the shrubbery got louder. A groan was followed by a pair of arms and legs flailing through the brush; then a body vaulted clumsily into the hot tub like a cannonball. Screams and shrieks filled the air. Frankie froze in place. Amy jumped out of the water, dragging Rachael with her. Nina was on her feet, staring down at the intruder. There it was: a blond wig floating in the water, and a woman with black hair and piercing blue eyes, looking up at her.

By the time anyone could comprehend what was going on, a dozen people, including two security officers, were on the scene.

"Jane! What are you doing here?" Nina screamed, while Amy and Rachael covered themselves with their robes. Frankie remained motionless, avoiding any movement that could hamper her recovery.

Jane was sputtering. "I . . . I wanted to talk to you."

"So why didn't you do that, instead of stalking me for two days?" Nina lashed out at her as never before. "How could you do this?" She was livid.

"Nina. I am so sorry." Jane pulled the floating wig from the water and tossed it on the patio while she attempted to get out of the tub. Her clothes clung to her body, and her shoes were flooded.

One of the security guards approached her. "Are you a guest here, miss?"

Jane cowered. "I'm not, sir."

"Then you are trespassing," he said. "You're going to have to come with me."

"Wait," Nina objected. "I know her. You can let her go."

The gentleman looked suspiciously at the women. "I take it, *all* of you are guests here?"

Amy raised her hand. Rachael nodded. Frankie gave him a thumbs-up. "Yes, we are," Nina answered.

More people from the hotel came out to see what the fuss was all about, including three men with similarly befuddled expressions on their faces. More noise ensued as names were called across the patio. "Frankie!" "Nina!" "Amy!" "Frankie!" "Richard"—and a few more "Frankie"s—while the rest of the assembled group shouted questions and greetings. Giovanni pushed past the gawkers as politely as he could to get to Frankie, who seemed to be holding her own. A slight look of amusement danced across her face. Finally, she wasn't the center of attention. She was now an observer of a different spectacle.

"Everybody settle down!" a sharp voice boomed over the clamor. "Can someone please explain what is going on here?" The man looked at Nina. "You seem to be the one with the answers."

Nina didn't quite know where to begin. Should she tell the guard this crazed woman had been following her for days? She thought better of it. "Sorry for the ruckus, folks. This is an old college friend who decided to surprise me." She gave

Jane a look that said, *If you didn't owe me before, you owe me big time right now.* "Apparently, she isn't so light on her feet, and fell into the hot tub."

The second security guard surveyed the crowd. "Show's over, folks. Everyone can go back to whatever they were doing." A few people hesitated. "As in now, please." The group slowly dispersed as the guests tried to figure out what had really happened.

Giovanni lifted Frankie from the edge of the tub, where she had been soaking her ankle. She flung her arms around him. "I think I need to ice it now." She giggled and pulled him closer.

Giovanni lifted her chin. "I cannot tell you how happy I am to see you. We were so worried." He brushed a strand of wet hair from her forehead and helped her into a robe. Nina took the remaining plush wrap, hanging Jane out to dry. Literally.

Nina didn't know what to do next: continue to give Jane a tongue lashing, or walk away. She picked walking away. She locked arms with Richard. "Thanks for coming. Sorry for all the drama."

"You've always been a good actress." He gave her a kiss on the top of her head. "You okay?" He knew there was a lot to unpack besides his two extra pairs of underwear and his toothbrush.

"I'm good." Nina smiled at him.

Amy was animated as she tried to catch Peter up with everything that had gone on. The elves, the mistletoe, Rachael, and the Frankie panic came gushing out of her mouth. "Hang on. Slow down." Peter rubbed her arms through the robe. "Let's get back to the room, and you can fill all of us in."

Frankie looked at Rachael. "What are you waiting for? Get over here!" Rachael scampered over to the waiting couple, and Giovanni put his free arm around her. He was pleased to see the two had put their quarrel behind them.

Amy and Peter led the wet and dampened troupe, followed by Giovanni, Frankie, and Rachael. Nina and Richard hung a few feet behind. Nina knew she couldn't just walk away without some closure. She turned to the shivering, humiliated Jane.

"What do you have to say for yourself? Explain all this if you don't mind. You owe me that much." Nina scowled.

"After you left Lois's office, she videoed me doing a cold read. I thought I did a pretty good job. When I was finished, she sent it to the director, who told her flat out he didn't want any changes."

"Right then and there?" Nina asked suspiciously.

"He was going on vacation and didn't want Lois or me to have to wait for a decision." Jane was sniveling.

"He didn't even look at your audition?"

"No. Case closed." Jane was wiping her nose with her sodden shirt.

"What did you think you would accomplish by following me all the way up here?"

"I thought maybe you told Jamie not to hire me."

"Wow, Jane, really? You think I would do something like that?"

"Honestly, no. It was a blow to my ego. I have credentials. Excellent reviews, yet he wouldn't even look at my tape."

Nina snickered. "Show business. Fun stuff."

"I never admitted this to you before, but I was jealous. Jealous of you. Your family. Your talent. Your wit."

"Let's not forget my hair." Nina smirked. "But jealous? Of me?"

"Look at you. Even when you got knocked down, you always got back up. You found ways to explore your talent. You were resilient." Jane sniffled again. "I, on the other hand, am not. I am not proud of the things I've done. Dumped friends. Drank too much. And you? You never took the low road. You were fiercely loyal, even to me. Me, who tried to sabotage you."

"Is that why you came all the way up here—to grovel?" Nina was leery of Jane's sincerity.

"At first, no. I wanted answers. But as I followed you, I was reminded of the friendships you forged over the years. Because you're loyal. You're dependable. You're generous. And you have integrity."

Nina was stunned by Jane's compliments. She couldn't recall any time in the past she'd heard Jane say a kind word about anyone. She searched her memory for a sliver of appreciation. Nothing. "Why now, Jane?"

"Because you deserve to hear the truth. I always felt that way about you and your talent. But most of all, it's the friendships and the love you have. I want that in my life, Nina." For the first time, Jane burst into real tears. Nina knew Jane was a good actress, but this was something different. She wasn't asking Nina. She was asking for it for herself and from a higher power.

"Jane, I really don't know what to say."

"Just please say you'll forgive me for everything I've done, and what I didn't do that I should have done."

"What do you mean?" Nina asked.

"When you first came to LA, I could have done more to help you, but I didn't. I didn't want you to outshine me."

Jane's eyes were filled with tears, turning that piercing blue into bloodshot red.

Nina was dumbfounded. Never, ever, did she think Jane would admit to something like this. Nina felt it in her bones, but this was an admission. A confession.

"Please, Nina, can you forgive me?"

Nina paused for a moment. How much did she really want to say to Jane? Something simple. "I forgive you, Jane."

Jane made an effort to give Nina a hug, but Richard was between them, and he maintained his stance. Jane might be sorry, and Nina might be forgiving, but that didn't erase the past. He knew Nina would need time to digest this newfound information.

Jane managed to grab Nina's hand. She looked her straight in the eyes. Her expression, instead of piercing, was humble. "Thank you."

"You are welcome." Nina managed a soft smile. "Just tell me one thing. Why the wig?"

"Because I wasn't sure if I would get up enough courage to talk to you. I thought if I followed you around, there might be a good opportunity."

Nina grunted. "You certainly made an impressive entrance."

Jane let out a slight laugh.

"You just can't help yourself, can you?" Nina was honestly teasing her. Jane would never try a gymnastic stunt. Not unless she was getting paid a lot of money. "It was memorable. Now *that* is something you should have on footage."

Richard looked up at the corner of the building. He pointed. "This may be your lucky day, Jane. Security camera."

"Oh no! That is something I would definitely not want to be aired in public."

"I'll check with security tomorrow morning," Richard offered.

"You may want a copy just for posterity." Nina was half serious. "You may never have the opportunity to try out for the Hot Tub Olympics again!"

Richard chuckled. "We got here after the event, so I wouldn't mind seeing it."

"Oh no. Please don't." Jane was almost begging.

Nina raised her eyebrows. "I think it may be worth watching. Everything happened so quickly. I wouldn't mind a replay."

Jane sighed. "I deserve every jab."

"I'll see how long they keep the footage," Richard said calmly.

"No!" Jane was now pleading.

Richard could feel Nina shivering. "Come on. Let's get you inside and into some dry clothes."

Nina turned to Jane. "Be kind to yourself, Jane, and to other people." Nina paused. "That would be the finest redemption. *Ciao*." Nina had used that salutation ever since she started spending more time with Frankie. She clutched Richard's arm as they briskly walked to the nearest entrance of the hotel.

"*Ciao*, Nina. Thank you," Jane called from behind.

Richard leaned closer to Nina's ear. "That was heavy duty."

"Sure was," Nina said emphatically.

"Do you believe her?"

"I think I just might." They scampered into the hallway, where they received peculiar glances. Both acted as if it were totally normal for a woman to be drenched, in a robe, and carrying her clothes in one hand. In the middle of the winter, no less.

When they entered the suite, Frankie was wearing a pair of flannel pajamas with her leg propped on the coffee table. A roaring fire gave the room a glow, and the warmth could be felt to the bone.

"What took you guys so long?" Frankie asked. "I thought you might be beating the snot out of her."

"I didn't have to. She had plenty of it running down her face."

"Ew!" Amy stuck her head out of her bedroom door. "What are you guys talking about?" She took a seat in one of the big overstuffed chairs.

"Let's wait for everyone to settle in. This is a story that bears repeating, but I only have the energy to tell it once."

There was a knock at the door. All eyes scanned the room. "Probably Rachael."

"What about food?" Richard asked as he went to answer it.

"Randy!" Amy cried out. "What brings you here so long after your shift?"

"Special delivery." He had two shopping bags in his hands. "Hotel management thought these items might be useful." He handed the bags to Richard. "But it was really my idea," he said in a loud whisper.

There was another knock at the door. This time it was Rachael, with an armful of grab-and-go sandwiches. "I know this isn't an ideal meal for you guys, but I figured you probably need to eat something."

"Oh, Rach, that is so sweet," Frankie said. Then she wanted to kick herself for not thinking of it herself. *Oh well, it's been some kind of day.*

"Hey, Randy. What brings you here?" Rachael gave him an elbow.

"Oh, just dropping off a few things."

Richard reached into one of the bags and pulled out a black jogging suit. "Huh. Just my size." It was amusing, because Richard and Giovanni had similar physiques, and Peter was just a tad shorter and thinner. "Oh, look. Peter, I think this might be for you." He handed over a navy-blue jogging suit. Then he checked the second bag. "Lookie here." He tossed a package of Fruit of the Loom underwear at Giovanni, who immediately put it behind his back. "I guess this is for you, too." Out came a gray jogging suit.

"When we found out you gentlemen were on a mission with only an overnight bag, we thought you might need a little something extra for the weather. We were also told Giovanni had absolutely nothing, ergo the unmentionables." He cleared his throat. "Rachael was good enough to guess at your sizes." He gave her a theatrical nod.

"My work here is done. See you at the party tomorrow."
He spun on his heel and left.

Nina got some plates from the cabinet and opened the
sandwiches. Amy helped her hand them out. "Glad we had
that big dinner." She was eyeing the ham and brie. "But I
could go for a little taste of something. I think I digested my
dinner jumping out of the tub!"

"Well, if there's enough, count me in!" Frankie gave a
shout from the sofa.

"There's plenty," Nina said. "Rachael, you did good, girlfriend."

Once everyone got settled, Nina explained the hot tub hul-
labaloo, starting with Jane's apology and ending with her
own final offer of forgiveness.

Richard was the first one to speak. "Nina, you are one of
the most generous people I know. Not only with things, but
with your spirit."

"That's why we are all besties." Amy grinned. "We are
soul travelers. Right, Frankie?"

"That's the theory," Frankie answered. "Like-minded people seek each other out, whether it's intentional or subcon-
sciously. I prefer to think it's a spiritual thing." She paused.
"It's not about religion. People can have any belief system
that works for them, but at the core, it's about love, kindness, and humanity."

Giovanni was leaning against the stone fireplace. He raised
his glass of wine. "Here's to our Frankie. She is the glue in
my life."

"She is the glue for all of us." Rachael spoke next. "I didn't
realize how much I needed my friend until she went missing."

Giovanni was still curious to learn more about the inter-
loper. "This woman, Jane. Does she still work in the movie
business?"

"Not lately. She has, or hopefully *had*, a self-destructive
streak and ruined a lot of opportunities."

"Maybe she'll be a better person for these shenanigans," Richard suggested.

"I hope so," Nina said thoughtfully. "We had a lot of fun when we weren't at odds. It was a roller-coaster relationship."

"And she flew right off the tracks and into the water!" Amy giggled.

Wanting to move on from the subject, Nina turned to the men. "Tell us about your flight. In a private jet."

"Mateo. He was most generous to make arrangements for us. Of course, I will pay him for the service and fuel," Giovanni said. "I understand why my Frankie has a big crush on him," he teased.

"Oh, stop!" She gave him a crooked eyebrow expression. "Speaking of Mateo, did anyone tell him I was okay?"

"Yes, when I finally got the news from Nina, I sent it to Mateo. He said to let him know if there's anything we need," Giovanni replied.

Frankie looked around the room. "And this is why I have a crush on Mateo."

Giovanni regretted his past jealousy. Somehow, he would find a way to make it up to Mateo.

"Any other bizarre stories?" Peter piped in.

"You mean the evil elves?" Amy's eyes widened.

"Evil elves?" Peter looked at her.

Amy took the lead and explained that an abundance of mistletoe had been appearing in the hallway and elevator. She went on to explain how two elves were placed outside their doorway. Then she repeated the lore about these creatures everyone associates with Santa. "It's all a big lie."

"We figure they are doing community service." Nina chortled.

"Or on parole," Frankie added.

Richard folded his arms. "I had no idea they were such malevolent beings."

"That's right. So whenever you see them, stay far away," Amy warned. "Even the inanimate kind. You don't know what wickedness they harbor." She sounded quite convincing.

"Duly noted," Richard replied, sounding very much like a lawyer.

"This is quite a story," Peter added. "One that ended with a big splash."

Groans emanated from everyone. "The vacation is not over yet. We still have two more days," Amy pointed out.

"Maybe we should lock ourselves in the suite," Giovanni joked.

"Uh, no," Frankie said, even though she knew he was kidding.

"What is on the agenda?" Richard asked.

"There's a New Year's Eve party tomorrow night. I invited Troy. And Duke, of course. Obviously, I will be hanging around here, but you guys can go off and enjoy this magnificent place."

"We can't leave you alone," Giovanni said.

"There's little I can do to get into trouble," Frankie said.

Nina, Amy, and Rachael rolled their eyes.

"Seriously. I'll sit by the fireplace and read a book. You know, one of those things I keep saying I will do when I have a chance?"

"You are an editor. Don't you read all the time?" Peter asked.

"Yes. My work. But it's not leisure reading. I think I might enjoy this forced lockdown." Frankie smiled.

Rachael yawned. "Okay, kids, bedtime for me. Way too much excitement for one day."

"Okay, honeybunch. Sleep well. See you for breakfast?" Nina said.

"Sure. The café? What time?" Frankie suggested.

Everyone was weary or jet lagged. "We're going to need at least eight hours' sleep. How's ten o'clock?" Nina suggested.

"Perfect," Rachael answered.

"Are you going to hit the slopes tomorrow?" Nina asked.

"I'll decide when I get up in the morning. I have to admit, every muscle in my body is annoyed right now. It's been a couple of years since I was out there, and I think I overdid it."

"You? Rachael? Overdoing something?" Frankie teased.

"Well, maybe if I didn't have to go out looking for you, my legs wouldn't be screaming right now."

"Sure. Blame me." Frankie laughed as Rachael proceeded toward the door. "Rach? Thanks. You know I love you."

"Love you more," Rachael said as she stepped out the door. "Sleep tight."

Everyone said their goodnights and retreated to their rooms. Giovanni arranged a pile of pillows for Frankie's ankle and helped her onto the bed. "Can I get you anything else?" he asked and handed her a glass of water and some Tylenol.

"How about a big hug?" She held out her arms, and he gently accommodated her.

# Chapter Thirteen

*New Year's Eve Day*

Frankie gingerly crawled out of bed, grabbed her crutches, and made it to the bathroom. She tried to put a little pressure on her lame ankle, but it still smarted. How she hated feeling compromised and limited. But then she realized how badly things could have ended, and she counted her blessings. She wanted Giovanni to go out with the guys and experience the magnitude of the glorious lake. The air. The sky. There was a house phone in the bathroom suite, and she asked to be connected to the spa. A massage was something she could do lying down, and there was an opening at one o'clock. Perfect. It would give everyone a chance to get outside while she was being pampered. Then she thought Nina might need a bit of the same, so she made two appointments. She knew Amy would want to spend time with Peter, and Giovanni and Richard could take a walk. Maybe buy some appropriate shoes and some extra clothes. They were going to be in Tahoe for a couple more days, and Giovanni couldn't be walking in the snow with his Mauri loafers. Come to think of it, Peter was the only one with appropriate footwear.

She'd noticed he was wearing a pair of Timberland boots. She chuckled at the idea that the men *had* to go shopping.

She gave Rachael a call.

"Why are you whispering?" Rachael asked.

"I'm in the bathroom, and Giovanni is still asleep. I am going to get a massage this afternoon. Have you decided what you want to do yet?"

Rachael hesitated. "Nah. But you go ahead and enjoy it. What about Nina?"

"I made an appointment for her, but I don't think she's up yet either."

"Okay. See you at ten!" Rachael said and hung up the phone. She had her own plans but, once again, she was not about to share them. One last surprise. She rubbed her hands together.

When Frankie went back into the bedroom, she could smell the rich, robust aroma of coffee. She moved quietly past Giovanni, who caught her arm. "Hey, I didn't mean to wake you," she whispered.

"I wanted to make sure it was really you and not a dream." He kissed her hand, rolled over, and dozed off.

Frankie made her way to the living room. Nina was making coffee at the murphy kitchen. She turned. "Well, if it isn't the Stumbling Snow Queen herself!"

"Already? It's not even eight o'clock." Frankie hopped over to the small café table. "Do you have plans for today? I made two appointments for massages."

"Oh, that sounds divine." Nina started another cup in the Nespresso machine. "What should I do about Richard?" She lowered her voice.

"He and Giovanni need clothes. They can't walk round in jogging suits with loafers!"

Nina snorted her coffee right out her nose! "That is a very

good point. Can you imagine? Talk about not dressing for the occasion."

"Peter is the only one with Timberland boots, and he has a pair of jeans. We can send the clothes they wore yesterday down to have them cleaned. Meanwhile, they can do some shopping."

"You think I should go with them?" Nina asked as she placed a fresh cup in front of Frankie.

"Would you want to be seen with them dressed like they just arrived from who knows where?"

"Good point." Nina took the seat across from Frankie. "When I was on my way back from hiking, I noticed a men's shop, and a Dick's Sporting Goods a few blocks away. I'm sure they can find something."

"Okay. So we shall send them on their way while you and I get pampered."

"What about Amy?"

"She mentioned she wanted to do a little hiking with Peter, and I think he's equipped to do that. Anything else could be a problem."

"And Rachael?" Nina asked.

"She said she wasn't sure what she was going to do today."

"Uh-oh. That could mean anything."

"That's for sure."

Frankie heard the shower running in her bathroom. "Giovanni must be up."

"I'll go check on Richard." Nina got up and went into their room.

Amy came bouncing from hers with Peter following behind. "Good morning, everyone!" Peter was wearing a robe over his pajamas, one of the few items he'd packed in his haste.

"Aren't you the perky one?" Nina chided.

"Aren't I always the perky one?" Amy's pink cheeks glowed.

She went over to the coffee maker and started a cup for herself, and then one for Peter.

Giovanni emerged from the bedroom with bare feet and wearing his new gray jogging suit. His hair was slicked back, the way Frankie liked it. Richard appeared next in his new outfit, wearing clean socks.

Frankie addressed the group. "Nina and I will be having massages this afternoon. Giovanni, you and Richard will go into the village and get some appropriate clothing, including boots." Frankie was in full Bossy Pants mode. "Rachael has something going on. She didn't care to share, which means it must be another one of her surprises. Amy? Peter? Do you have a plan?"

"We thought we'd take a short hike," Amy replied. She looked out the glass patio doors. "It looks like we might get some snow."

Peter added, "According to my weather app, they are predicting flurries later this afternoon."

"All the more reason to get yourselves suited up for the weather," Frankie said sternly.

"As you wish, madame." Giovanni gave her a slight bow.

"It's really in your best interest. You don't want to ruin your loafers. And you certainly don't want to be mocked."

"Mocked?" He squinted.

"You realize how ridiculous you are going to look wearing your shoes with the tracksuit."

"I'll say it's the new style!" he replied.

"Yeah, no, don't." Frankie knew he was kidding.

"She's right," Richard said. "We're going to look like a couple of dimwits walking down the street. First thing is to find boots."

"There's a Dick's Sporting Goods a few blocks away. Maybe you can hustle before anyone catches a glimpse of your fashion faux pas."

Amy giggled. "And to think, just a few days ago I was on the Ten Most Wanted by the Fashion Police!"

The mood was upbeat now that the traumas of the prior day were behind them.

"Sounds like we have a working plan," Nina said. "We'll meet back here later this afternoon, have a hot toddy in front of the fireplace, go down to dinner, and then to the party."

"Bravo!" Giovanni said.

Setting a slow pace this morning was exactly what everyone needed. Frankie thought she was still running on adrenaline. Nina's amperage was above normal, too.

The seven of them met for breakfast, which was at an equally unhurried pace. The day before was a lot to process. Until Frankie could ditch the crutches, each step was a reminder of how lucky she was. And that was all that mattered. When someone said, "You could have been . . ." she politely replied, "But I wasn't."

When they finished, they agreed to meet at the fireplace lounge in the lobby at seven o'clock. That would give everyone plenty of time to get ready for dinner.

Rachael walked up to Randy's desk with a prankish look on her face. Randy propped his elbows on his desk and rested his chin on his knuckles. "What have you been up to, Missy? With all the mishigas that has gone on, I would think you'd retire your crown."

"Frankie assumed a new royal title: The Stumbling Snow Queen!" She snickered.

"Don't be sassy. Your friend had a terrible scare yesterday."

"For sure. I wasn't the one who gave her the title, just to be clear."

"Crystal. So what is up your petite sleeve?" Randy cocked his head.

Rachael gave him a short recap of the cruise she and her

friends had gone on two years before. She'd been taking a class with the guest choreographer on the ship. "That's Henry. The guy I just broke up with."

"Wait. When?" Randy asked.

"When I was swooshing down the slope."

"Wait. You called him? Pulled a Frankie?"

"No, silly. I had an epiphany. I realized we were already over. I put the lid on it and set it on the curb."

"Is that some new metaphor?" He sat up as some guests came through.

"It's my metaphor. I don't mean as in trash, but it's done. What do you do with things that are done? You don't keep them stashed under your bed. You have to make room for new things."

"Huh." Randy was intrigued.

"This has nothing to do with Henry personally. It has to do with me. It serves neither of us if I keep nagging him to please spend time with me. Please talk to me."

"And you've asked him, correct?"

"Numerous times." Rachael appeared calm and collected. "The answer was always the same. He was either busy or had an appointment, or something. I don't think we've seen each other more than three times in the past four months. I don't need a building to fall on me to get that he's over me.

"I've sent him many messages, and stupidly, I wasn't getting his, if you get my drift. No pun intended." She huffed. "Anyway . . ."

"Okay. What is going on in that cute little head of yours?"

"We pull a few pranks. You are familiar with Bruno Mars, correct?"

He nodded. "Of course!"

She looked around, pretending she was about to reveal Colonel Sanders's Famous Recipe, then whispered, "Uptown Funk."

"Love it!" Randy leaned in again. "Details, please."

Rachael whispered the details of her plan, and Randy was all in. "One thing, though. My brother is coming in from San Fran late this afternoon."

"I think we can work this out by then. See ya!" She turned and left through the front entrance.

Randy leaned on his elbow again and sighed. "I'm going to miss her."

Rachael walked into the village and procured the item she needed. She hurried back to the hotel before anyone spotted her with the big package. When she got back to her room, she unpacked the box, plugged it in, activated the Bluetooth, and hit a button from her music playlist. All was in working order.

She'd heard boom boxes were back, but now they had much more advanced technology. Pretty cool. She'd also heard cassette tapes were making a comeback. Why not? Vinyl did. She disliked the phrase *Old School*. How about *Smart School* or *We Did a Lot of Stuff Before You Were Born School*?

Grinning, she began practicing her steps. Next up was finding Marlena and Carrie, two of the housekeepers. According to Randy, they would be up for something like this.

Before Giovanni and Richard left the hotel, they debated whether they should wear their coats. Giovanni had a black camel hair, and Richard had a bright blue anorak. Neither of them would get past the fashion police. They briskly walked down the street to the sports shop, doing their best not to attract too much attention to themselves. Richard stifled a laugh as they passed their reflection in a store window. "We are quite a pair."

"*Presto! Presto!*" Giovanni urged him to move quickly.

A totally geared-up dude greeted them as they entered the store. He gave them the once-over, and then once again. He stared at their feet. "I bet you're looking for boots?"

"Yes, thank you, Captain Obvious," Richard retorted.

"Right this way, gentlemen." Richard spotted the young man making a subtle mocking gesture to one of his colleagues and nodded at their feet.

"It was an emergency. We had to come without luggage," Giovanni tried to explain.

"No worries, man." The dude showed them displays of dozens of boots. "What are you looking for?"

"We are going to be here for two and a half more days." Richard lifted a pair of black Merrell boots off the shelf. "Got these in a size ten?"

Giovanni chose a pair of Danner boots. "Eleven?" They were lightweight with a low profile and good traction. Four hundred dollars was more than he'd expected to spend, but he could wear them when he was working. They paid for the boots and put them on immediately, packing their shoes in the boot boxes.

On to clothes. Were they going to spend any time on the slopes? Not Giovanni. Not Richard, either, so they opted for jogging suits similar to what they were wearing. At one point, Giovanni realized he'd picked the same suit in a different color. "I suspect this is where Randy found the clothes for us." By the time they were finished, both men had to purchase duffel bags for the trip home.

Giovanni had pointed out that they needed something for the party. Something for dinners. Something to lounge in. Something for outside walking. That meant Giovanni needed a jacket. He went for a traditional cotton duck jacket with a light removable sherpa lining. Socks, underwear, slippers, and pajamas.

They put everything into the duffel bags and walked proudly back to the hotel in their hiking boots, Tek Gear running suits, and jackets. "I don't think I've ever shopped like this before," Richard said. "I go through my closet every season and decide what to keep and what to toss. It's pretty easy since all my shirts fall into two categories: work, and not work."

"Yes. I think I own thirty-five white dress shirts. I wear one every day."

They rustled past Randy, who was listening to something with an earbud in one ear. "Nicely done, gentlemen." He nodded, but did not continue with any further conversation.

Richard gave Giovanni a shrug. This wasn't the effusive Randy they had grown to love over the past eighteen hours.

The foyer of the spa was otherworldly. The scent of lavender wafting through the air greeted them, as gentle relaxing strains of a harp blended with the sound of a soft waterfall. They could feel the tension begin to melt away. Nina whispered, "Brilliant idea, my friend."

As they were escorted to a private changing area, the lavender scent and harp followed them. They wrapped themselves in lavish robes and slippers and then moved to a waiting area with another waterfall, teak lounge chairs, and an attendant who served herbal tea. The music and scent were ever present.

Two women in white uniforms guided them to their individual massage rooms, each of which had a view of the lake.

Frankie's masseuse lowered the table with the push of a button and helped her on. She asked Frankie what kind of pressure she preferred, to which Frankie replied, "Until I scream."

Nina had comparable tolerance for deep-tissue massage and gave her masseuse similar instructions.

The experience touched many senses, and two hours later, they emerged like blobs of jelly.

Once again, they were directed to the lounge chairs to allow their bodies to acclimate and release toxins while they sipped another serving of herbal tea. Within minutes, they both dozed off.

Nina jumped when the attendant touched her shoulder. She was deep in la-la land. Frankie merely stirred. She wasn't ready to come back from wherever she was visiting, but Nina gently nudged her. "Sweetcakes. Come. These fine ladies want to get out of here."

Frankie blinked several times. "Wow. Where in the heck did I go?"

"The Garden of Life," one of the attendants replied.

Frankie shook the sleep from her head as best she could. "That was amazing, but I think I need a nap."

"We were both out cold for over an hour." Nina smiled.

"I need more. Please, may I have some more?"

Nina asked the attendant what time it was. "Just past four."

"Oh, good. We have a couple of hours before dinner, so you can take another snooze. That means you have to get up, though."

"Waahh . . ." Frankie feigned displeasure.

"Come on, kiddo." Nina helped her up, positioning the crutches under each arm.

Amy and Peter took a leisurely stroll through town and then along a local path near the lake. "This is quite beautiful," Peter said in a hushed voice.

"Right?" Amy locked arms with him. "I'm kinda, sorta glad you're here. I don't mean kinda. I mean I really am glad you're here. I'm just sorry it was under such scary circumstances."

"I'm kinda, sorta glad I'm here too," Peter replied. "I have to admit, you have an interesting group of friends. I haven't had this much excitement since I got my CPA."

Amy laughed out loud. "I thought you were going to say since you met me."

"That was truly a special moment, above and beyond all

else. Meeting you brought something into my life that was missing: fun."

"So accountants really live dull lives, do they?" Amy prodded.

"Not anymore." Peter placed his arm around her shoulders. "We had such a good time on the cruise. I couldn't believe my luck. I really had absolutely no expectations whatsoever. It was just something to do besides watching the ball drop while people made spectacles of themselves on TV."

"Well, I'm glad you were just a few cabins away from us. I don't know if I would have had the nerve to talk to you otherwise," Amy admitted.

"You mean you would never have talked to me?"

"I'm really kind of shy when it comes to that sort of thing."

"I think you can thank your friends for bringing the best out in you. They are a bunch of crazy, entertaining, wonderful women."

"Yes, they are. They accepted me when everyone else made fun of me. I was a bookworm. Geek. Dweeb. But they embraced my idiosyncratic personality."

"And I think you round out this quartet quite nicely. Each of you has something to give. Something to offer."

"It's the friendship and support we give each other," Amy said.

"That's exactly what I'm talking about. You are patient and kind and are willing to do whatever you can to help your friends, and they feel the same way about you."

"They were very supportive when my parents split up. It was tough with my mother trying to drive a wedge between me and my father, but Frankie and Nina kept me on track. Then I moved to Silicon Valley, Nina moved to LA, Rachael was having her usual turmoil, and Frankie moved to the city and worked her way to the top of a publishing company. If it hadn't been for that reunion, I might never have reconnected with them." Amy took a breath. "And trust me, I was very nervous about going, but my dad practically shoved me out the door. Well, he drove me to the reunion. And then shoved me out the door." She giggled.

"And then the four of you went on a cruise. And you didn't know your father was also aboard the ship."

"Crazy stuff. It always seems to happen when the four of us are together."

"I can attest to that!" Peter smiled. "Since I met you, I feel like my life has gotten better. Lighter. Happier."

"I know we only see each other on weekends, but I feel the same way. I love that we're both obsessed with puzzles. And watch British mysteries."

"Me, too." Peter hesitated. "Amy, what if I told you I had a job offer in Boston?"

"Really?" Amy's eyes grew wide.

"Yes, the firm I work for is expanding their offices in Boston and asked me if I was interested in relocating."

"Well, are you?" Amy asked, on pins and needles.

"Most definitely," Peter said.

"We could see more of each other." Amy held her breath.

"That would be the only reason I would consider moving. I don't know anyone in Boston, so you'd be my only friend."

"Peter, you'll make friends." Amy was slipping into absent-minded professor mode.

"That's not what I meant." He cleared his throat. "We've been seeing each other for two years. What do you say we put both our names on a mailbox?"

"Like live together?" Amy asked.

"For a start. We can figure out things as we go along."

"Do you like cats?" Amy asked, even though she knew the answer.

"Blinky and Gimpy? My favs." He chuckled. "Actually, that's who I really want to live with. Your fur babies."

Amy laughed out loud and then snuggled closer to him.

"When you sent me that text about Frankie being missing, and Giovanni went above and beyond to get here, it made me think. I would have done the same for you."

"Really, Peter?" Amy looked up at him with big eyes.

"Really, Amy, my little brainiac." Peter gave her an affectionate hug. "We should head back. I think they're right about snow coming."

Giovanni and Richard changed their morning attire and dressed in something appropriate to check out the hotel and the lake. There was a walking path that ran along the shore. It had been cleared, but there was still a lot of ice and snow to navigate. "Good thing we got these boots," Richard said as he stomped some of the snow off the bottom of them.

"Yes. And they are very warm, too." Giovanni nodded in agreement. "I used to ski when I was a boy. I loved being outside in the snow. Now? Not so much." He laughed. "Maybe I am too old."

"Nah. We're just smarter. Why freeze your you-know-what off if you don't have to?"

"People love it. Me? I prefer warmth and sunshine. Where I grew up, it was sunny most of the time, but the summers were very hot. We didn't seem to mind. We would go to swim in a river."

"We belonged to a pool club," Richard said. "Growing up in Philadelphia, there weren't many options. And no ocean. But every summer, my folks would rent a house at the Jersey Shore."

"Not like the television show?" Giovanni was half serious.

"Nothing like it. We went to Long Beach Island. Mostly summer houses, rentals. Not too much riffraff. My brother and I would hit the beach first thing in the morning, go home and get sandwiches that my mom had ready for us, and then go back to the beach. I became a decent surfer at one point."

"No kidding? You? Corabunga?" Giovanni's accent made Richard laugh.

"Cowabunga. But no. I don't think I ever uttered that word."

"You don't like snowboard?" Giovanni asked as they strolled along the crystal-clear lake.

"By the time I went to college, it was all books and studying. I didn't have time to explore more outdoor sports. And, as you said, it's too cold."

Giovanni looked up as clouds began to cover the clear blue sky. "I think snow is coming. I can smell it."

"I think you're right. We should probably head back."

When they returned to the hotel lobby, Randy was not at his post. Instead, it was manned by a young woman who looked completely befuddled with two phones ringing at the same time and several people standing in line before the concierge station. Richard and Giovanni edged closer to see what the commotion was all about. One guest was complaining, "But I made a reservation for dinner three days ago."

The woman apologized. "I am sorry, sir, but there seems to be a problem with the kitchen staff."

Giovanni's ears perked up. He stepped forward. "Excuse me. I couldn't help overhearing there is a problem with the kitchen staff?"

"Yes, sir, and if you have a reservation for dinner, we will have to cancel it."

"What seems to be the trouble?"

"Our kitchen crew lives a little way up the mountain, and with the warm weather, they had a bit of a snow slide that dumped several feet of snow on their street, their driveways, and on their cars. They can't get out of the neighborhood, and it's beginning to snow at the higher elevations. The road crews have to start salting the main roads first. As long as our workers are safe and inside their homes, digging them out isn't a priority right now."

"I see. Can you tell me who is in charge of the kitchen?" Giovanni asked politely.

"It won't help. He's ready to close it down."

"Please. May I speak with him? My brother and I own a restaurant in New York. Maybe I can be of assistance."

Richard put his hand on Giovanni's shoulder. "Count me in, if you need help."

The flustered woman dialed the kitchen manager. "Sir, there is someone who would like to speak to you."

"I told you I don't have anyone to cover. Tell them to try the grab-and-go."

"But, sir, he owns a restaurant and said he might be able to help."

"Unless he can produce a half dozen people, I don't know what he'll be able to do." His voice was so loud everyone could hear it coming through the receiver of the phone.

Giovanni turned to Richard. "You, me, Peter. That's three. Nina, Amy, Rachael. That's six." He leaned closer to the woman, who was listening to the man screeching on the other end. He made a gesture to hand the phone over to him. "Signore. My name is Giovanni Lombardi. Please may I come and talk to you?"

The man huffed. "Sure. I don't know what you can do, but yeah. Sure. Come on back."

Giovanni and Richard made their way through the dining room and into the kitchen. Giovanni tilted his head at the man with the red face and bulging eyes.

"Signore? I am Giovanni Lombardi." He put his hand out.

"You own a restaurant?" the cranky man asked.

"Yes. In New York. With my brother." He looked around the kitchen.

"We have reservations for sixty people." The man eyed Giovanni skeptically.

"Yes. We've done it before. Can you show me what the

purveyors brought today? Your inventory? Maybe we can do a prix fixe menu?"

The manager showed him around the large walk-in refrigerator. There was beef, chicken, pork; another rack held a multitude of vegetables, and another had bags of shrimp and scallops. "Pasta?" Giovanni asked.

"Got plenty of that." Mr. Cranky Pants showed him the pantry.

Giovanni did some calculations in his head. "What if we make it a tasting menu? Four courses? First, we serve sauteed shrimp and scallops over greens. Then a pasta dish. Then a choice of beef, chicken, pork. We can make the different sauces ahead of time. Finish with dessert."

The man looked at Giovanni in amazement. "You can do that?"

Giovanni tilted his head to one side, then the other. "We can try."

Richard stepped in at this point. "Better to serve people food and have them complain about the food than complain that the hotel couldn't accommodate them on New Year's Eve."

Giovanni gave him a look. "Complain?"

"Sorry, I didn't mean that the way it came out. People love your food."

Mr. Cranky Pants threw up his hands and tossed Giovanni an apron. "It's all yours." Then he marched out.

Richard and Giovanni stared at each other. "Another fine mess you've gotten me into, Ollie," Richard said with a bit of levity. "What's the worst that can happen?"

Giovanni started speaking to himself in Italian, and Richard was glad he didn't understand a word of it.

"First course is at seven-thirty." Richard checked the big clock on the wall. "We have two and a half hours to figure this out."

Three people emerged from the back room. "Hello. I hope you are here to help us?" Giovanni pleaded.

One of the men spoke. "Yes, I work the line." He pointed to a young woman standing next to him. "She does the salad. I'm the sauté guy. He works the grill." He nodded to the third person.

"I'm the pasta man," Giovanni said. "Richard, you can help prep."

The three kitchen workers stood with their arms folded. The first one spoke again. "You think we can pull this off?"

"We can try," Giovanni said. "We are going to round up a few more people to help, but we need to change the menu. Who can get new menus printed?"

The young woman raised her hand. "I'm Becky. I can go to the front desk and have them print up menus for tonight. Just tell me what you want them to say. We have the hotel logo. All that stuff."

Giovanni grabbed a clipboard off the wall and wrote down:


New Year's Eve Tasting Menu

First Course
Grilled Shrimp & Scallop Scampi Served over Wilted Greens
Served with a Crisp Sauvignon Blanc

Second Course
Fettuccini with Peas and Mushrooms in a Light Cream Sauce
Served with a Pinot Gris


Third Course
Your Choice
Filet Mignon with Béarnaise Sauce

Chicken Marsala
Pork Tenderloin in a Port Wine Sauce
Choice of Cabernet Sauvignon or White Bordeaux


He studied the menu. It was doable. "What do we have for dessert?" he asked the others.

"We have a slew of profiteroles, gelato, and sorbet."

"Okay. Add:


Fourth Course
Dessert Assortment
Coffee — Tea
Port or Brandy


Giovanni looked at Richard. "*Si?*"

"Looks good to me. We should round up the others. Pronto!" Richard grinned.

Giovanni turned to the three people with blank stares on their faces. "You get things ready. I will be back in an hour." One by one, he put his hands on each of their shoulders and looked them in the eye. "I know we can do this."

The three gave each other dubious looks, but they'd showed up to work tonight, and they would, even if they were thrust into creating an impromptu tasting dinner for New Year's Eve.

Giovanni and Richard stopped at the concierge desk on their way to the suite. Randy was consoling the young woman, who was being verbally battered by irate guests.

"We have the situation under control," Richard announced. "I mean, Giovanni has the situation under control. Becky is going to have new menus made up for a tasting dinner. Giovanni will be executive chef; I'll be the bozo he'll be shouting out orders to."

Randy's eyes went wide. "For real?"

"*Si*. We met with Mister Pantaloni Irritabili in the kitchen. He has three people ready to work, and we have six. It will be a tasting menu, so we won't have to worry about making too many different meals. The guests will choose their main course from only three options."

"Genius!" Randy said in awe. "See?" He turned to the tearful woman. "You handled it the best you could. People can be mean, especially when it comes to food."

Giovanni cracked a smile. "*Capisce?*"

She nodded and wiped her nose with a tissue.

"Now go. Take a break." Randy gave her a gentle tap.

Once she was out of earshot, Randy leaned in. "She'll never make it in this job. Poor thing." He sat down. "So what do you need from me?"

"Nothing," Richard replied. "As soon as Becky gets the new menus printed, she can give one to you in case anyone asks."

"Limited seating, of course?" Randy asked.

"Of course," Giovanni answered. "Not to worry, Randy."

"If you say so."

"I say so!" Giovanni laughed.

The two men headed to their suite. "Who is going to break the news to the girls?"

Giovanni raised his eyebrows. "We may need to do it together, no?"

"I'd say 'no,' but that wouldn't help, now, would it?" Richard guffawed.

"No. 'No' would not help."

When they entered the suite, Nina was lounging on the sofa in front of the fireplace. Amy and Peter had returned from their walk.

"Frankie?" Giovanni asked. Nina pointed to the bedroom.

Giovanni stepped quietly to where Frankie was resting.

She opened her sleepy eyes. "Hey. Where've you been? I would have thought you'd be back before now."

"Ah. Yes. We have what you call a 'glitch' in tonight's plans."

Frankie sat up and rubbed her face. "What kind of glitch?"

"The warm weather made some of the snow melt. Most of the kitchen workers cannot get to the hotel because the street where they live is full of snow right now."

"Don't they have plows for that?" Frankie asked with a puzzled look.

"Yes, but they are predicting snow later, and the plows have to be on standby."

She closed one eye. "And?"

"And, well, they were going to have to cancel all the dinner reservations for tonight."

"And?" She had a pretty good idea where this might be going.

"And I said I would handle it."

"You are going to handle it," she repeated in a neutral tone. It was more of an announcement than a question.

"Yes, me. And Richard, and Peter, and Nina, and Amy, and Rachael."

"Have you told them about your plan to prepare dinner for . . . how many people?"

"Sixty," Giovanni stated.

Frankie's mouth dropped. "You're going to prepare sixty dinners? Alone?"

"No, cara. Everyone is going to help. I have three people already in the kitchen who work here." He was more excited about the task at hand than he was worried.

He lowered himself on the bed. "Frankie, I know this will be a little tricky, but I believe it can be done."

Frankie did not want to challenge Giovanni. He was a master in the kitchen. He had years of experience, from busing tables to acting as executive chef to co-managing the family restaurant. She took his hand. "If anyone can do it, you can."

"*Grazie*. Your confidence in me gives me more confidence." He held out his arms to help her up. "Come. We need to tell everyone."

The buzz in the living room was lively. "I hear we are going to be kitchen help tonight?" Nina said lightly. "Do you really think we can pull this off?"

"We have to try. People want to celebrate New Year's Eve. I've done this many times," he said without the least bit of concern.

"Yeah, but not with our crew." Nina laughed.

"But I have faith. You are very smart people. I know you can follow directions. Trust me, please. It will be a memorable night. I promise."

"Memorable for sure!" Amy was delighted at this new monkey wrench in their plans. "Heck, nothing has gone according to plan, but everything's worked out so far, right?"

"Excellent observation, Amy," Richard said.

"Where's Rachael?" Frankie asked.

"She's doing something," Nina said.

"No doubt. But what?" Frankie asked suspiciously.

"I guess we'll find out, but in the meantime, I'll leave her a voice mail in her room and send a text," Nina said. "Details, please?" She looked at Giovanni.

"Everyone meet in the kitchen at five-thirty. Wear comfortable shoes." He raised one of his legs to show off his new purchase. "See? I knew these would be good."

Richard spoke next. "I know this is a curve ball, but in the spirit of kindness, I think it's worth the effort. We'll be doing something good." He paused. "Or not." He laughed.

"I'm all in," Nina said.

"This will be a night to remember," Amy cheered.

"Okay. Everyone start to get ready. I have a few notes I

must make." Giovanni hung up his jacket and went to the small café table, the clipboard under his arm. He drew a sketch of the kitchen layout and made an X where people were going to stand to perform their jobs. If everyone had one or two simple tasks, the prep should go smoothly, provided they were quick. Pushing out sixty dinners at one time meant there would be a lot of balls in the air.

Fortunately, the waitstaff hadn't been affected by the snow slide and the forthcoming storm. But if the roads weren't cleared by the end of the night, there could be a few people sharing rooms or sleeping in the lobby. But that wasn't a problem for Giovanni to solve. He had other fish to fry. Or sauté.

Just after five o'clock, Giovanni put on his laundered white shirt and slacks and his new boots. "I'm going to the kitchen now. Frankie, do you want to come with me?"

"Yes, I do." As much of a tease as Frankie could be, she didn't want to do anything to deflate Giovanni's resolve and enthusiasm. She was moving much better than the day before and was hopeful she could walk on her own before they left Tahoe.

When they arrived in the kitchen, the paltry staff stood in a row, wearing their uniforms. "Good evening, chef," they said with respect.

"*Grazie*. Good evening. Are there more uniforms here?"

"We have jackets in the locker room. I think there are six or seven."

"Perfecto." He looked at Frankie, who was helplessly leaning on her crutches. "*Cara*, let me find you a place to sit, a knife, and some mushrooms. Okay?"

"Okay!" Frankie knew she could manage that.

The rest of the group arrived, including Rachael. "What's the deal?" she asked, looking around the sparsely staffed kitchen.

"We are the deal," Nina said as she put her arm around Rachael. "We are going to be serving a tasting menu."

"You mean as in *we*?" She pointed to everyone.

"Yes, ma'am," Amy replied and handed Rachael a white jacket and a chef's hat.

"Really? A hat?" she whined.

"Health laws," Richard answered.

Rachael slipped on the jacket, which was clearly two sizes too big. The sleeves ended at her fingertips. "Oh, swell."

Nina helped Rachael fold her cuffs. "Don't be such a baby." She plopped the hat on Rachael's head. "Adorable," Nina said as she went through the same paces.

Giovanni checked the dining room. The tables were ready with the new menus at each place setting. Then he gasped. Dishwashers! Were they here? He ran back into the kitchen in a panic. "Do we have dishwashers?"

Becky pointed at a large machine in the far corner. "Do we have someone who can operate them?"

Becky looked a little confused. Then it dawned on her that he was asking about people. "Yes. They should be here by six."

Giovanni took several breaths. He was almost on the verge of a panic attack.

He went over the menu with everyone and asked which dish or job each of them thought they could handle, minus the mushrooms. That had already been assigned to Frankie, who chirped, "I can also peel potatoes."

Once Giovanni had finished handing out assignments, he spoke to the waitstaff. "I know some people may complain, but this menu is what we have to offer under the circumstances. If they wish to cancel their reservation, they may do so without any penalty. You should also tell them we cannot offer any special requests, such as gluten-free pasta. And if they are vegetarian, they can have an extra serving of pasta or a plate of vegetables."

Everyone nodded. "Any questions?"

There were none. "Thank you in advance for your patience and willingness to go along with this experiment. If you run into any trouble, please come directly to me. Even if I am shouting, it's only because I want someone to be able to hear my instructions. Not because I am angry. *Capisce?*"

A few giggled "*Capisce*" in return.

"And serve everyone a glass of Prosecco as soon as they're seated. That should make them, how you say, loosey-goosey?"

A few laughed out loud. "Yes, Chef!"

Giovanni went back into the kitchen. "May I have everyone come over to me for a minute?" His small army of friends and the three regulars formed a circle. "Please humor me. Everyone take hands." He bowed his head. "Heavenly father, mother, all the saints, and heavenly angels, bless us with speed, good will, and good food. Amen." A very loud *amen* rang through the kitchen.

Giovanni asked Becky if they usually played music in the kitchen. "It depends on his mood."

"The chef?"

"No, the manager."

"Ah. I understand. He is always a little cranky?"

Becky nodded. "Yep!"

"Do you have favorite music here?"

"Usually some George Benson, eighties R&B, Billy Ocean, stuff like that gets us moving in a nice groove."

"Then your other job is to find that music so we can dance and sing as we work!"

"Perfecto!" She gave him a big smile.

A few minutes later, the strong bass line and familiar sound of the great guitarist George Benson filled the room with "Give Me the Night." On cue, everyone was swaying to the easy, upbeat music. Nina and Frankie were prompted to sing the backup melody together. Things were cooking. Literally. If they plated ten dishes at a time, they could move the first course out in six rounds.

Giovanni surveyed the kitchen. People were smiling, chopping, singing, braising, wilting, and sautéing. They were all moving with the same rhythm. Music. *Molto bene.*

The pasta was fresh, so it would take only a few minutes to cook. The sauce was a bit delicate, and Giovanni nurtured it, stirring gently as he slowly added mounds of Parmigiana Reggiano to the mixture. He looked at the checks for the third course. Mostly beef and pork.

The next song was "Just the Two of Us" by Bill Withers and Grover Washington, Jr., followed by "Isn't She Lovely" by Stevie Wonder. The singing continued, and the food was miraculously on time. It was the magic of the music that kept everyone in sync.

The first two courses went out without a hitch. If they could get through the next one, the night would be a huge success. Up until that moment, there hadn't been one complaint, one broken glass, and so far, no one was wearing food. But it wouldn't be a normal day in any kitchen if there wasn't at least one disgruntled patron. Sure enough, someone complained his chicken was too dry, and he made a big stink about how he was paying good money for a rubber chicken. Giovanni had the team prepare another, and he personally brought it to the table. "My apologies, sir. It has been a very challenging evening. This is my first time in this kitchen. And because of the snow, we're working with a reduced staff. So please accept my apology for your disappointment."

Half the dining room could hear the interaction. Whispers of awe and surprise went around the room. One gentleman stood and raised his glass. "Bravo! The dinner was stupendous! Thank you. Happy New Year!" The rest of the diners joined in, leaving the complainer a bit shamefaced.

Once the dinner dishes were cleared, dessert was served with the after-dinner libation. People lingered and chatted about the food, the predicted snowstorm.

Giovanni stuck his head out the door to listen to what

people were saying. "Wonderful idea. Each plate was just enough to taste and savor. And the wine pairing was perfect."

"I loved that pasta dish. Never had anything like it before," a woman said.

Giovanni was elated. And proud. Proud of the effort everyone had made to pull it off. He went back into the kitchen, where everyone was waiting for a reaction. "*Bellissimo*! *Bravo*! I make you come work in my kitchen!" He hugged Frankie, then Nina; then everyone was hugging everyone else. Rachael threw her hat up in the air and bolted out the door.

"Where is she going?" Nina wondered out loud.

"I'm sure we will find out."

Jane stood in the cold, watching the enormous effort going on in the kitchen. They were dancing, singing, shouting, cooking. There was an indelible bond between them. What she'd said to Nina was true. She'd felt jealous all these years. Now she felt admiration. Jane truly wanted to have one last goodbye.

The gourmet group went back to their suite to clean up and change. The cocktail party was to start at ten o'clock. Frankie pulled on a pair of leggings and a white turtleneck tunic sweater, pulled her hair back in a ponytail. She looked refreshed and relaxed. No one would ever guess she had had an accident the day before, a quick trip to the hospital, and just finished working as a cook's assistant for sixty people.

Within the hour, everyone was spiffed, smiling, and ready to celebrate the New Year and their impromptu accomplishment.

When they arrived in the lobby, the snow was falling thickly outside, and a man was leaning against the fireplace. Frankie and Nina thought they recognized him, then realized it was Troy. A clean-shaven Troy. A showered, hair-combed-back Troy. The sight of Duke at his side was a good hint, too. Nina walked over to him. "You clean up real good."

"Why, thank you, ma'am," he said, pretending to tip an invisible hat.

"And Duke. You look very handsome, too."

He gave her his paw.

Frankie hobbled over to say hello and pet the dog who'd saved her. Then she noticed he was guarding a small basket near the hearth. "What you got there, boy?"

He nudged her arm. "You want me to take a look?"

She lifted the lid, and two green eyes looked back at her. She was startled for a brief moment. Then she realized the eyes were surrounded by black fur, and the creature had two ears, four paws, and whiskers. "Oh, my. How cute. Who does she belong to?" She looked around. Duke gave a slight woof. "Me? No, it doesn't belong to me." She turned to Troy. "Is this little baby yours?"

"Not really. I found her on the edge of the property this morning, and I didn't want to leave her alone. She's my plus one?" He smirked.

"Are you going to keep her?" Frankie asked. "Duke seems to like her."

"Right now, my place isn't good for a young kitten like this. Duke is fine in the cold. This little girlie needs a regular home. Plus, I don't know where I am going to end up."

Frankie made a decision right there on the spot. This little thing was going home with her. She would be Bandit's new bestie.

Nina wasn't the least surprised when Frankie scooped up the kitten. "Now about that land of yours?"

"Like I told you guys, it's not mine. Or so they say."

"Wait right here." Nina moved through the small crowd and found Richard. She gave him a brief explanation of Troy's situation, and Richard said he would be happy to hear what her friend had to say and see if he could be of any help. The two inched their way back to where Troy was standing, and Nina introduced them. She left the two men alone while she and Frankie talked a mile a minute about everything that had transpired that night.

"It has been crazy. Nothing like I expected," Frankie said as she cuddled the little furball.

"Not expected, but not surprising," Nina said. "I hope Richard can help Troy."

"Yeah, me too. He deserves some good karma for rescuing me."

"Interesting, my dear." Nina looked at her. "What if Richard is able to help Troy? But he would never have met Troy if you hadn't fallen."

"I told you we'll get six degrees of separation by the time we leave." Frankie laughed.

Giovanni came over with two glasses of wine. He handed one to Nina and the other to Frankie, who was leaning against the stone wall of the fireplace. "You have a new friend?" he asked. "Who does he or she belong to?"

"You're looking at her." Nina smirked.

"Frankie? You are going to take this kitten home?" he asked with delight.

"I promised Bandit I would bring him a present." Frankie rubbed her face against the kitten's coat. The kitten responded by purring up a storm.

Nina noticed Richard and Troy were wrapping up their conversation. She also spotted a guitar near where they were standing. She elbowed Frankie. "Check it out. We've got to get him to play something."

"I don't think he brought it here to sell it." Frankie's response was lighthearted.

Nina walked over, picked the instrument up, and handed it to Troy. "Play, sir." He was taken aback.

"Please?" She gave him a coy look.

"Okay. Twist my arm." He moved over to a big mission-style chair and sat on the armrest. He began with "Wichita Lineman," a song from the late 1960s recorded by Glen Campbell and considered one of the most haunting ballads of its time.

Frankie turned to Nina. "Troy does the song justice. Not many can sing it well. Even if you never met a lineman, the ballad somehow gets into your core." Nina put her arm around Frankie as the crowd hooted and applauded.

Troy's next song was "Whenever You Come Around" by Vince Gill. The two women looked at each other and made their way over to Troy, Frankie hobbling with the kitten in one arm. Before anyone could say a word, the two began to sing harmony with Troy. Another resounding cheer for the trio.

In the distance stood the woman with the blue eyes. She'd come to say one last goodbye to Nina and apologize one more time to the others. When she heard the voice coming across the room, she froze. She couldn't see his face and didn't want to believe it could be Troy, but she knew it was. After two more songs, he put the guitar down and went to the bar to get a drink. As he was about to take his first sip, a voice called his name. It was a ghost from his past. He turned slowly and was face-to-face with the woman who'd torn his heart out.

"Jane?" he said, mystified.

"Troy," she replied softly. "Can we talk?"

He was stunned. "Uh, yes. Sure." They found a quiet place to sit.

Nina noticed Troy was engrossed in a heavy conversation. Then she realized he was talking to Jane. "What in the . . ."

Frankie leaned to look in the same direction. "Whoa. Is that who I think it is?"

"Yes, it is," Nina said.

"What are you going to do?"

"Not a thing." Nina still had mixed feelings about Jane. It was more important to her to enjoy the rest of the evening with her significant other.

Giovanni gave Frankie a kiss on the cheek. "Your voices sounded so good together."

"Thank you. Nina and I used to sing harmonies when we were kids. We'd always sing along with the radio in the car. Drove my mother nuts." She chuckled. "It wasn't that we were bad. It was just she didn't like our music."

It was getting close to midnight, and people were filling their glasses with champagne. There was a large-screen television on the far side of the room that had been set with a three-hour delay for the ball drop in Times Square. Everyone started shouting "Five! Four! Three! Two! One! Happy New Year!"

Giovanni gave Frankie a warm, loving kiss while she held the little fur baby close to her chest.

Once the merriment died down, Troy walked over to Nina. "Jane wants to apologize before she leaves."

"Uh. Okay. And what about you?"

"We've made peace."

"Really?" Nina asked warily.

"Yes. I told you I was over our breakup, and I am willing to accept her apology. She actually seems sincere."

"I think she just might be," Nina said as Jane approached gingerly.

"Nina, I truly am sorry for all the disrespect and abuse. I realize now that jealousy is only admiration turned inside out."

"Well said." Nina hugged her. "Thank you."

Suddenly, the thump of a bass and the sounds of *doot-doot, doot-doo-doot* were blaring through a boom box. It was the introduction to "Uptown Funk" by Mark Ronson and Bruno Mars, and Rachael was about to reprise the flash-mob dance she'd created on the cruise. Behind her danced Randy and several other people Rachael had cajoled into joining the fun. They trotted to the middle of the lobby and finished the dance with flair, more hoots, whistles, and applause.

At that point, Frankie was ready for slumber. She, Giovanni, and her new family member made their way to the suite. Giovanni pulled out a small plastic bag. It contained some chopped chicken. He spread it on a paper towel. "I think she might be hungry, no?"

"You are the best." Frankie set the kitten down on the bed. She figured the cat was about eight weeks old. "Who would leave such a sweet thing on the side of the road?" And that's when she decided to call her Sweet P.

"What about a litter box?" Giovanni had become rather adept at catsitting. "Ah, the shoebox my boots came in." Then he shredded some toilet paper to act as litter until they could get the proper feline necessities. The rest of the crew meandered in shortly thereafter, all vowing to sleep until noon.

# Chapter Fourteen

*New Year's Day*

By the time everyone crawled out of slumberland, the streets had been plowed, sidewalks shoveled, and ice melt sprinkled in strategic places. The plan was for Troy to meet everyone for lunch. He would discuss his situation with Richard afterwards. The big question was, would there be food?

The staff that had worked the night before had been given rooms to stay over, and they were able to offer steak sandwiches, chicken sandwiches, or salad topped with shrimp, beef, or chicken.

"Leftovers!" Giovanni exclaimed. He stuck his head in the kitchen and gave them a thumbs-up. Then he gave each of them a one-hundred-dollar bill. They were overjoyed. Giovanni knew the hotel wouldn't pay them for doubling up jobs, and he was grateful they were able to save him from embarrassment. He would have been mortified if things had gone awry.

When they finished lunch, Frankie got a text from Mateo:
**How are things? How are you?**
**What are your plans?**

She replied:

**All good here. Heading back to NYC day after tomorrow.**

He asked:

**Need a ride?**

She replied with a

**???**

**Jet is still in Tahoe. Weather issues. Supposed to return to-morrow if you don't mind leaving early.**

Frankie turned to the others. "Mateo is offering his jet, but we would have to leave tomorrow."

She was almost bowled over by the *yes*es and *count me in*s. She sent a text back:

**Wheels up?**

He replied:

**11:00**

She sent him a thumbs-up and a big red heart. She was relieved she wouldn't have to ride a shuttle to Reno and navigate through an airport. "This is a blessing."

"Amen to that!"

# Epilogue

The flight home was uneventful, a nice respite considering the past few days. They were in total agreement that a lot can be accomplished when people work together, show kindness, and are willing to help one another. It was the essence of what brought them closer together. So they made a pact that they would reconvene every year at a new location to share the fun and excitement. A little "drama" was a given, considering this distinct group of friends.

Throughout the year, they kept each other up-to-date on their day-to-day lives.

Richard reviewed all of Troy's paperwork. There were enough loopholes to sink a ship. Richard told Troy to tell the developers to make him an offer, no ifs, ands, or buts. They settled on two million dollars. It was more than enough for Troy and Duke to start a new life. He was only thirty-eight. There were many roads ahead, including the one to Nashville, and farther along the highway, to visit his friend Nina and her pals on the East Coast.

When Rachael and Henry finally had that awkward conversation, he was pleasantly surprised at Rachael's approach. *No hard feelings. Let's keep in touch.* Her generosity guilted Henry into finding work for Randy in a Broadway show.

Rachael wheedled Randy into ballroom dancing competitions while she made valiant efforts to be more discerning when it came to men. But with Rachael, anything could change in five minutes, and she would pull a number of shenanigans over the next year.

Nina phoned Michael Powell and accepted his offer to produce her own radio show. Whatever the subject. She decided to call the show *You Can't Be Serious*. Each week, she would tackle social issues, family issues, and interview people on those topics. They would tape the shows, edit them, and turn them into podcasts.

Within a month, it was one of the most listened-to programs in the country. She once told Frankie, "The best part is, I don't have to think about my hair!" Richard became her manager and opened an office in New York, spending half his time there and half in Philadelphia. But there were many stories Nina wanted to tell, and she planned on pulling her BFF, Frankie, into the mix. Where it would lead was anybody's guess, and a lot can happen in a year.

Peter took the job in Boston, and he and Amy set up house. The spare bedroom was arranged with a table for jigsaw puzzles and another one for board games. Of course, Blinky and Gimpy had to get their paws into everything. Amy's new research project could prove to be beneficial when the four met up again next season.

Giovanni became a member of Mateo's Share a Meal charity and hosted fundraisers at his restaurant, encouraging other restaurateurs to do the same. He was able to curtail Frankie's insecurities by moving in with her, Bandit, and Sweet P.

Frankie had such great success with Mateo's book and his mission that her publishing company created her own imprint, called Cooking for a Cause. She began developing cookbooks with celebrity chefs who had their own personal charities. A portion of the proceeds would go to the charity, and the charities could sell the cookbooks through their donor networks. By next year, she planned to have her "Cook Force" in full swing, finding fun and exciting ways for people to break bread together. And she would be sure to bring her gal pals into the mix, for better or otherwise.

The wheels were already in motion for their next reunion, guaranteeing there would be more tricks up their sleeves, new dance moves, and surprises they never imagined. But only if Frankie promised to never, ever go snowshoeing again.